WARNING!

Adult Fiction
Sexually Exquisite

*If you are not eighteen or older,
do not, seriously, do not read this book.*

HoneyB

Married on Mondays
Single Husbands
Sexcapades

HoneyB writing as Mary B. Morrison

If I Can't Have You
The Eternal Engagement
Darius Jones
Unconditionally Single
Maneater (with Noire)
Who's Loving You
Sweeter Than Honey
When Somebody Loves You Back
Nothing Has Ever Felt Like This
Somebody's Gotta Be on Top
He's Just a Friend
Never Again Once More
Soulmates Dissipate
Who's Making Love
Justice Just Us Just Me

Coauthored with Carl Weber

She Ain't the One

Presented by Mary B. Morrison

Diverse Stories: From the Imaginations of Sixth Graders,
an anthology written by thirty-three sixth graders

THE
RICH GIRLS'
CLUB

GRAND CENTRAL
PUBLISHING

NEW YORK   BOSTON

Excerpt from *If I Can't Have You* by Mary B. Morrison copyright © 2012 by Mary B. Morrison. Published by arrangement with Dafina Books, an imprint of Kensington Publishing Corp. All rights reserved.

Grand Central Publishing
Hachette Book Group
237 Park Avenue
New York, NY 10017

www.HachetteBookGroup.com

Printed in the United States of America

RRD-C

First Edition: March 2013
10 9 8 7 6 5 4 3 2 1

Grand Central Publishing is a division of Hachette Book Group, Inc.
The Grand Central Publishing name and logo is a trademark of Hachette Book Group, Inc.

The Hachette Speakers Bureau provides a wide range of authors for speaking events. To find out more, go to www.hachettespeakersbureau.com or call (866) 376-6591.

The publisher is not responsible for websites (or their content) that are not owned by the publisher.

Library of Congress Cataloging-in-Publication Data
HoneyB.
    The rich girls' club / HoneyB. — 1st ed.
        p. cm.
    ISBN 978-0-446-58473-9 (hardcover) — ISBN 978-1-4555-1091-7 (ebook)
    1. African Americans—Fiction. I. Title.
    PS3563.O87477R53 2013
    813'.54—dc23
                                    2012027208

You're a Rich Girl

Date:

Given To:

Given By:

Personal Message:

Barbara H. Cooper
Brenetta Fisher
Dawn C. Mallory
Marissa Monteilh
Andrea Morrison
Regina Morrison
Elizabeth Norris-Baines
Margie Rickerson
Stella Morrison, and
Debra Noel

You are truly worthy!

Pussy is best served... Ice Cold

Every Dick has its Day

Women Rule

MUTUAL MASTURBATION

*A*hh...have you ever teased your clit while watching your man stroke his dick?

I know some ladies are uncomfortable with touching their pussy and others have never seen their vagina. In addition to not seeing what's between your legs, some women don't know they urinate and can ejaculate from their urethra. The two types of fluids are very different. Also, the clitoris has six to eight thousand nerve endings that make it easier for some women to experience oral orgasms versus vaginal orgasms.

It's not okay for a woman not to know her body. If you're like me, I was reared in a household where talking about sex was taboo, yet going to church every Sunday was mandatory. Ladies, you have to take ownership of your climaxes and understand the various types of orgasms—clitoral, vaginal, anal, breast stimulation, mental (absent being touched), etc. Educate yourself.

At the age of fourteen I took to the streets, got me a sixteen-year-old boyfriend, and lost my virginity all for the desire to have a feeling I'd heard of but knew nothing about. He didn't know much more than I did, and it took two additional years for me to meet a twenty-one-year-old that gave me my first orgasm. The explosion was unbelievable! Immediately I felt sexually liberated.

It's never too late to say, "Hello," to your kitty. Take a close-up picture of her, save it in your cell phone or in a special place. Compliment your kitty often. Every pussy looks different. Make sure you groom her, wax, trim, or shave. To avoid in-grown hairs, I recommend waxing for women with coarse hair and wearing elastic-free panties.

Get real comfortable with your punany, and you'll discover a new side of your sexuality and personality. Your walk will evolve into a confident strut that quietly gestures to the world you've got good pussy and you know it. Men will notice the sway in your hips and the difference in your attitude without your having to say a word.

Learning to enjoy masturbating with your guy will turn him on. He'll start making requests like, "Baby, play with your pussy for me." If he's not sexually inhibited, trust me, he'll willingly follow your lead.

Sex doesn't always have to be a contact sport. Ladies, your initiating mutual masturbation (MM) is a healthy way to climax with your partner because most men are visual creatures. They love to watch their women get off. Letting him see you in action will definitely enhance his and your creativity.

Please let your sex toys sit this one out. It's not that he wouldn't like to see you use your F—Kin Rabbit, lipstick vibrator, or your amazing G-Spot penetrator with anal and clitoral stimulators, but you don't want to show off; you want his undivided attention. That, and you want to level the playing field during MM. Well, honestly the playing field can never be leveled because women, by nature, have an advantage I'll mention in detail later.

Men won't admit it. In fact they want women to believe they should be crowned king when it comes to sex, but the truth is their equipment comes packaged with less options. Sex is the only arena where the queen can dethrone her king largely because most men undervalue their manhood. There's nothing we can do about that. But you can make your man a better lover and make him earn his crown.

Ladies, I told you earlier your clitoris has six to eight thousand nerve endings. You read this right; thousands of nerve endings are in your precious tiny pearl. Couple that clit sensation with a G-spot that, when massaged properly, allows a woman to ejaculate from her urethra like a man, and you should always come first. With proper foreplay we can cross the finish line before a man is out of the gate. So why are we the ones waiting on them to cum when after they cum they leave us hanging? We're capable of having vaginal, clitoral, and anal orgasms and we can squirt.

Okay, I'm getting off track here. I've already talked about this but wanted to make certain women understand what I am communicating. Back to MM.

Why do you think some women can cum in less than sixty seconds, then cum again and again? And don't mention those women that can have the hour long and total body orgasms. Whew! Your pussy is beautiful. Being a woman is amazing. But only if you understand what God has blessed you with. It won't benefit you to have the winning lotto numbers if you never check your ticket. Ladies, please learn your body so you can satisfy yourself first, then teach your man how to fully satisfy you.

Now, when a man ejaculates quickly, afterward he's dissatisfied and you're pissed the fuck off because you have all these revved-up orgasmic fluids ready to shoot a ten-gun salute and you haven't fired off your first round.

Most women who climax are multi-orgasmic. And if you've

never had one, read *Married on Mondays* by HoneyB. Don't leave it up to your man to figure you out. Play with your pussy in front of his face until you have the big screaming O.

Once both of you cum from MM, you'll crave having his hard dick inside your throbbing vagina, but he might be in recovery. If he falls asleep, damn girl—you're so hot you wore him out by showing him your pussy. Pat yourself on the back for that accomplishment, let him take a thirty-minute nap, give or take five, then wake his ass up by riding or sucking his dick, or sitting your punany on his face. It's penetration time.

Moan in his ear, "Wake up, daddy, and fuck this good pussy. You've got me so wet I want to feel you deep inside of me." You know your man best. Say whatever it takes to get him ready for round two.

MM empowers a woman.

Have you witnessed your guy ejaculating? If you haven't, please do. This is some sexxxy shit! I know some of you have but it's usually when he pulls out and squirts his semen on your pussy, titties, in your face, on your ass, or somewhere else on your body. That's cool. Actually that's fantastic. Let him do his thing while you pay attention to his fast, slow, long, and short strokes. Whatever he does to himself is what he likes most from a hand job. Try to mimic his rhythm.

HoneyB wants more women to get comfortable with touching their pussies. It's your pussy and you don't need permission to develop a one-on-one relationship with her. Get up close and personal with your punany. Put that chick in front of a magnified mirror. Spread your lips. Watch her become engorged. When she pouts, don't stop. When she puckers, keep going. Touch her, rub her, spank her, stroke her, open her up, stick your finger inside then rub your juices on your clit, use lubrication if you want, and don't stop teasing her until you're done cumming.

Fellas generally have this area covered, as the majority, if not all of them, masturbate at an early age. Most men continue to do it but they do so while they're alone. If a woman is present, the man feels obligated to penetrate her. This is not necessary all the time, ladies, so it's up to you to create the MM platform.

Masturbating is similar to a woman riding a dick in that there is no wrong way to enjoy the moment. Don't overthink the situation. Do what *feels* good. Sex is not a guilty pleasure. Sexual satisfaction is a man's privilege and a woman's right.

Erotic talk is encouraged. Go with the flow. Focus on sounding seductive. The tone of your voice is more important than what you're actually saying. If the dialogue doesn't fit, don't force it. Moan, groan, and grunt, but don't overdo it. Here's one example of how you can initiate mutual masturbation with your partner.

I sit next to him. We're having a good time, enjoying one another's company. My pussy is puckering, but he doesn't know it. A rerun of *Love and Hip Hop* is getting ready to come on in ten minutes. It's one of the few shows we both like; the other is *The Game* on BET. I'm thankful it's not a new episode or what I have planned for my man would have to wait at least an hour.

"Baby, you want a glass of wine?" I ask him.

"Sure, but hurry up," he says, flipping through the channels, his eyes fixed on the flat screen.

I retreat to the bedroom, freshen up my kitty with a quick shower, then change into a thong and a spaghetti strap T-shirt.

I ditch the thong and tee for a see-through nightie but that's not the look I'm going for. I toss the nightie in the drawer and step into a pair of lace boy shorts, and a push-up bra. A dab of perfume behind my ears, on my bra straps, and the scent awakens my senses.

"This is it!" I say, slapping my ass then admiring myself in the mirror. I love the way I smell. I feel sexy and desirable.

En route back to the living room, I grab two glasses and a bottle of wine.

"Hey, babe. Here," I say, handing him the glasses.

Reaching, still focusing on the flat screen, he leans forward to set the goblets on the coffee table. "Sit down, it just started."

I whisper, "Baby."

He looks at me. One of the glasses tilts sideways. He fumbles but catches it before it crashes to the floor. His mouth is open, eyelids are stretching.

"Wow. What did I do to deserve this?" he says, staring at my juicy cleavage. Slowly his eyes trail to my navel, then my shorts.

I stand there letting my man drool.

"Come here." His hands settle on my hips as he tugs on my shorts.

I turn around, bend over, pour wine into my glass, then his. Before setting the bottle on the table, I face him, splash my pussy with the wine. Just enough to get her moist. I don't have to say, "Taste me," because his lips are already gnawing through the lace. He pulls my panties to one side and his lips are all over mine.

Removing my boy shorts, I take a few sips of wine. I pull up a stool from my bar. I position the chair on the other side of the coffee table in front of the television. I want my pussy close enough for him to see, but far enough for him to have to reach out in order to touch her. I sit in front of him, spread my thighs, then touch myself.

He drinks from the wine bottle, comes to me, kisses me, then swallows.

I back him up to the sofa, unzip his pants, pull out his dick, gently push him down, then I sit my wet pussy back on the cool leather stool. Opening and closing my thighs, I begin to play with my punany.

My man doesn't need instructions. He admires what he knows is his stuff as he grips his dick. Reclining into the sofa, he holds himself. "Open your legs a little wider," he says, easing his hand up his shaft.

I do as he asks. My finger trails the rim of my lips. I dip it in, pull it out, look into his eyes, then I ease my finger in my mouth and taste myself. I moan, leave it there for a little while before sliding it out.

I lust to have his hard dick inside me and begin to stroke myself in small circles. His chest heaves up and down. I dip my finger again, except this time I kneel on the coffee table. Ass tilted in the air, I lean toward him. He licks his lips, meets me halfway. I swipe my fingertip under his nose, then trace my finger along his lips.

His tongue slides out of his mouth, savoring my juices. He smiles at me. "I don't know what made you do this, but damn, baby, you're hot."

"Indeed I am . . . and I'm so hot for you, baby," I say, sitting on the stool as I slip my hand deep into my walls. I squirm, wiggle my hips, finger-fuck myself for a moment. Then I prop my foot on the coffee table and spread my lips so he can see all of his glory.

"Damn, she's beautiful."

He proceeds to stand, remove his jeans, throw them to the floor. I love what I see.

His dick is hard, standing tall. He places his hands on his hips. Stares at me then smiles. He picks up his pants, shoves his hand in the pocket, pulls out a condom.

Shaking my head, I begin massaging my clit. "You don't need that condom. Not yet. I want you to sit back down and stroke your dick for me. I want to see *you* cum for me, baby."

Closing then opening my legs, I cup my vagina, then play peekaboo with my pussy. I rub her while looking at him stroking his dick. "Damn, you feel so good," I say, imagining him deep inside of me.

Faster and faster his hand moves in short strokes from the top to the bottom of his bulging head. He's giving special attention to his frenulum. When he slides his hands to the base of his shaft then resumes short fast strokes, I tease my clit to his rhythm.

I want to cum so hard. I feel my face tightening as his brows draw closer together. Our eyes meet and our spines arch at the same time. My man looks so sexy I can't hold back. My feet touch the floor as my ass slides to the edge of the stool.

He's breathing heavily while stroking long, short, fast and faster. His hand tightens around his dick. White fluid squirts in spurts. I see his cum flow over his fist and my pussy begs to explode. Rushing to him, I'm panting. I squat over him. He wiggles his dick head up and down my clit, making me cum all over him. I hug him tight; I can't let go. The faster he wiggles, the more I cum. The orgasmic sensation lingers even after I stop cumming.

Slowly, I sit beside him on the sofa. *Love and Hip Hop* is going off. Intoxicated with my man's energy, I lay my head on his shoulder. He holds me in his arms, and for a moment the two of us become one.

THE RICH GIRLS' CLUB

CHAPTER 1

Storm

Y ou'd better fuck this good pussy or I'm going to fuck the shit out of you."

She bounced on his dick, the way she'd done when riding her award-winning thoroughbred. The mayor's ass slammed against her mattress. Problem was, the rhythm between them was solely created by her fading enthusiasm.

"Fuck me harder, you filthy bastard...harder...harder!" she pleaded, staring down at him.

She'd never talked that way to her horses. But men were different from stallions, harder to train, nearly impossible to have follow commands. Grinding her pussy into the depths of his shaft, she desperately tried to make herself cum all over his nuts.

His lips tightened as his eyes closed. She watched in amazement as his brows moved closer together. His dick hardened, butt cheeks lifted, then contracted.

"So it's like that, huh?" she said, slowing her pace.

Lazy fucker. I swear the more successful this man becomes, the harder it is for me to get him to get me off. He's laying here letting my hard-earned sweat drench his body and he's seriously trying to ejaculate on the under. I know him too well. When I'm done exhaust-ing myself for his pleasure, he'll brag about how he gave me the dick so good I couldn't take it anymore. Or say something selfish like, "I thought you came." Forget this. I've got something special for him today.

Red platform stilettos dug into the mattress as she rode him one last time, then stopped. "Okay, I'm not doing this again this morning. It's too damn early for me to be sexually frustrated. I quit. Go fuck your wife." She slapped his face, dismounted him, then paced the floor beside her canopy sex bed.

Opening his eyes wide, he held his jaw. "Ow! What's wrong, babycakes? I was almost about to give you the grand prize." Limp dick in hand, vigorously he started stroking himself.

Yeah, like the useless surprise in the bottom of a box of caramel popcorn with peanuts. "If I'm not busting a big O up in this bitch, neither are you. Get your lazy ass up," she demanded, pushing him to the floor. He was lucky she didn't use all of her one hun-dred and twenty-two pounds to jump up and down on him.

He landed on his knees in a praying position. Braced his el-bows on the edge of the mattress. "For a little woman you're strong like a man."

All she wanted was one head-to-toe orgasm . . . one. Somehow she doubted he cared enough to fulfill her deep desire to have her pussy explode with pleasure. She shouldn't have to have a boy do a man's job. Her twenty-one-year-old boyfriend Chancelor was nine years younger than her with the stamina of her favorite racehorse. That's the kind of *man* she needed.

Lying on the bed, she spread her firm thighs wide. "You see this here pretty pussy?"

The mayor exhaled, stared into her eyes. His lips tensed. He didn't blink.

She scooted closer to him. The brief pause between each word was due to her Asian accent. "Look at her when I'm talking to you."

Placing her five-inch heels over his shoulders, she parted her lips for him to see how dry her pink flesh was from the constant friction. "All that riding and my pussy is dryer than stale rice."

Dragging the tip of her finger up her pasty engorged shaft, she felt the swelling expand then pulsate. With a little saliva and masturbation she could make herself cum but that would defeat the purpose of having him there. And doing herself would make her madder at him.

She released her ponytail, fingered her brow-length bang. "You might be in charge when you're running the city of Los Angeles, but there's only one boss and one bitch in this bed. Got that?"

The mayor should've been at his office preparing for his nine o'clock meeting but sexing her was a standard Wednesday appointment he hadn't missed in half a decade. She had more money than he did; he had more political power than she did. His influence had helped many of her people become United States citizens, including his wife.

The mayor's trophy Mrs., the same age as Storm, was one of those stay-at-home, go-to-every-PTA-meeting-and-soccer-game-for-their-kid kind of moms. No one in LA seemed to care that the mayor was twice the age of his beautiful second wife. The woman had probably spoiled him in many ways, including allowing him to lay on his ass while she did him and all the household chores. And while the Mrs. kept decent watch over her husband, he still managed to find time to cheat on her.

Most evenings, after leaving the office, his time was consumed by dinner meetings that made late nights impossible for him to steal away without being missed by his wife and kid. So one day a week, like clockwork, he showed up at her door at the break of dawn with an erection and a wide smile. *But he'd better not confuse fucking his wife with their sexing one another, or he'd start taking his ass straight to work on Wednesday mornings.*

Pushing him backward, she lowered her legs, stood over him, and commanded, "Get your ass up."

He sprang to his feet, straightened his spine, then saluted her. "Yes, captain. Whatever you say. You're the boss and the bitch, right?" Holding his stomach, he laughed.

She didn't need to confirm what he already knew. She shoved him onto the thousand-thread-count, sky blue sheet, opened the pleasure chest at the foot of her bed and pulled out an eighteen-inch, double-headed dildo. She stood beside the bed and repeatedly slapped the dick against her palm. His smile faded into a frown.

"I'm not playing with you. No more letting you lay in my bed and leaving me with a wet ass." She was ready to end their weekly affair and focus all of her attention on her boyfriend. What she was going to do to the mayor would make their breakup his idea.

Slowly her tongue circled the silicone tip, then spiraled down the shaft. His eyes widened with excitement. If he knew what she was going to do with the dick in her hands, he'd head for the door, get in his car, and drive off.

"You like watching me take this dick into my . . . wet . . . hot . . . juicy mouth, don't you?" Suctioning one side into her throat a little at a time, she took in a few inches as she stroked the other end while keeping her eyes on his growing erection.

The mayor held his penis tight, then began massaging himself as he watched her slip the silicone in and out of her drooling mouth. "Damn, you are so freaky," he said, panting with his tongue hanging out. "This is why I can't stop fucking you."

His last comment made her eyes roll toward the ceiling, then back to him.

His chest heaved high, paused, then flattened as he closed his lips, then exhaled through his nostrils like a bull. "Come here, Storm Dangerfield." He leaned forward, reached for her. She shoved him back on the bed, then stepped away as he begged. "I want your sexy juices rolling down my cock. Damn it, I want you to do to me what you're doing to that. This here is real, babycakes."

Inches from his face, she paused. Wiggling the head out of her mouth like a rattlesnake's tail, she positioned her tongue over his balls, then spat on his dick.

"Oh, yeah. That's it. Treat me like the dog I am. Spit on me again," he pleaded.

Storm raised the dildo above her head, then lowered her arm. *Smack!*

"Ow! What the hell was that for? Don't do that again!" he protested, cupping his erection. "You almost hit my cock."

She whispered, "I missed on purpose," then told him, "Shut the fuck up and listen." She grabbed his ankles and pulled his body to her. She slammed his feet against the edge of the bed where they dangled off the edge.

"What's gotten into you, woman?"

Waving the eighteen inches in front of his face, she calmly said, "One of these dicks is going to fuck me the way I need to be fucked. I'm tired of doing all the work. And I haven't forgotten those lies you were shoo-shooing in my ear at campaign headquarters when I helped you get re-elected. 'Baby, I want to eat your pussy forever until you cream all over my face. I want to bury my face in your double-Ds and bite your nipples until you cream. Then I'm going to drink your juices, and screw you so good with this big cock you're going to gush all over me, then fall asleep with a smile on your face.' So far you've proven to be a real politician. All smoke and mirrors. Because we both know you haven't made me cream, gush, or put me to sleep with a smile. And your *cock* ain't bigger than my dick. So make me cum or shut up and roll over. Somebody's getting fucked in here this morning."

And no one would hear him scream.

Her nearest neighbor was a half mile downhill. Tall evergreen trees surrounded the front of her mansion. A high, sparkling, gold-toned electronic gate guarded the entrance. Two six-foot-tall golden dragon statues with hidden cameras inside the eyes captured his goings and comings, so if the mayor ever tried the unthinkable, she had enough proof to make his life miserable. Open backfields stretched for an acre, housing her stable, swimming pool, Jacuzzi, and tennis court.

He sat on the edge of the bed facing her. His hand rested on her thigh. "Look here. I forgive you. Just suck me off and I promise I—"

The silicone in her hand plugged his mouth, forcing him to swallow words she didn't care to hear. "This is non-negotiable. When I pull this dick from between your lips, you've got exactly five seconds to start fucking me or your ass will wish that you had."

Chapter 2

Morgan

S he lived for Saturdays.

Not because it was her day off from the five-star hotel she owned in the heart of Beverly Hills. Not because her husband worked for her, managing Angels Hotel and Spa, or that he stayed overnight at her establishment on weekends. Having their house to herself Fridays, Saturdays, and Sundays made her appreciate seeing her husband on Mondays and happy to kiss him good-bye on Friday mornings.

She loved Magnum but being with him seven days a week irritated her. Listening to him debate trivial things that didn't make any sense forced her to either challenge his point of view or totally ignore him. Morgan didn't love her husband any less but her decision to give him something constructive to do three days a week had worked exceptionally well over the last four years of their eight-year marriage.

The reason she loved Saturdays so much was because every Saturday her girls, the exclusive members of the group she'd founded—the Rich Girls' Club—came together to have fun, talk shit about men, and discuss ways to make more money. Today she was hosting their most important meeting ever.

Glad she lived far from the congested city's smog, Morgan opened the front door and filled her lungs with fresh air. Stretching her arms to the rolling mountains, she said, "I need all of you to back me up on this one." Admittedly, she didn't label herself as a Christian but she was a believer in the higher power and prayed all of her neighbors would support her on what she was about to unveil. She took another deep breath before going inside and sitting on the bench in the foyer as she waited for her girls to walk in.

Brooks was the first to arrive. Strolling in wearing elegant, winter white wool slacks and a powder-blue, buttoned-up cashmere sweater, her best friend struck a diva pose.

"Hey, girl, you look fabulous as always. Fresh tan?"

Morgan smiled then nodded at Brooks. "I could save a lot of money if I were born with your complexion."

"Mz. Bronze and Blonde—tanned or not—you're always flawless."

All of the girls were stellar, on the outside.

Proudly, the Rich Girls flaunted their wealth and their wisdom. A smart woman afraid to speak her mind underserved everyone around her. The confidence each of the girls exhibited was the reason Morgan had handpicked them from the most elite women's-only establishment in Beverly Hills, where the membership fee was one hundred thousand dollars a year. Money could gain the right woman access to the Beverly Hills group, but membership into the Rich Girls' Club was limited to the four of them and closed for life. Any other women desiring to start their own RGC had to do just that.

Brooks sniffed the air. "Umm," she moaned, inhaled long and

slow, then continued, "It smells delicious in here, girlfriend. The scent alone makes me feel guilty for what I'm thinking about eating. What's that sexy-ass cook of yours making?"

Giving Brooks a kiss on the lips, Morgan said, "You know Bo; he's in the kitchen preparing his special crepes, homegrown apples with fresh ground cinnamon, his version of grilled smoked pineapple chicken sausage, and lots of other fresh goodies using vegetables that he hand-picked from my garden this morning. He's amazing. That's why I keep him on payroll."

Bo was so fantastic with his culinary skills he deserved his own cable television show. Morgan was appreciative to have him prepare their brunch each week. He was the best chef she'd ever hired and the most handsome black man she'd ever laid her jade-colored eyes upon. Well, second most attractive African American. Her husband was the first. Like Michael Jackson sang, "It don't matter if you're black or white." She'd also dated white, Cuban, Latino, Iranian, and Egyptian men.

Though the two men—Magnum and Bo—had never met, Morgan knew she had to make sure they never did. One look at Bo and Magnum would fire him on the spot. Men didn't like to admit it but they were jealous of attractive men, the same way most women were jealous of gorgeous women, who were hired to work inside their home.

Interrupting her thoughts, Brooks said, "If I weren't already—" then abruptly stopped.

Morgan stared at her friend. "Already what, girl? Don't stand there with your mouth hanging open. Say it."

"Nothing. It's not like my dickless life matters to anyone except me." Brooks's eyes rolled toward the ceiling, then back to Morgan. "Maybe I should buy me some good dick of my own that's attached to a real man, girl. It's not like I couldn't afford to take care of one...or two." Brooks laughed then shook her head.

"There's nothing wrong with being dickless for a few weeks, but it's been years," Morgan said. Reaching between Brooks's thighs, she strummed her girlfriend's clit.

Brooks jumped back, swatting Morgan's hand away. "Don't do that. What if someone sees you?"

"Sorry girl, I couldn't help it," Morgan told her. "Besides, celibacy does have some advantages. Maybe I should add getting you laid to today's agenda."

One day her friend would get some good dick and get married again. Next time, to the right man. Not to some loser boasting about her success while splurging her money on a gold digger. If Magnum ever cheated on Morgan, he might not live to regret it, or she'd probably pay someone to break all three of his legs. She rattled her head, shaking away the horrible vision in her mind. She loved her husband too much to hurt him but then again she did believe in an eye for an eye.

"Go enjoy a cocktail, girl, for the both of us. I moved the bar. The champagne, orange juice, and Bloody Mary ingredients are set up near the window overlooking the pools."

Routine bored Morgan. Sex. Business. Décor. Each week she had the furniture in their clubroom rearranged. Her bedroom was redecorated monthly with new linens, drapes, a decorative comforter, and lots of throw pillows. Her designer bath towels were changed weekly. The only thing that remained consistent in Morgan's life was her friendship with her girlfriends and her marriage.

"Well, to the bar! That's where you'll find me," Brooks said, walking in the direction of the west wing.

"Brooks, wait. Giving you a heads up, honey. I have a serious proposition for you but I'll announce it when Storm and Hope get here. And no, I'm not going to tell you now so go have that drink and relax."

"Morgan, trust me, with all the LA drama I've heard at my coffee shop this week—from basketball wives to housewives, sweetheart, I will happily wait while I'm enjoying a much needed drink," Brooks said, resuming her stride.

Morgan sat on the bench in the foyer smiling as she watched Brooks strut down the hallway like it was a runway. There was something special about the sway in a black woman's hips that conveyed her confidence. What Morgan had in mind for Brooks would certainly please the Rich Girls. This was the opportunity of their lifetimes and the time to implement her idea was now.

Brooks, the most conservative amongst them, hadn't dated since her divorce five years ago. Thanks to her loyal customers, Brooks owned the most popular twenty-four hour café in LA— BK Brew. Brooks constantly met attractive eligible bachelors, so there was no reason for her girlfriend not to have a man. Netting an annual revenue in excess of three million dollars, Brooks literally had men and money at her fingertips. Brooks knew most, if not all, of the regulars by their first and last names but Morgan wasn't sure why her friend refused to go out on dates with any of them. Had something earth-shattering happened during Brooks's childhood? Rape? Molestation? Heaven forbid if Brooks had had an abortion and never told anyone. They'd both be devastated.

Morgan glanced up from the files in her lap.

Hope Andrews, the well-kept daughter of a billionaire Native American Tribal Leader who owned several casinos on reservations throughout California, strolled in wearing a mink shawl and a pink, knee-length, halter dress with a plunging V-neckline.

"Hey, Mrs. Childs," Hope beamed with a wide smile. Proudly she adjusted her double-Es. "It sure smells good in here! What's on the menu?"

A brilliant pink diamond choker complimented her pink emerald-cut earrings. From her heart to her head to her feet, Morgan loved that nothing about Hope was fake. The breast enhancements didn't count. The way the Rich Girls saw it, the implants were an investment in Hope's happiness.

Closing the folder, Morgan replied, "Big business, babe. You look stunning as always. Brooks is already here. Go join her. Get comfortable. Have a drink. I'll be in as soon as Storm arrives."

"You don't have to tell me twice," Hope said, laying her mink over her arm. She jiggled her voluptuous buttocks down the hall.

The three-thousand square-foot, oval-shaped clubroom that Hope was headed toward was an area designated to fornicate and to facilitate the Rich Girls' life-altering decisions. For years, beginning early in her marriage, the room was Morgan's hideaway. A place where she'd escape to meditate or unwind while reading her favorite authors, like Marissa Monteilh, Pynk, and Mary B. Morrison.

Morgan refused to buy books written by reformed doggish men telling women how to date. A woman didn't need a man's advice on much, and surely the Rich Girls didn't allow men to tell them when to open or close their legs.

To enhance the peaceful aura of the west wing, Morgan had hired the same architects that had renovated her hotel to remodel the entire area. A one-million dollar upgrade had been a small price to pay to enjoy a special space with her friends: A Jacuzzi filled with herbal teas and hot mineral water was built into the hillside, and down a flight of stairs the indoor/outdoor swimming pool had been built with a view overlooking the valley.

For the Rich Girls, anything was attainable. Any man any of them desired could be had. And the men that they were proud to call their own knew their places. None of them were allowed to linger in the west wing or socialize in the clubroom, including Morgan's husband. As for Bo, his job was to set up the food then leave immediately.

A square ivory conference table with four high-backed plum, leather roller chairs was on the opposite end of the room from the bar. High arched openings led to the adjacent bedroom and other rooms. While Morgan did have a few secrets, she didn't have internal doors anywhere in her home. The only exceptions were the bathrooms.

She was clever. Since most people overlooked the obvious, all the things she should've hidden were transparent. Friends loved her magnetic personality. When she'd elected herself as their investment broker, none of The Girls protested. The Rich Girls' Club's portfolio, which had started out five years ago with an initial contribution of a half million dollars each, was now valued at over twenty million. On paper.

As outgoing as Morgan was, Storm was the most extroverted of the four. She always had the juiciest sexcapades to share, though all of the girls were sexy. Storm and Hope had breasts big enough to feed all the men in LA County and Morgan and Brooks's C-cups were a perfect match for one another.

Having money really did make all of them happier, but emotionally supporting each other made them the happiest. Nothing made Morgan feel more complete than the relationships she'd established with her girls, not even her marriage to Magnum Childs. Having a husband was nice and gave her the stability she hadn't had when she'd been single, but having girlfriends that trusted her was priceless.

Morgan continued thumbing through the proposals for each of the girls, making certain every "i" was dotted and every "t" was crossed. Careless mistakes were truly a sign of incompetence and she had a strong disdain for them.

Storm breezed through the door. "Girl, you are always working on something. Put those files down because you won't believe what I did to Mr. Mayor this past Wednesday."

With her growing political affiliations, Storm might prove to be the most valuable asset for Morgan's plan. Unbeknownst to Storm, her promiscuous ways had helped Morgan formulate her strategy.

"Lord, I hope you didn't violate that man's anal rights."

Storm laughed out loud.

"Yeah, you did. And you know I want to hear every detail but it'll have to wait until after my big announcement," Morgan said, waving the files in her hand. "Let's go."

Strolling down the corridor, Storm said, "I just love that painting hanging in the foyer of you and Magnum on your wedding day. You were smart to hire an artist to capture the moment you exchanged vows at the altar. When I get married, I'm going to do that, too."

The painting was indeed Morgan's favorite. It was the first visual she wanted each time she walked through her front door. She was the only rich girl in the group that was married, and the love she had for Magnum had grown stronger every year. He was her backbone, her foundation, her everything. The best part of her relationships with her girls was there was no competition. They loved Magnum and he loved them, too.

In the clubroom, a hint of ginger, raspberry, and cinnamon

filled the air. Morgan entered and placed the four files at the foot of her chaise. Four plush, lavender leather chaise lounges formed a circle near the floor-to-ceiling sliding glass windows. The seating allowed the girls to enjoy the sunshine while discussing business and pleasure.

"Ladies, you know I'm full of surprises but you'll never guess what I've orchestrated for the Rich Girls' Club this year." Morgan's brilliant smile lit the entire room, causing the other women to beam with curiosity.

Taking one last moment before revealing her big secret, Morgan tucked her blond hair behind her ears, stood in the window and stared down the hillside. She'd accomplished a lot in her thirty-seven years of living. An only child born to wealthy parents, Morgan had been reared and was married in a small town where everyone knew her. And Morgan appreciated the quality of life her mother and father had given her.

She'd moved to the City of Angels for her husband. When she relocated, the big city life didn't change the wild country girl inside of her. She missed hunting, fishing, and riding horses, but she loved him so much she'd go wherever he wanted. She had enjoyed Lake Charles, Louisiana, but he hadn't liked the place at all.

Opening a lavish hotel had been her way of providing Southern hospitality to celebrities with deep pockets. Living in Calabasas, right outside of Los Angeles, provided an escape from the busy streets and congested freeways.

"Girl, how long are you going to stare out of that window?" Storm asked. "We are on our second drink and you haven't had one. And I'm ready to tell y'all the good gushy gushy about my pussy."

Morgan rattled her head. "You're right," she responded,

scooping up the files. Quickly she handed Brooks, Storm, and Hope a folder each before sitting on her chaise. "Don't open it until I tell you to.

"This year, ladies, the Rich Girls' Club is doing what no other female organization is brilliant enough to orchestrate or bold enough to execute. And that includes the women's club in BH," Morgan said, tapping on her file. "The entire BH group will end up being our biggest supporters, but what is discussed in this room today remains between us."

Morgan glanced at the folders in each of the women's hands. She'd tailored each task specifically. "This being the first Saturday in January, we have to work hard and fast but we wait to make our announcement until right before the deadline. Once we go public, we have seven months to execute this plan. The biggest part of this assignment is reserved for Brooks Kennedy."

Brooks swept her shoulder-length, chestnut hair behind her ear, then glanced at the other members. Her big brown eyes expanded with excitement, then narrowed with curiosity. Her mocha skin flushed red. "Why me? And you'd better not say it's because I'm the oldest," she said, pursing her full lips.

Storm laughed.

Always thinking before opening her mouth, Hope remained quiet. She was a thinker and deemed herself the moral conscience of the group. If there were any resistance to, or holes in, the plan, Hope would wait until the others spoke then share her thoughts.

Brooks cleared her throat and said, "Morgan, you treated each of us to an all-expense paid vacation to Sydney for Christmas and you gave us a full year of complimentary spa services. Now what are you up to?"

Morgan nodded. "I saved the best to kickoff the New Year.

You'll see things my way in a moment. Open your folders. Read the content in its entirety. When you're done, close your file. Then we'll discuss the specifics."

Soft swishes, strong flipping; page by page Morgan observed the ladies reading, smiling, gasping, and shaking their heads until the very last word.

Brooks quietly set her folder beside her. "Whenever you're ready to explain this Morgan, I'm all ears."

Snap! Slap! Hope closed then placed her file in her lap.

"Hell, yeah!" Storm said, waving her folder high in the air. "Everybody dies but not everybody lives, baby. Power to the pussy! This is what I call living it up!"

Morgan calmly commented, "Trust me, ladies. This plan will position us to rule the state of California for decades to come. Now is our time to seize this opportunity. We have to take immediate action. Hope, are you in?"

Hope nodded. "The only concern I have is about the ten million dollars it's going to cost us."

"I'll explain that later. Storm, what about you?"

"You know it! I'm cool with everything except the part that says we have to let go of all of our indoor staff. Who's going to clean our houses?"

"You'll be fine," Hope said. "It'll do you some good to learn how to clean up. My house is bigger than yours and I'll manage."

"Good, then when you're done cleaning your house, come and do mine."

"Ladies, please," Morgan said. "Focus."

All members had answered in favor but without Brooks's approval the plan would perish. Slowly, Morgan said, "Brooks, can we count on you?"

"Well," Brooks said, then paused.

Morgan interrupted. "I know it's a lot to ask. Perhaps seemingly impossible, but you're the only one of us without a man."

"What's that supposed to mean? You're the married one. Wouldn't that make you a better candidate?" Brooks fired back, her voice escalating.

"On the surface, yes. But I'm a better organizer than you."

"That's true," Hope and Storm agreed simultaneously.

Besides, Morgan had no desire to be in front of a camera, podium, or crowd. She didn't want to travel away from her husband or relocate from Los Angeles to Sacramento, but she knew she'd do all of those things if she had to in support of the plan. Brooks was the friendliest, most social of them all, and the fact that she was unattached didn't matter. "Trust me," Morgan said. "If I didn't think you could do this, I wouldn't have proposed it. We're in this together. We've got you. All you have do is say *yes*."

CHAPTER 3

Brooks

What would her parents think? Brooks, the daughter of an affluent African-American couple, refused to tarnish her family's name. On one hand, her parents, would be extremely proud of her. On the other hand, if her secrets surfaced and publicly humiliated them all, Morgan's plan would crush the entire Kennedy family. Brooks doubted that Morgan had given any thought to the worst possible outcome.

"Saying yes is the easy part, but what about..." Brooks's words trailed off into deeper thoughts.

Having the media uncover every mistake she'd made in her entire life and use those mistakes against her was not something she wanted to experience at forty-five years of age. Plus, most politicians were married. If only for media purposes, and not necessarily because they unconditionally loved their spouses, their images were a factor.

Flashbacks of her kissing an underage boy over twenty years ago came to mind. She'd been twenty-five. He was seventeen. She hadn't had sex with him even though she'd wanted to. What if he still had those naked photos of her? The media would throw her under the bus and a jury might have enough evidence to prove she'd had sex with a minor.

No fucking way, Brooks thought, then began, "You know—"

Morgan quickly interrupted. "That's between us. Yes, you can do this."

"If she won't do it, I sure as hell will," Storm said.

Revealing her affair with Morgan wasn't where Brooks had been headed, but maybe that was what Morgan thought she was going to say. And that was another reason why Brooks had to say, "No."

"What's between you two?" Hope asked.

Good ole Hope always tried to figure out what wasn't being said. Ignoring Hope's valid question, Brooks addressed her own concerns. "Me? Run for governor? Of the state of California? This year?" She swallowed the tension in her throat. "I'm not so sure about that. My opponents are going to strip me naked." One of them already had. It was just that none of the girls knew she was sexing Governor Bailey Goodman.

"Better me than you," Storm replied. "I enjoy being naked. But seriously, Brooks, did you read Morgan's plan? It doesn't matter what they find, we'll have a trump card for their every move."

Storm, the daughter of an Asian family that assisted immigrants with gaining U.S. citizenship, stared at the folder as though it were a photo of her favorite thoroughbred horse. Her natural double-Ds made her a standout from most Asian women with considerably smaller breasts; her twins made her a highly sought-after bed partner for men of every ethnicity. Storm loved three things—her horses, sexing younger men, and helping disadvantaged people.

Hope opened her mouth and everyone stared in her direction. "Pause for a minute, Storm. I don't know what Brooks and Morgan are keeping from us but as long as it doesn't interfere with this agenda, it's fine for now. The plan is brilliant and will definitely work. Think about it, Brooks. How many female politicians have been accused of infidelity or caught cheating? Now, think about how many male politicians, from President Clinton to Arnold Schwarzenegger to John Edwards, to that governor that left his state unattended, and not to mention—heaven help him—that Weiner guy. You did watch *Celebrity Cheaters*, right? All of those men were publicly humiliated for their indiscretions."

"Exactly," Storm said. "Dicks are dumb. Pussies are," she purred like a kitten then said, "not."

Hope continued. "Good observation. With this plan, we don't even have to fuck your opponents—"

Storm interrupted, "Speak for yourself. Brooks's opponents that are assigned to me, I'm fucking them, videotaping the shit, taking pictures, and making sure I collect and preserve their DNA. Hair, semen, underwear, I want it all. There'll be no way they'll be able to deny the sex scandal. And if all else fails, crying rape is an option that never fails for a rich lady."

Storm claimed she'd never been in love, and that could explain her emotional detachment from men. Hope had been in love before, but not with the man she was currently dating.

"Minus the rape part, that's exactly the attitude we need," Hope said. "But we only go public with blackmail if Brooks's opponents refuse to do what we demand of them. Exposing them publicly will be our last resort. We'll force the weakest ones to drop out first. The strongest ones, we'll make sure they scale back on their campaigning. And Brooks darling, I'll write all of your campaign speeches for you."

Brooks frowned but she did like Hope's approach. But what if...?

Morgan looked at her. "Brooks? You in, babe?"

Maybe Morgan had a full-proof execution to make sure nothing backfired. Wasn't like Brooks was squeaky clean. She was human and had sexual needs to satisfy so she couldn't give up her secret lovers. The girls didn't need to know everything about her. No one did.

Hunching her shoulders, Brooks exhaled, nodded, then said, "Fine. Let's do it."

"Great!" Morgan danced to the mimosa bar, poured four glasses of champagne and handed each of the girls a flute. "A toast is definitely in order." She tipped her glass to Hope. "Ms. Andrews, would you like to do the honors?"

They gathered in a circle, stood near the window overlooking the indoor pool, then held their crystal flutes toward the clear blue sky.

"A toast to the Rich Girls' Club. When women come together, there's nothing men can do to divide us. Brooks, you will become the first female and first African-American governor of the state of California. We salute you, honey."

Brooks felt confident she'd do a better job of running the state than the current celebrity governor; he was currently preoccupied with getting his own reality TV show. Bailey Goodman was a different kind of politician, and he'd prove to be her biggest competitor for one reason. Californians loved celebs. Since voters weren't fed up with his spending most of his time in front of the camera instead of behind a desk making decisions in their best interests, the only way she could beat him would be to implement Morgan's plan.

Bailey was a movie star first and a governor somewhere down

the line. However, the bad decisions he'd made wouldn't be enough to stop voters from reelecting him. How would the Rich Girls frame Goodman without incriminating her? Hopefully Bailey had a few hidden sexcapades with other mistresses that would decrease his votes and allow his affair with her to remain a secret.

"Thanks for trusting me, ladies," Brooks finally said. "I pray I won't disappoint you."

She hoped she was right. She silently prayed to God that Morgan was discreet enough to make sure their sexual encounters remained sacred, and that she never found the one hidden skeleton in Brooks's closet that would not only destroy their friendship, but ultimately dissolve the Rich Girls' Club.

"Let's change the subject," Brooks insisted. "I want to hear what Storm did to the mayor."

Hope interrupted. "Not just yet. Morgan, I need to understand why we have to contribute two and a half million dollars each to implement this plan. Why aren't we using money from the Rich Girls' Club fund? We have more than enough and we might not need ten million to fund Brooks's campaign and blackmail her opponents. It's not like we won't get contributions."

"Let's table that discussion for our next meeting. Right now, I'm with Brooks." Morgan's smile beamed as she turned her back to Hope. Facing Storm, she said, "Tell us what happened and don't leave out any of the dirty details."

Brooks stood beside Hope. Why couldn't they use part of the twenty million dollars they had in investments?

CHAPTER 4

Hope

Hope drove along the Interstate with both hands on the steering wheel of her ruby red Porsche 911 GT2 RS. A visual of Storm inserting that dildo into the mayor's ass made her smile. Only Storm could get away with doing such a thing. Hope would never attempt that with her man. Stanley only liked three things near his asshole: water, soap and toilet tissue.

Hope focused on the road ahead as she commanded her car's Bluetooth. "Dial . . . Darius Jones."

She glanced in her rearview mirror. This was her third and final customer of the morning. As her own boss, Hope strived to end each workday by noon. The sports car she drove was one of eleven vehicles she owned, part of her customized auto collection that was valued at over five million dollars.

Darius answered, "What's up?"

"Hello, Mr. Jones. This is Hope. I'm approximately fifteen minutes away from your house, with an on-time delivery of the newest addition to your family."

Hope cruised at twenty miles an hour until she approached the street leading to her client's home. Slowing through the curvy mountain roadways, trees lined what would've been side-walks in a regular neighborhood. Darius' private road was not pedestrian-friendly.

The eighteen-wheeler trailed at a safe distance. What was inside the metal container was guaranteed to please any man, especially the man on the other end of the line.

"Damn, I didn't realize you were coming today. I thought we were scheduled for next week."

"What do you mean, you didn't realize I was coming today? I left you a message, sent you a text and an e-mail. But you're the customer and I stand by my 'satisfaction guaranteed' clause. What would you like me to do, Mr. Jones?"

Anytime a man forgot about a nearly half million-dollar purchase, he needed to donate more of his money to charity and spend less on expensive toys. Hope made a mental note to ask Darius for a healthy donation to Brooks's campaign fund, but timing was important and asking right now would be inappropriate. She'd mention it later on her follow-up call.

He laughed, then said, "Wait, son. Give me a minute, I'm on the phone. . . . Ms. Andrews, did you make sure all of my requests were met?"

"Absolutely. I personally verified all the upgrades on your Lamborghini Gallardo Superleggera are as you specified." He'd spent more money on customizing the car than the retail price of two-hundred and thirty-eight thousand dollars for the standard version of the vehicle.

"When you see the newest addition to your collection, you're going to be speechless for at least two minutes. She's metallic red. Hotter than fire. Fabulous, one of a kind, and all yours! I promise you, it'll be love at first sight." Hope increased the volume on the Bluetooth to magnify his excitement.

"Damn, I wish I was there. Gotta fly to Atlanta tomorrow for practice but I'm in D.C. right now with my son." He exhaled then said, "Long story."

Decreasing the volume, Hope tapped on her brakes. Great. Darius was over three thousand miles away from his house and he'd forgotten today was the scheduled delivery. Hope supposed parenting emergencies could've drastically changed his plans.

A child's voice whined. "Daddy!"

Hope quickly asked, "Okay, so is anybody home?"

"Son, please, stop. Look, my wife Fancy is at the house. I bought the car for her. It's a surprise."

Gently pressing the accelerator, Hope resumed her speed. "Well, with your permission, I can have the driver unload the car in the driveway, uncover it in front of your wife, and have her sign off on the paperwork." Hope said, crossing her fingers. It was his purchase and she needed his blessing. Either way, she was departing for San Francisco today, but delaying the delivery would mean she'd have to return from San Francisco earlier than scheduled.

"Daddy, get off the phone!"

"My man, give me a few more minutes. I'm almost done. . . . That sounds good, Ms. Andrews."

Quietly, Hope exhaled. "Great. Now, remember. No sales are final with Andrews Luxury Concierge. If for any reason you're not completely satisfied, you can return the car, no questions asked." Hope said with a cheerful chuckle. "Call me after your wife takes you for a ride." Oh, damn. That didn't come out right.

"Thanks. I gotta go."

"You're welcome. Bye," Hope said, then waited for Darius to end the call.

Damn. Of all her clients that would've found that statement amusing, he was not the one. She was fortunate Darius didn't cancel his purchase right then and there. Every woman wanted him, and she didn't want Darius to think she was coming on to him. The media was always right there to slander his name, but they couldn't dispute Darius' talent on the basketball court. As a starter for Atlanta, he had a house in Georgia, but considered LA his home.

Soon, Hope was ready to get on with her last delivery so she could meet up with Stanley. She had plans to ride her man's dick in celebration of another lucrative day. Though she was currently in the middle of a rush, Hope's business wasn't usually demanding. Ever since she was a little girl her father's fast cars had excited her. Over time her dad had taught her everything he knew, and now she was more knowledgeable than he was about cars. She had turned her knowledge into a profitable business.

Owning a door-to-door automobile service for multimillionaires granted her access to invitation-only celebrity events. Between the gamblers, ballers, politicians, family members, and friends, she never had to solicit for business. Her company thrived on referrals.

For instance, the athletes she serviced loved competition. Hope was sure that once Fancy's girlfriends saw her car they'd have their husbands call with even more expensive requests. Rich people, especially those living the Hollywood lifestyle with seven-, eight-, and nine-figure checks rolling in, had egos bigger than their bank accounts. They wanted everything either done to or for them.

Hope laughed at another flashback of what Storm had done to the mayor. He probably had a cushion in his chair right now.

Poor thing might not be able to comfortably sit down for a week. Fortunately for him, he had an assistant to run his errands.

From personal shoppers to caterers to gardeners to masseuses or fitness trainers, the one thing wealthy folks did not want was to be inconvenienced. For Hope, the key to her success was constantly learning all she could about expensive automobiles, especially the newest models. Knowing more than most men about the Ferrari 599 GTB Fiarano, the Mercedes-Benz SLR McLaren, and the Buggati Veyron made her the envy of many girlfriends and wives.

Now that her work was done, the paperwork signed, her ten percent commission check in her purse, Hope headed to the London Hotel for some afternoon delight on the rooftop with her number one man Stanley Perkins.

After sexing Stanley, she was off for a trip to the Bay Area to meet with the top Republican candidate, Johnathon Waters, about supporting his campaign. According to Morgan's plan, Brooks's opponents had to be blackmailed before Brooks made her announcement to run in late March. Starting with Hope's meeting with Johnathon, the Rich Girls had exactly two months to frame all the candidates. Offering hefty financial contributions was their bait. What politician would turn down a million dollars?

Once Hope was done with Johnathon, she would meet with Laura Littleton in Sacramento to hand her a check. Since Laura had a wife instead of a husband, she might prove to be the most difficult opponent to set up.

Who really cared about a woman cheating on a woman? Or a woman cheating on a man? Hope would have to create a different kind of scandal to tarnish Laura's image.

Hope's heels clicked along the marble tiles as she strolled into the hotel's entrance. She stopped at the front desk, reserved a suite, got her room key, then headed for the rooftop.

Stanley greeted her with a juicy kiss that made her pussy pucker. Didn't take much for him to excite her. She loved the way Stanley made her feel.

He was six-two with almost flat abs and a dazzling smile with nearly straight teeth. The fullness of his chest pressed hard against her cleavage, making her nipples harden.

"Hey, babe. It's so good to see you." He sniffed her hair. "Wow, the way you smell drives me crazy. How are you? You all set for our trip to Paris next week?" he asked in a charming, articulate manner. Pulling out her chair, he continued, "We're overdue for this vacation."

Stanley was the whitest black man she'd ever met. In fact, when she'd initially met him over the phone, she thought he was white. He worked for the Passport Agency in Los Angeles but what had impressed her most was that he was the boss and he personally serviced all her needs.

Oh, damn. After Morgan announced the plan, Hope had forgotten about their trip and how much money he'd spent. It had taken him six months to save up for her all-expenses-paid birthday gift. Exhaling, Hope slid her sunglasses atop her head and placed her purse on the empty chair between them.

"Baby, I'm really sorry but I can't go. I just found out that I have to help my father with a huge project. He's planning to open another casino," she lied. "I'm not sure exactly how long it's going to take but . . . it'll be at least twelve months before I can leave the country." By then the election would be over, Brooks would be sworn in, and Hope would *need* a vacation in Paris.

"What!" he shouted. "Do you have any—?"

"Lower your voice; you're embarrassing me. Yes, I do know,

baby, but it's not like we won't still go to Paris. I just can't go next week or next month. Reschedule it for this time next year, baby."

Stanley slumped in his seat, staring her in the eyes. "Hope, I can tell you're being dishonest. Share the truth with me, baby. What are you up to?"

Hope shook her head, slid her sunglasses over her eyes. "I've told you as much as I can. I can't discuss the details of my dad's plans but," she paused then motioned for the waiter. "We'll order room service."

"Baby, let's go," Hope said, leading the way. "I don't want to talk. I need to feel you inside me." They stepped onto the elevator, and she pressed the button for their floor. Like most men, Stanley could be distracted with sex. A temporary detour from the conversation was all she wanted right now.

Soon as the doors opened Hope marched ahead of Stanley. Her eyes rolled left to right.

"I'm sure your dad will understand my side. Tell your dad we'll be back in three weeks. I've planned this vacation for—"

"I know," Hope interrupted, unlocking the door. During the three years she'd dated Stanley he'd met her dad three times, and truthfully he'd possibly never meet him again. She believed women, like men, shouldn't welcome their mates into their family circle unless they were sure he was the one.

The suite was large enough to comfortably accommodate four people. She had exactly three hours to eat lunch, devour Stanley, and make it to LAX for her flight to SFO. She mixed two vodka and cranberry cocktails from the minibar.

Stanley took a huge gulp of his drink. "So are you going to tell me the truth or not? You want me to call your dad? I insist we go to France as originally planned."

She thought it was cute how Stanley was trying to take charge. "You go. Take your mom. But I'm not going and I can't discuss the details. You can't speak with my father, so please just let it go and take off your clothes," Hope said, removing her canary wraparound dress. She hung it in the closet and joined Stanley on the sofa in the living area.

His hand caressed the side of her face. He trailed his tense finger from her temple to her cheek.

Hope turned her face, sucked his finger into her mouth. Slowly her lips slid up to his knuckles. She tightened her jaws for him, clenched her pussy for herself. "Mmm."

Stanley bit her nipple through her lace bra, squeezed her breasts together, then bit the other nipple. "These are the most perfect breasts I've ever seen. And they're all mine." His laugh was hearty, possessive. There was no need to tell him otherwise.

Whispering in his ear, Hope said, "Take my bra and thong off, then suck my nipples until I cum."

One unsnap in the front and her bra was released. He tossed it on the arm of the couch then eased her thong from between her cheeks. He placed it near her bra.

She straddled him, jiggled her titties in his face, then fed her man ... one fifty-cent piece-sized areola at a time. She swore he knew a silent language that spoke to every part her body.

"Ah, yes. Right there. Right there. Yes," she exhaled, grinding her pussy along his hard shaft.

Stanley was so hard it felt like she was riding a piece of steel. She fed him her other nipple.

"Bite it, baby," she said, leaning her head back. "Ah, yes. Like that. Mama can hold this titty for you." She shoved as much of her breast as she could into his mouth then moaned in his ear. "I want you to take your dick, put it inside me, and give me every inch of you." Exhaling, she continued, "Don't stop until you feel your nuts touch my lips."

When she felt his head press against her opening, she whispered, "Go slow, daddy. Penetrate me slow...and deep. I want to feel all of this good dick."

Stanley did as she asked. When she felt his bulging head part her inner lips, her juices flowed.

"Right there, baby. Pause right there for me," she moaned. "Now suck my nipple and let me do the work."

Hope lowered her hips onto his dick then rose to his head and stopped. She kneeled over him. "Bite me, baby. Now," she pleaded as more juices flowed.

"Get up," Stanley said. "I've got to get this sweetness from behind."

She was ready for whatever he wanted. Vaginal. Anal. Whatever. She knelt on the sofa, then braced herself across the back. Her titties rested over the edge. Massaging her breasts she looked over her shoulder at him.

He stared into her eyes, spread her butt cheeks wide, licked his fingers, then rubbed her pussy. Licking his fingers again, he strummed her clit like the strings on a guitar.

"You ready for this cock?"

"I stay ready for you, baby," she said.

"You don't sound like you're ready for me. I'm going to ask you again." *Smack!* His hand tapped her ass. "Are you ready for your man's cock?"

Hope grunted. "Fuck me, dammit! I'm ready to cum again."

Stanley slid his dick up and down her pussy. Hope tried to align his head with her opening then pushed back onto him but he pulled away.

"Keep still. You've controlled enough. I'm in charge of this."

As he said the word "this", he slid his manhood deep inside her. "You already screwed up my birthday gift to you. Don't mess this up, too."

Hope's head fell back. She squeezed her nipples and smiled as Stanley pounded her with the pleasure she could never get enough of. Maybe she should piss him off more often. With one hand pinching her nipple, she slid her other hand between her legs and massaged her clit.

"Where you want this cum?" he asked. "I should release myself all over your face."

When Stanley asked, Hope leaned her hips against the edge of the sofa. She tried to move fast enough to eject his shaft, but Stanley leaned with her, shoving his dick deeper. Then he leaned back a little and inserted his finger in her asshole.

Her fluids gushed into the sofa's cushion. "Oh my god," she screamed.

Forcing his dick and finger deeper, Stanley pressed his palm into the small of her back. "That's it, baby. Let yourself go. You know I love it when you squirt for me." He pulled out of both holes at the same time. "Suck me."

Hope sat on the edge of the wet sofa and opened her mouth wide. Aiming the eye toward her throat, Stanley moved his hips. She sucked him until the remaining sweet cum spilled into her mouth. She licked her lips, then kissed his head.

Stanley sat on the sofa beside her. He spread his thighs wide. His dick stood high like an eighteen-year-old's that couldn't lose an erection. "You know what time it is," he said.

Indeed she did. Stanley loved having multiple orgasms. Hope squatted on his shaft and bounced. This was the beginning of what would soon become a non-stop fucking session until she came all over him again.

CHAPTER 5

Storm

Seven days had passed since Hope's visit to San Francisco. She'd made contact with Johnathon but with no concrete plan for Laura, she'd decided to postpone their face-to-face. The girls had nine weeks left to secure proof and present evidence that none of the other candidates were worthy of being governor. But the plan had to be flawless, making sure none of them appeared attached to any of the scandals.

Everyone was happy that Hope had made a strong initial connection with Republican Johnathon Waters. Payment had been promised to him but had not yet been delivered. The exchange, of his being blackmailed and his receiving money, had to happen simultaneously.

Each politician on the Rich Girls' list would receive the same amount but each would have a different price to pay. The Girls had agreed to donate—make that *invest*—a million dollars to Johnathon and Laura's campaigns. These contributions would not be in their club's name, not in Hope's company name, but in Hope's father's business' name. Morgan had explained it would be best to seem to draw from larger resources, knowing Brooks's opponents might eventually trace the funds.

Storm was excited for Hope's success and couldn't wait to start having fun with her own targeted men. Later this month Storm was having her meetings with Randall "Randy" Wallace and Anthony "Tony" Dennison. She predicted Randy would be the easier to frame, with his crooked cynical smile, seedy eyes, and dingy beige hair. It wouldn't surprise her if he was the kind of guy who sex texted and sent photos of his manhood to women he'd fucked, believing he'd never get caught with his pants down.

Storm figured that like a jack-in-the-box, there'd eventually be one girl too many and Randy's dick pics would pop-up online. Storm had a few favors she could count on from members of the women's club in Beverly Hills that would help her to bury Randy and Tony deeper in scandal.

Even if Storm misjudged Randy, she was convinced that once he saw her perky identical twins Joy and Pleasure, he'd eagerly want to slide his dick between her breasts. She probably wouldn't have to suck Randy's dick or ride him hard, but given the chance she'd definitely want to make him scream like a bitch.

Enough dwelling on Randy. Storm interlocked her fingers with Chancelor's as they strolled the open green fields behind her home. A wooden log fence bordered the perimeter to keep her animals from roaming off the property. A few of her horses trotted alongside one another. Owners paid upward of a hundred thousand dollars for her stallions to stud their mares, in hopes of producing the next Derby winner. Even if a horse placed fourth in that race, the owner would break even, but $1.24 million plus the gold trophy awaited the first-place winner. Storm's horses had cashed in on first-place six times before she'd retired them.

Now, Storm yelled out to her caretaker, "Take excellent care of my babies!"

"Indeed, Ms. Dangerfield. These are my babies, too!" he responded.

According to the plan, the outdoor help was permitted to stay, but Storm needed someone to at least clean her bathrooms. It would be degrading to ask her lover but if he truly cared for her she could persuade him tidy up the toilets.

High noon had her spirit warmer than the seventy-degree fresh air and California sunshine greeting their bodies. She kissed the back of Chancelor's hand.

"Baby, where do you see yourself in, say, two years?" she asked him.

His loose-fitted blue jeans hung well below his slender waist-line, clinging to his pelvis. His dark pubic hairs, generously exposed, made her pussy twitch with the anticipation of having him sex her.

Making love with Chancelor was incredible. His stamina, eagerness to learn, willingness to please, and faithfulness were unmatched by any of her older suitors, like Mr. Mayor. But how long could her fantasy romance with a younger man last?

Scooping her into his arms, he twirled her around. "I see myself with you forever."

Forever? That's a long time.

"Eventually I'll live here full-time instead of sometimes. Of course I'll make a respectable woman out of you as your husband," he said with a smile brighter than the rays beaming down on them.

"Put me down, Chancelor."

Comments like the ones he'd just made reminded Storm of their age difference. They'd been together for three years but Chancelor Beaver wasn't her future. He was too young. Besides, neither Chancelor nor any other man could make her what she already was.

He was going to make a respectable woman out of her? Really? Was that how he saw it? All that she had accomplished didn't seem to mean anything to him until she carried his last name. What did having his last name mean to her?

Why did men think women were desperate to wear their ring, birth their babies, and carry their last names? Maybe that was true for other women, but not for Storm. Getting hitched was easier than picking out a pair of designer shoes. To her, marriage was overrated and definitely undervalued by almost every man that said "I do." As far as she was concerned, not many couples, wedded or not, seemed truly happy in their relationships.

Rich girls deserved to have boy toys, sports cars, vacation homes, and the same finer things that wealthy men possessed. Whatever a woman earned she'd worked harder than a man to get. Even if that woman was a gold digger, she had to do more than a gigolo.

Unlike men with money, women with it knew how to appreciate what they acquired. For men, their acquisitions, including women and property, were constant ego boosters. Stroke a man's ego; watch him thrive. Starve his ego; see his enthusiasm—and his dick—become flaccid.

"Think about what I ask and tell me next time we see one other," she told him. "It's time you start thinking about your, not our, future. If you want to go to grad school, I'll pay for that, too."

Chancelor's hazel eyes stared at her then his gaze darted in the direction of one of her horses that galloped by. He nodded. Exhaled. "You're right. I don't want to live my life without you but I do need to have a life of my own. I should take advantage of your offer to continue to pay for my education. I mean, I can't afford to pay for college or keep accompanying you to events and not have the ability to hold intellectually stimulating conversations with your peers. I mean, I need to represent you the same way you make me shine. Physically, I know I'm that man. Mentally, I can hold my own. Financially, I don't measure up. Maybe I'll go to law school. That way I can represent you if anyone tries to take advantage of you."

That won't happen in either of our lifetimes. Storm didn't understand why accomplished women allowed their husbands or even their newly found men to manage their money or their careers. Then, when their men started fucking other women they'd hired with their woman's money, the fiancées and wives felt betrayed. How many men allowed their wives or women to manage them? Not many.

"Law school is a great choice for you, Chancelor. You're handsome, tall, and with the right firm and mentors, you'll do well," Storm said, then pressed her lips to the back of his hand and held them there. "Remember this: a man doesn't become a man until he can support himself, respect himself, and love himself."

They'd strolled far enough from the caretaker to enjoy one another outdoors. Lowering Chancelor's arm, she knelt before him, then kissed each of his fingertips. Resting his hand by his hip, Storm slowly unzipped his denims and removed his pants. Then she eased his beautiful dick in and out of her mouth.

"Whose dick is this?" she asked, sucking him slowly.

Chancelor stared down at her. His soft, gentle gaze penetrated hers as she looked up at him. "Why madam, this dick is yours any time you want it," he said, swinging his hips side-to-side. The left and right parts of his head slapped his stomach. "Any way you want this, I'll give it to you real good. You do so much for me. Tell me, Storm. What can I do to please you?" he asked, roaming his fingers through her hair.

She stood, removed her clothes as she motioned for him to kneel before her. His tender lips caressed her outer labia as his tongue explored her inner walls, teasing up one side then down the other. The tip of his tongue swept her clit and wiggled along her shaft.

She grabbed two fistfuls of his curls, jerked his head back. He resisted and found his way back to her pearl. This time he sucked harder. His middle finger slid deep inside her pussy then furiously fondled her G-spot.

"Oh my gosh, Chancelor, stop it. You're about to make me gush all over you. I don't want to . . . aw damn! I can't hold back. Fuck you, Chancelor."

Sucking her clit and stroking her spot, he steadied the rhythm and pressure.

Storm held her breasts. Teased her nipples. "Oh, god! Yes, right there. Right there," she moaned as fluids ejected from her urethra, showering his face.

Chancelor rubbed his eyes then stretched his body on the lawn. He held his dick in his hand. "You know what I want you to do," he said, then smiled wide.

Indeed she did. It was time for her to pony up. She became his jockey and he was her stallion.

CHAPTER 6

Morgan

E very girl has got a secret.

Watching her husband sleep, Morgan struggled to rid herself of her guilt. If she woke Magnum and told him part of the truth, she could peacefully close her eyes.

Which was hardest? Telling her husband about the plan, telling the Rich Girls she'd made a few terrible investments, or telling her husband for the first time in their marriage she was going to sex another man? Or was it best not to tell him or the girls anything?

Quietly exhaling, Morgan couldn't believe she was going to let the incumbent, Bailey Goodman, penetrate her sexually. It definitely would not be raw. Infidelity was one thing. Not protecting her husband and herself was incomprehensible. Storm could've taken Bailey on as a third client, but Morgan was committed to the girls and felt she had to do her part, too.

The current governor was Brooks's strongest opponent, but he wouldn't be for long. To ensure he was not reelected, Morgan planned to take their sexual encounter all the way and collect lots of his sperm from the condom for an undeniable DNA match.

She felt sorry for her husband. Poor guy was clueless. Thankfully he was still asleep.

Two weeks into the plan, Magnum still didn't know what was happening around him, in his home, or what was going to take place in his bed. Revealing the details to her husband could destroy all the Rich Girls had accomplished thus far. Then again, not disclosing the details to her husband could end her marriage. She had eight weeks left to come up with something before the announcement.

Giving herself most of the credit, Morgan was pleased with the girls' progress. Storm had scheduled lunch with Randall. Hope's brunch date with Johnathon was finally on the calendar. And Morgan had made certain that Brooks had direct access to the best advisors on health care, education, immigration, and environmental issues. Their allies would be the members of the women's club in Beverly Hills. While they didn't know the details of the Rich Girls' devious plan, each member of BH, including the president, would most likely support Brooks.

If Morgan creatively managed Brooks's political contributions, the Rich Girls' investment fund could recover from her stupid mistake without any of them knowing she'd lost the entire twenty million dollars.

Hope had prioritized the agenda for Brooks's campaign and Storm was documenting the long list of promises the incumbent had made before the last election but still hadn't accomplished.

"Morning, beautiful," Magnum said, rolling over facing her.

Morgan leaned toward him then kissed her husband. "Morning, handsome. What's on your schedule for today?"

He smiled. "Golfing, golfing, and more—"

Morgan interrupted, "And more golfing with the fellas. That's great honey...hmm."

"Hmm what?" he said, raising a brow.

The thoughts in her head had translated into a *hmm* not intended for her husband to hear. Morgan braced her back against the headboard. She couldn't tell him everything at once. Magnum would become outraged.

She'd once watched him pick up a floor lamp and slam it into their television, then punch the wall until his knuckles bled, when she'd told him they'd lost their first and only unborn child. After her dilation and curettage procedure, he claimed he never wanted kids because he didn't know what he'd do if he lost another one. To keep his word, against her desire, her husband had a vasectomy.

If she had decided to abort their baby or have her tubes tied without consulting him, he probably would've never forgiven her or worse, divorced her. But his decision to terminate the possibility of their ever starting a family of their own was no big deal for him.

"Well, I want to run something by you," she said, pulling the sheet over her legs.

Morgan couldn't afford to take a chance on getting pregnant when she fucked the governor. What if the condom broke? Birth control pills might take too long to work. An IUD might slip out while having sex with her husband. The Plan B pill was not her Plan A but it was an option.

Magnum propped himself beside her. He shoved two king-sized pillows behind his back. "Shoot, babe."

Strumming the soft hairs on his chest, Morgan exhaled, then looked into his eyes.

"Wow, this is serious. Just give it to me straight. If it's bad news, tell me after I get back from golfing. Don't want to hit balls while I'm angry."

Exhaling again, Morgan said, "I think you should know that Brooks is going to run for governor."

Magnum belted with laughter and whacked Morgan with a pillow. He leaned forward, held his stomach, and continued laughing in her face. "Governor of what?" he asked, as if there was more than one position.

"California, honey. I'm serious. This is not a joke."

"Depends on who you ask." Magnum leaned back, stretched his neck to one side then the other. Sternly he said, "If you're serious, Brooks can't do that. That's a horrible idea. I mean, who would vote for an unmarried woman to run any state? The Rich Girls have accomplished a lot of great things with the women of Beverly Hills. Stick with helping immigrants, rebuilding schools, and teaching young girls how to become women. Babe, there's never been an African-American or female governor of California and that's the way it should stay. Whose stupid idea was this? Hope's, I bet."

"Have you looked in the mirror lately? You're black! Why would you say something ignorant like that?"

"Yes, I'm black, but I'm a man. I didn't mean a black man shouldn't become governor. In fact, I'm voting for Anthony Dennison. In case you haven't noticed, he's black. If Brooks were a man I'd agree with you, but this entire idea is preposterous. It's plain stupid, babe," he said, shaking his head.

Morgan countered. "It's not stupid. And if the governor was a man of his word, where is all the lottery money that the state is supposed to get? Certainly not in the public schools that we financially support."

"Oh, so it was your idea. You should've consulted with me first. Squash it, babe," he said, kissing her cheek. "End of discussion."

Morgan was so angry she was close to telling her husband everything. She wanted to piss him off the way he'd done her. "Like it or not, we have a foolproof plan. Trust me. Brooks is going to win. Besides, it's time for California to give a female the chance to pull this state out of the financial pit these men keep digging."

Magnum peeled back the sheet, revealing his erection. "End of discussion, babe. Let it go. But seeing you upset has made me horny as hell. Let me boar a hole so deep in your pussy that when you regain consciousness you'll have forgotten all about this ludicrous idea of yours."

Although she didn't agree with her husband's opposition to Brooks's candidacy, she needed to fuck off her frustrations. Morgan turned over, braced herself on her hands and knees, then glanced over her shoulder. Her husband hadn't changed her mind but she could use a nice orgasm to replace her frown with a smile.

"Since you're acting like a dog, hump this pussy from behind. And I want you to bark the entire time," she told him.

Being that her husband was an Omega, barking was second nature to him, just like stomping. Fucking lots of women had been part of his DNA until she'd tamed and trained him not to roam.

Magnum leaned his head back and howled, "Ow...ah-ruff, ruff, ruff." He growled a gurgling sound slow and deep in his throat, then released another, "Ruff!"

Spreading her cheeks, he repeatedly spanked her clit. *Slap!* His hand landed on her ass. "Get out the bed. I want you on the floor," he commanded.

She obeyed, crawled away from him. "Come get this pussy. Give me that big beautiful dick," she demanded. The only thing she loved more than his gorgeous chocolate cock inside her vanilla vagina was a clit in her mouth.

Magnum held her hips then slid all the way inside her. His thrusting started immediately. The crown of her head bobbed across the floor until it banged against the wall.

She didn't need anything to add to the headache he'd already given her. She pushed on his dick, slamming her pussy against her husband's balls, backing him up. There was nothing she wouldn't do with or for Magnum.

Slap. His hand landed on her ass again. Her butt stung with pleasure. "Can I have some of this sweet ass, baby?"

Morgan crawled to the nightstand drawer and handed him the anal lube. Anal sex was the one thing she wouldn't allow Goodman to do to her. That would remain reserved for her husband.

Once a woman granted a man access to fuck her in the ass, their connection became stronger. Most women, especially black women, were anal virgins. Giving up their anal virginity to a man opened a door that no man had entered before. Morgan hadn't been an anal virgin with Magnum but she'd lied and told him she was the first time she'd let him in. Unlike with the vagina, unless a woman had anal sex frequently, men couldn't tell because there was no tissue to break through, like a woman's hymen. If a man broke tissue during anal sex, he was an amateur and the woman should never let him fuck her again.

"You can put that beautiful cock wherever you'd like, handsome."

CHAPTER 7

Brooks

*S*ituations are going to get complicated real fast...if I can't cover my ass!

Three weeks had passed since Morgan had revealed her plan in early January. Only seven weeks remained before Brooks had to go public with her candidacy in late March.

The closer it came to Brooks making her announcement to enter the race, the more she thought about the people she'd randomly sexed over the past twelve months. She'd had more one-night stands than she could remember. And they were meant to be that way—buried in the back of her mind. She didn't care to see those men again. For Brooks, sometimes it just seemed best to sex married men. She doubted any of them would jeopardize their relationships to slander her.

The more she told herself, "Think like a dick. Keep your emotions out of the race," the more she worried about being the primary candidate exposed.

Her broke and broken down ex-husband, along with the media, could prove to become her worst enemies. Brooks sat in her home office all morning and afternoon carefully studying each document before her. Information began taking longer to digest than it should. She found herself re-reading the same sentences but nothing registered. Removing her glasses, she rubbed her eyes. Her hands flopped to her lap.

She'd barely slept last night, and tonight would be the same if she didn't uninvite her married lover, who was in town on business. But with her mounting stress, she needed his stiff dick deep inside her to release her endorphins.

They'd been sexing one another going on two years. No one knew but them. Brooks liked their secret affair. He provided the companionship she needed and she gave him the orgasmic pleasure his wife didn't.

Pussy was a terrible thing to waste. A week without seeing one of her lovers was too long. She enjoyed this man because he knew all of her erogenous zones. He could make her cum just by sucking her fingers or licking her toes. But how could she continue seeing him for the next nine months, until Election Day, without her other opponents finding out? Worse, how could she keep the girls from discovering she was doing him?

The cup of coffee on her desk was cold. Brooks stumbled to the kitchen to brew a fresh pot. She'd seen commercials and propaganda gone wrong. If that should happen to her, by the time they aired there wouldn't be anything to do except fight back in self-defense then pray the voters believed her. Starting a fight was much better than defending herself.

Maybe she should rethink that. Obama never started a nasty debate but he always finished the strongest. Perhaps finishing strong should be her approach.

Grinding Columbian beans, she envisioned her opponents, and frail seniors with walkers and wheelchairs outside her mansion holding signs that read, "Kennedy claims she's for healthcare but voted against hospitalization for the uninsured elderly." Brooks knew what she'd really voted against was the hospitals' practice of double-billing the elderly's private providers and Medicare. Hospitals collected money from seniors' healthcare plans and those institutions were charging Medicare for the same services and getting away with it.

The "what ifs" cluttering her mind about pharmaceutical drugs versus the legalization of medical marijuana were exhausting. While Hope, Storm, and Morgan slept peacefully, she hadn't gotten a good night's rest since she'd agreed to run for governor. Brooks prayed she could keep her eyes open while making her press announcement two months from now with Morgan standing by her side. Then she'd have to keep moving until she crossed the finish line in November.

Her cell phone rang. She closed the bag of coffee beans, set the package on the counter. Dragging her feet back to her office, she saw on the caller-ID that it was Morgan.

"Hey," she exhaled, sitting on the edge of her desk.

"Hey, Brooks, sweetie, I'm calling to check on you. How are you doing, honey?"

"Tired. Managing."

"Did Bo deliver your lunch and dinner? He said he would do me that personal favor."

Brooks was too tired to eat, too hungry to sleep, but if Bo had licked her pussy before his handsome behind left she'd be horizontal. If she'd had a few vitamin B-Complex tablets in her system she would've had enough energy to devour Bo. But none of the girls drooled over Bo because he was the cook and no matter how sexy he was, the Rich Girls didn't fuck the help.

Maybe Morgan's enthusiasm could revive her. "Yes, and

thanks but I haven't eaten any of it yet. I was just about to take a break. You want to come over?"

Damn, she really was tired. Why did she ask Morgan that? Morgan couldn't come over. If her lover arrived while Morgan was there, Morgan would cancel her brilliant plan. Maybe that wasn't a bad idea. Then Brooks could resume a normal life without being subjected to having others judge her.

"I'd love to come but I'm headed to Sacramento. I can't wait to get my foot in Goodman's door before I put it up his ass. I have a meeting with his assistant tomorrow." Morgan sounded refreshed, chipper. Her excitement drained Brooks even more.

Brooks knew Morgan was meeting with Goodman tomorrow but Brooks was more concerned with wrapping her legs and locking her feet around Goodman's sexy white ass tonight. She was Bailey's lover, but it was best if Morgan did the dirty work. If Brooks exposed Bailey, her confession would admit to their double affair and give the other party an advantage.

"You can do this, honey. Everything is on track. Hang in there. I'll book you a two-hour massage with my personal masseuse, Nathaniel Brown, when I get back. He'll come to you. He's the absolute best. All the celebrities hire him. I'll check on you later sweetie. Bye."

That was what Brooks needed: to marry a massage therapist. That way she could have all her physical needs met by one man.

Sighing heavily, Brooks ended the call. "Now, where was I? Oh, yeah. That's right. Coffee. No . . . food," she mumbled, stumbling back to the kitchen.

She stood at the marbled island in the middle of the floor, opened the vegetable tray, and began eating her first piece of food for the day, a carrot stick. The dark blue island, that doubled as a wet bar, was the main place where the girls gathered when they were at her home. Four plush chocolate-colored swivel barstools lined the sides, two on each. Unlike at Morgan's place, not much cooking happened in Brooks's kitchen.

Her doorbell rang. *Can't be.* "Don't tell me he's early?" Brooks looked at the time on her cell: 4:00 p.m.

Hurrying to her office, she closed the door then rushed to the living room. She entered the foyer, and peeped through the view hole. Yep, he was early. She knew she looked a hot mess but when she sniffed under her armpit—"damn"—she smelled like sour milk. If she didn't know him so well, she would've walked away and pretended she wasn't home.

Opening the door, she asked, "Why didn't you call first? I need to shower. Don't get too close," She dodged his kiss. "You should've called or at least texted me . . . something."

"I apologize, sweetheart. My meeting ended early so I thought I'd surprise you," he said, handing her a bouquet of red roses. "Are you going to move so I can come in?"

She stepped aside. "Yes. Of course. Come in. Make yourself comfortable in the bedroom. I'm going to take a bath right now," she said, closing the door behind him.

Passing by her office, Brooks pulled the handle to make certain the door was completely closed. She made a mental note to have a lock installed as soon as possible.

"I've never seen you look this tired," he said, following her. "Are you okay? Maybe you need to get your thyroid checked."

Thyroid . . . right. What did he know or care about her thyroid?

"Maybe you're right. I'll have my thyroid checked out," she agreed in order to pacify him. It was best not to tell him why she was exhausted. Now wasn't the right time.

Seeing him made her realize he was exactly what she needed.

His silver hair had a hint of pepper sprinkled throughout. He was twenty years older than she was but his sixty-five-year-old body could compete with any fifty-year-old's. The golden tone of his smooth skin and his perfect Hollywood veneers could've easily allowed him to star in *An Officer and A Gentleman*. Now he could double for Richard Gere in *The Double*. Bailey Goodman was probably every woman's fantasy.

Brooks headed to the bathroom, turned on the hot and cold water to her spa tub, removed her clothes, then quickly tossed them in the hamper. Generously she added lavender crystals. Covering her hair with a plastic cap, she folded a bath towel in half, then rolled it up. Settling in the tub she leaned her neck against the towel and closed her eyes.

Her body struggled to relax in the warm water as she inhaled the calming fragrance bursting from the bubbles. She was stiff, feeling like her weight was sinking to the bottom of the rose-colored porcelain. For the first time today she noticed how much her muscles ached from countless hours of sitting in the same position.

Suddenly, she felt his gentle touch. His hand slid between her breasts, over her navel and pubic hairs, then between her thighs. He pressed a finger against her clit and held it there.

She opened her eyes long enough to see him sitting on the edge of the tub. He whispered, "Relax. Let go of all the stress. I've got you. That's why I'm here."

She inhaled deeply, her eyes closed, and she allowed her head, toes, and every part of her body in between to submit to his touch as she slowly inhaled then exhaled. Why couldn't her ex-husband have been this attentive before they'd separated?

Was he still living with his mistress, now his forty-something girlfriend? If he were, she could hardly consider the woman

a mistress at this point. But if he weren't, for all she knew...
Brooks's eyelids flashed upward. "That's it!"

"What's 'it'? You okay?" Bailey asked.

Brooks closed her eyes without answering then exhaled a sigh of relief.

When her ex-husband had left her twenty years ago, Brooks had never mentioned him again, but there were times she'd thought about him. Back then, when they'd stood at the altar, they were both young, barely twenty-one. Neither of them had known much about being married. But now, if they could somehow re-marry before the election, Brooks thought she could win the hearts and votes of hopeless romantics.

"Mmm, that feels so good," she moaned to let her lover know he was stroking her nicely.

Having been cheated on during her marriage, Brooks knew how horrible that felt. Based on the numerous stories she'd heard at her coffee shop, Brooks knew how other women shared her pain of infidelity. Many of them, despite being cheated on, wanted to reunite with their husbands or boyfriends. Forgiving her ex would encourage other women to do the same and possibly win her votes as long as the ladies never found out she was also a potential home wrecker.

Sexing another woman's husband for sexual gratification was wrong. Period. But now she understood how easily affairs happened when neither person exercised control. Brooks wondered if Bailey pleased his wife at all.

"You want me to go faster or slower?" he asked.

"A little slower would be nice."

The first notch of his finger penetrated her opening ever so gently. He paused, allowing her to relax. Her libido spiked. A small fluttering orgasm stimulated the lining of her uterus. She inhaled again. No matter what he did to her, it always felt so right and something that felt so right couldn't be totally wrong. If she were his wife, would he be stroking someone else? Should she tell him now?

What she had to say would ruin not only the moment but definitely terminate their relationship. Brooks wondered if there would be a way for them to remain lovers after she'd claimed his seat.

His middle finger eased all the way inside her pussy, pressing upward against her G-spot. He held his finger there. She squirmed, lowering her hips, then moaned with pleasure.

"That's it. Let it go," he whispered. Leaning forward he kissed her ear.

The sensation of his lips to her earlobe made her cum again. She knew she had to tell him the news before the press conference but now wasn't a good time. She stepped out of the tub. Dripping wet, she led him to her bed. His dick had to finish what his finger had started.

She imagined the conversation going something like, "Bailey, I need to tell you that I'm going to be your opponent. I'm running for governor and I'm going to win."

Perhaps he'd respond, "Is this some sort of a joke? You can't be serious."

She'd have to tell him at some point, "I am serious. Dead serious."

Whenever that confession happened, it would kill more than his career.

CHAPTER 8

Hope

Next to Manhattan, San Francisco was Hope's favorite city, ranking above Chicago and Atlanta. What she liked most about southern California was the weather. Temperatures were warm enough to enjoy year-round tanning by her pool. The only downside was that it was seldom cold enough to wear any of her mink coats. Yet out of all the places she'd traveled, the only area she comfortably called home was Los Angeles.

Today, things were strategically in place and she didn't have to fly to meet him. He'd come to her town. Brooks's big announcement was six weeks away, and what Hope had to accomplish didn't require clothing or a trip outdoors. If she were meeting Stanley, all she would've worn was a mink and her stilettos.

But she wasn't meeting Stanley.

Hope roamed her luxury suite at the Beverly Hills Hotel, checking each of the hidden cameras she'd placed in the living, bed, and bathroom areas. BHH was her number one choice for many reasons: the décor and exterior were her favorite color, pink. The five-star accommodations were available for those who could afford it. Celebrity sightings were common at the hotel, although that didn't mean much to her. Hell, she had more money than most celebs she knew.

"It's show time," Hope said, jiggling her perky titties in the mirror. Instantly her nipples became erect. Now all she had to do was get Johnathon back to her room after their luncheon and fuck him senseless.

Her cell phone rang, reminding her to power it off later. But before she did, she answered, "Hey, Stanley. No, I haven't changed my mind about rescheduling the vacation any time soon."

"But I postponed Paris just for you. When are we going to go, Hope?"

"I'm busy right now. I'll call you later, baby. Bye."

"Hope, don't hang up on—"

She ended the call and turned off her phone. She understood Stanley's frustrations but it wasn't like he was going to give up the best pussy he ever had. Stanley would get over it eventually. Hope smiled a devious smile. "Now, where was I?

"There's no way any man can resist all of this." Hope slapped her own juicy booty. Her butt wasn't flat like a pancake. It was hump-a-licious. She had the kind of ass a man could easily cuddle up against and part from behind, cup a handful and squeeze it tight. The best view for her man was when she bent over for Stanley—he could see her hair-free ass and pussy.

Dropping three strong peppermints in an empty wine goblet, she added a half an ounce of bottled water. Upon their return, she'd drink the mixture before French kissing and sucking Mr. Water's dick. The cooling sensation was sure to get him hard and the minty freshness was guaranteed to keep him close.

Massaging her breasts, ass, vagina, stomach, arms, legs, and feet with shea butter, she toweled off the excess, leaving the right amount to make her skin radiant but not too slippery. She tied the sash on her red halter wrap dress. Although she preferred pink, when it came to seducing men a sexy red outfit was always best.

Allowing her pussy freedom, she passed on wearing the red thong. She'd slip it on when she returned so he could ease it to the side and slip his dick into her slick pussy.

Hope dabbed perfume behind each ear and between her breasts. Bright red lipstick highlighted her warm vanilla-toned face. Long luxurious strip lashes made her brown eyes captivating. She stepped into her leopard platform sling-backs, making sure her perfectly pedicured toes were visible.

Easing her arms into her fluffy, white, wide-sleeved ankle-length mink, she admired the pink diamond solitaire on her right ring finger. Her earrings, necklace, and tennis bracelet were flooded with pink diamonds, too. Everything about her was real, including her intentions of deception.

"Damn, I love being a woman," she said, closing the hotel room door. Hope rode the elevator to the top floor. She was fifteen minutes late but with a million-dollar check in her purse she was certain Mr. Waters would wait if he had to.

Her grand entrance into The Polo Lounge commanded everyone's attention. All eyes, especially the men's, were on her before she assumed her diva pose—tall stance, navel to the spine, ass tilted backward, one foot slightly in front the other. The stares from the women made it clear, although they didn't know her, that they hated her.

For Hope, men mattered; women that didn't know her... did not.

"Welcome, madam. What can *I* do for *you*?" the host asked in a high-pitched tone, like he was going through puberty.

She looked directly into his eyes, thrust her breasts forward, then smiled. Hope placed the tip of her manicured nail between her teeth, then slid her finger from the corner of her mouth to her chin. "I'm here to dine with—"

Johnathon quickly appeared. "Yes, ye-yes," he stuttered in a soft, sexy kind of way. "She's the one I've been waiting for," he drooled. "Come with me."

His eagerness seemed personal. The thrusting of his chest and squaring of his shoulders as he turned his back to the host resembled what a man would do if she were his date. That or he was already interested in marking his territory.

"May I please take your coat, madam?"

Hope slowly eased the soft fluffy collar down her back. The host nodded at Johnathon, an unspoken signal that said, "Damn! Man, now I really see why you got your ass up here in a hurry," but he remained professional.

"I've got it," Johnathon said, taking her mink from the host. He tossed it across his arm, clenched it to his side.

Hope nodded toward her coat, gesturing for the host to take it right away.

The host nodded back at her then said to Johnathon, "Sir, please, allow me."

Before Johnathon could respond, Hope thanked the host then told Johnathon, "You are quite the gentleman. Thanks, Mr. Waters, but my coat will be properly stored. A mink should never lay." Her eyes trailed from his face to his chest. "A real mink is always hung."

"Oh, please, call me Johnathon," he said with a brilliant smile that already proved to outshine his intellect.

Men were clueless when it came to valuing the precious belongings of a woman. Unfortunately, that sometimes included what was between her ears and thighs.

Hope's coat wasn't some three-thousand-dollar knock-off. The price tag had been fifty grand, pre-tax. But there was no need to chastise him. She was sure his ego was like most men's... fragile. As with Stanley, sometimes it was best to quietly correct a man's mistakes to keep the pendulum, and the dick, swinging in her direction.

Hope fluffed then shook her hair in front of him. Men loved a slightly untamed look. It was more appealing than the stiffness of having every strand in place. Boring hair implied an equally boring woman.

Johnathon Waters looked good enough to suck his dick in the middle of the restaurant. His navy suit, white-collared shirt, and solid blue tie were crisp. He was on our party's side, along with Brooks and Bailey. The light fragrance hovering around him made her pussy notice the swollen imprint in his pants that peeked between the opening in his jacket. Indeed, he was very well-endowed.

The waiter motioned to pull out her chair. Johnathon beat him to it, waited until she was seated, then sat across from her. His dark wavy hair was tapered on the sides, fuller on top, not a gray strand in sight. A clean shave highlighted his left dimple. The bridge of his nose extended forward, his nostrils flared wide. Lips thin and sexy as hell when he smiled.

"Please, move his chair next to mine," Hope told the waiter. "And bring us a bottle of your finest champagne. We're having a celebration."

"If you prefer, madam, I can relocate you to a private booth," the waiter said, then asked, "What's the occasion?"

"Thanks, but that won't be necessary," Hope replied, not answering his question.

Staring into her eyes, Johnathon said, "Well, I must admit I had no idea you were so, um, attractive."

That wasn't what he really wanted to say, was it? He'd seen her before. What he hadn't witnessed was the size of her breasts without a bra.

Beauty was a woman's trump card. Good looks could yield good favor, open closed doors, and garner respect even when unwarranted. Gorgeous women made men do dumb things, but only when the woman was intelligent enough to know she was in charge.

Hope smiled, placing her hand on his knee under the table. Her fingernails lightly scraped his thigh. "I'm Native American and look just like my mother." And she had the ruthless, cutthroat characteristics of her father. "But we're here to discuss business."

"Yes, ye-yes. We are. So, are you a lobbyist or a philanthropist, or are you a member of an organization that wants to support my campaign because you want me to push your agenda?" he asked. The lust in his eyes shifted to curiosity.

"I'll get straight to the point, Mr.—" she paused then continued, "I mean, Johnathon. It's no secret who my father is or that the Andrews family—"

"I apologize for interrupting, but how are you Native American yet your last name is Andrews?"

"It's about Christopher Columbus claiming he discovered America, the Pilgrims betraying the Indians, and the U.S. stealing this great state from the Mexicans then denying them citizenship. What's in a name? Pick one. You are seeking to represent California, aren't you?"

His thick brows drew close together. "Didn't mean to put my foot in my mouth. I apologize."

"Accepted. Now please, I'm the one asking the questions, but if you don't want the million dollar donation, I'll let you ask all the questions you'd like."

Johnathon's lips tightened as he nodded. Occasionally a woman had to slip a man a little bitch to hold her position.

He definitely wasn't as smart as Hope had anticipated, but she wasn't here to be impressed by his intellect. The waiter placed the silver stand holding an ice bucket and the bottle of champagne by the table.

"Please, send this to my Presidential suite. Hope Andrews." She looked at Johnathon. "Why don't we continue this conversation where no one will overhear us? Can't be too trusting of people around you. Wouldn't want any paparazzi taking pictures of us at this innocent luncheon then plastering them online."

They retrieved her coat from the host, then went back to her room.

"Make yourself comfortable."

"Impressive," he said, sitting on the sofa near the fireplace.

The champagne arrived. Hope instructed the waiter to set up everything by the bar then tipped him accordingly. If Johnathon had had real class, Hope thought, he would've tipped the waiter instead of letting her do it.

She filled two flutes, handed one to Johnathon, sat beside him then crossed her legs. The opening in her wraparound dress exposed her overlapping thighs. Noticing was his job. Pretending not to notice was hers.

"You know, by accepting this donation," Hope paused. Opened her purse and handed him the check payable to the

Johnathon Waters Campaign Fund. "We are counting on you to make sure an initiative to tax casinos on reservations will never pass if you're elected and as long as you're in office. Never."

Nodding at the contribution, Johnathon said, "I reassure you that will never happen when I'm elected." He stared at the check, folded it, then stuffed it in his wallet as though it would be deposited into his personal account.

He scooted to the edge of the sofa. Glancing between his legs, he said, "Yes. Yes. Well, I thank you but I should be going." The imprint in his pants grew larger.

Hope thrust her breasts toward him, held up her glass. "There's more where that came from if you do the right things."

Johnathon paused, picked up his flute, held it next to hers. "How rude of me; we should toast."

His glass tilted toward his lap. Champagne spilled onto the erection bulging in his pants. He sprang to his feet. "Oh, damn. I guess I'm so excited," he said, placing the glass on the table.

"Of course you are. A million dollars is a lot of money and you deserve every penny," she lied. "You can't leave like this. What would people think?" Standing beside him, Hope unbuckled his belt, unzipped, then removed his pants. "It's a good thing we came up here," she said, parting her red lips just enough for him to imagine sliding his dick inside.

A real woman could undress a man before he realized he was naked. "I'll tidy these up for you." She selected a bottle of soda water from the bar, got a hanger from the closet, then took his pants into the bathroom and hung them behind the door. She spot-cleaned the outline so when the champagne dried it wouldn't leave a watermark.

Hope dipped her fingers into the wine glass she'd set aside earlier, smeared a little peppermint mixture on her pussy, downed the rest like a shot, then returned to the living room. "We'll need to let those air-dry for about thirty minutes then I'll blow it with the hair dryer," she said, refilling his champagne glass before sitting beside him on the sofa.

"Yes, ye-yes; where were we?" he asked, appearing very comfortable in his black cotton boxer briefs.

She could tell he was proud of his protruding manhood. Hope touched his knee, massaging his inner thigh. "You tell me."

"Be careful," he said, moving her hand. "If I spill this again, I'll have to remove my underwear." His smile sparkled, matching the light in his eyes. Men had a price just like women.

Hope tilted her glass toward his. Champagne spilled onto his boxers. She looked into his eyes and smiled. "Oops. Now this is crazy. I didn't mean to do that."

Johnathon took her glass and his, placing them on the table. His thin lips perched in her direction. She met him halfway.

"I've been wanting to taste these all day," he said, lowering her halter over her breasts.

"Oh, wow. Is this what happens behind closed doors with politicians? I've heard quite a few stories." She thrust her titties forward.

"I don't do this kind of thing, but I find you so hot."

"It's okay. You deserve this, Johnathon," she said, feeding him one nipple, then the other. "Oh, yes. Bite a little harder. You are the man and a man in your position shouldn't be denied any woman he desires."

Johnathon removed his briefs. His dick was big, beautiful, and circumcised just the way Hope liked them. She untied the sash on her dress and dropped it on the sofa so she wouldn't have to pick it up off the floor. She didn't want him to have a Monica Lewinsky flashback and end their session early.

"Keep on the leopard heels. They're so fucking hot on you," he said. "Damn, you have a pretty pussy." It was good she hadn't put on her thong. Right now it would be in their way.

Hope picked up the bottle of champagne, splashing the liquid on her pussy. "A toast. To Johnathon Waters. Our next governor." Hope did a Wonder Woman stance in front of him. "Well, if you're going to get a taste of this sweet pussy, now is the time. Later you'll be too busy."

He parted her lips, licked the opening of her vagina, then sucked her clit. "You're right. This pussy is tasty." He buried his face deeper. His tongue stroked hard, like she was the lunch and dessert he hadn't had.

"Oh, yes. You're getting my pussy all wet." Hope grabbed the back of his head, pulled him closer, then whispered, "Fuck me, Johnathon. I want to feel your huge cock inside me." She gripped a fistful of his hair, then jerked his head back.

"Let me get on top," she insisted, motioning for him to lie on the sofa. Before straddling him, she opened her purse and retrieved a condom. She sucked the latex into her mouth, put her mouth over his head, then rolled the condom down his shaft.

Hope positioned her pussy over his dick. *Here we go.* Slowly she lowered herself onto him. "Aw, yes." He felt great.

"Grab my ass, Johnathon," she moaned, placing his hands on her hips. "Yeah, like that."

"You're amazing," he said, staring up at her. His face was exactly where she wanted. In front of the hidden camera buried in the chandelier.

"I'm about to cum. You ready for it?" he asked.

What? Already?

His eyes rolled toward the top of his head. Bouncing her peppermint pussy up and down his shaft, she fucked him fast . . . then slow. The coolness stimulated her. She massaged her clit with one hand, his balls with the other, as she continued riding him.

His urgency to ejaculate could've been overexcitement or due to his reservations about being in her room too long. Didn't matter. Her job was done.

"I'm ready for it," she moaned.

They came together and it wasn't electrifying but it was pleasant. Too bad she had to use the evidence against him. He seemed like a nice guy.

Softly, she said, "I needed that." Removing the condom, she made sure his cum dripped onto her red dress before handing the condom to him.

"Flush this down the toilet."

Taking it from her, he said, "Promise me you'll keep this between us," then headed to the bathroom with his underwear in the other hand.

"I promise."

CHAPTER 9

Storm

T he quaint three-bedroom, three-bathroom house in Del
Mar Estates was her hideaway when she desired a break
from networking, her boyfriend, and assisting her parents in
LA. Helping her fellow Asians to get citizenship was at times a
twenty-four-hour job. An unexpected call could come at noon
or midnight.

Meeting with the girls was fun but tending to the details
for Brooks's upcoming campaign was weighing Storm down.
Saturdays were seemingly growing closer together, and March
was fast approaching. With five and a half weeks left before
the big announcement, at least everything was going as
planned.

Storm loved laying with Chancelor, but having him around
in her spare time left little quality time for herself. Thankfully,
when she really needed relaxation or in the event of an emergency, she had this place to escape the madness.

Like men with money, she believed that rich women should
own more than one residence, sex more than one lover and
not feel guilty about their pleasures. Now Storm was in the San

Diego area, because that's where she'd agreed to meet Randy since his schedule didn't permit him to meet her in LA.

She sat on a blanket, legs folded, palms faced up on her thighs, giving thanks as she admired the world-famous thoroughbreds exercising along the shore. Storm smiled, reminiscing about when her parents had bought her first horse, for her thirteenth birthday. She missed going to the Del Mar Race Track. Maybe she'd go before her return to LA but definitely not before entrapping Randy. Randall Wallace would be at her house in a few hours.

Inhaling the fresh morning breeze, her eyes trailed the sun rising from the horizon. Layers of orange, red, and yellow blended like the perfect portrait, illuminating the sky. Her days of racing were behind her. The competitions for her retired award-winning horses were over. She gazed out over the Pacific Ocean, wishing there were more moments when she could enjoy her solitude. Embracing nature's beauty fed her soul. Yet, as breathtaking as the morning was, Storm realized everything that was good could also be bad.

Too much water could drown. Too much air could suffocate. Too much sun could burn. Too much love could...wow. She shook her head at an astonishing epiphany.

Storm had never been in love.

Sure her parents loved her, but their love was tough. "No man wants to marry a not so smart woman. You must get straight A's," her father had always demanded. "Nothing less. And your mother will teach you how to please a man in and out of bed. That's your real job. Rich black man, wealthy white man, Asian man with lots of money, they all love beautiful Asian woman. You give them happy ending they love you more. Always let them love you more. You manage all the money...

you'll be happy and never broke. That's how your marriage will last. Even if he divorces you, you might get heartbroken, but like Jordan's ex-wife, you be happy you not broke. Woman happy. Husband happy. Woman no happy. Husband no happy."

Her mother's thoughts had been the same but her approach was different. "You love horses, honey. That's your passion. Let's learn how horses can make you money." And riding horses was a good way to learn how to please a man.

The thought of marrying for love was discouraged. Her mother would say, "Do not marry a man unless he has millions with an 's.' Your money is your money and *his* money is your money."

Storm wanted to know what being in love felt like. She thought she'd come close once in college. Thought he was the man she'd marry despite her parents' disapproval. She'd dreamt of giving birth to his babies. But when she realized she was committed to him but he was busy showing other girls the sex skills she'd taught him, the fairy tale crumbled.

Men, politics, and sex blended more smoothly than flour, eggs, and milk. Men were slick like butter, or so they thought, but they couldn't outsmart her. And Storm's mother's recipe for how to sex a man senseless was easier to follow than her grandmother's instructions on how to make funky chicken with sesame noodles. Too bad she didn't have a recipe for love or a prevention for heartache.

Storm stood, shook her blanket and folded it, then headed to her black convertible Corvette. Del Mar was only 2.1 square miles with less than five thousand residents. It was a safe place to live. She could come and go without worrying about her neighbors spying on her or about burglars breaking into her home when she was away.

She parked in her garage, lowered the door behind her car, then opened one of the other garage doors for Randy to park his car. She decided to leave the kitchen door leading into the house ajar so he could let himself in.

Randy had briefly informed her he had had other obligations and couldn't stay at her house long. Storm didn't want to risk letting him leave before she had what she needed so her plot to entrap him was elevated.

Filling a flute with chilled champagne she added a splash of orange juice to her glass then filled a large crystal pitcher with the remaining juice. She dissolved a sedative in water, stirred it into the juice, placed the pitcher in the freezer, then headed to the bathroom and filled her deep tub with cool water.

It was noon and the temperature was already seventy-five degrees with a projected high of eighty. With her guest's arrival only an hour away, Storm removed her clothes and relaxed in the tub, thinking about her girls.

Being a member of the Rich Girls' Club gave her what money couldn't: sisterhood. She didn't see Brooks as African-American, Morgan as Caucasian, Hope as Native American, or herself as Asian. Collectively they were the most powerful foursome in Los Angeles. The best part of their sisterhood was they had nothing to hide and they accepted one another's flaws. Some women would consider her high sex drive and the outrageous things she did to men degrading, but her sisters didn't. They understood that she loved giving pleasure to others and having multiple orgasms herself.

Storm inserted her finger deep into her vagina and twirled it around several times. In small circular motions she gently rubbed lemongrass body scrub over her arms, breasts, stomach, between her thighs, and down her legs to her feet.

Damn, my pussy feels good. But there was no time to masturbate or call her man for phone sex. Sometimes it was better to wait. She'd save her sexual energy for when she got back to LA and saw Chancelor.

She rinsed in the shower, dried off, then selected a few sex toys to use on Randall. By the time she was done with him, like a black widow spider she'd screw him then politically devour him.

Storm eased into her bright red bikini and tied the bottom on each end. She looped the halter straps around her neck, and the other two straps in front underneath her breasts. A woman couldn't go wrong with red. The Rich Girls knew that hues of red excited men—lipstick, polish, lingerie, shoes—and especially thongs. The brighter the better. But like a matador tempting a bull, the alluring movement of the woman was the main attraction for the man.

Massaging tanning oil on her arms and legs, she'd ask Randall to cover her back when he arrived. Storm checked the security monitor in her office. All of the indoor and outdoor cameras were functioning properly.

"Hello," a manly voice called from her kitchen.

She wrapped a sheer sash about her waist before trotting in the direction of his voice. "Hey, Mr. Wallace, glad you could make it. I'm excited about supporting your campaign. My family is excited as well." Storm removed the pitcher of juice from the freezer. "Grab those two glasses for me, will you?"

Randy was comfortably dressed in a navy polo shirt, neatly tucked inside khaki pants, and casual shoes. His Padres baseball cap was creased in the center of the bill. Placing his shades on the brim of his cap he picked up the glasses. "Just a reminder that I can't stay long. I have to catch up to a few other contributors. We're teeing off at three. I love golfing."

Following her to the patio, he sat on the edge of the cushioned seat, interlocked his fingers, then placed his elbows on his knees. His short black hair was tapered, sideburns well-trimmed against his pale complexion. He appeared somewhat unorthodox for a Republican with his extra facial hair.

"Your acceptance of this generous donation means you will keep your promise to make immigration a priority?" she asked, standing a few feet away, fingering her sash. She poured him a tall glass of orange juice before sitting sideways on a lounge chair across from him. Hopefully it wouldn't take long for him to pass out.

"Sure. Of course," he said, taking several gulps of juice. He looked around. "Excuse me for asking but why do you have four beach chairs? And you're wearing a swimsuit—which looks great on you, by the way—but where's the pool?"

Storm smiled, watching him down the rest of his juice. He refilled his glass. Randy was making this easy.

"This must be freshly squeezed. It's amazing." The second glass of juice slid down his throat faster than the first as he leaned back against the chair. "Aw, man. All of a sudden I can barely feel my legs. What's in this juice? I know I ran five miles this morning but—*whoa*—what's happening to—?"

"To answer your questions, yes, it is freshly squeezed, and with the beach so close by," she said reclining on the lounge chair, "I don't need a pool." She raised her leg in the air, pointed her toes, and layered on more tanning oil. "You mind getting my back?"

Randy placed his cap and glasses on the table. His eyes widened, his body swayed to the left. He rubbed at his eyes and looked around as if looking for something or someone. Did he think he was being watched?

"Not at," he yawned, stretching his arms above his head, "all." He staggered toward her.

Handing him the bottle, Storm lay face down. "Oh, and that's your check on the table in the white envelope," she said, pointing next to the half-empty pitcher of orange juice. "I know you have to leave so when you're done with my back you can see yourself out. I'll be in touch."

His ass plunked down beside her. His slippery hand roamed up and down her back. His palms dug a little deep. "What the hell. I think I'm having...call 9-1-1." With each stroke, his touch slowed, became heavier.

"Whoa," he said, slipping and falling across her back. "Sorry about that. I don't know what just happened. Please call for—" His body slumped on top of hers and stayed there.

Storm eased out from under Randy and rolled him over. His eyes were shut. "Randy," she sang, waving her hand in front his face. He didn't respond, didn't flinch. She wasn't trying to kill him. Perhaps the sedative had made his heart race.

Just to be sure, Storm checked his pulse; it was normal. She removed his shoes, then undressed him from head to toe. "Cute purple boxers, little dick, though. You never know," she murmured to herself. If she tried riding him, her pussy would swallow his walnut-sized balls.

After neatly placing his clothes on an adjacent lounge chair, she removed her swimsuit, letting it drop to the ground. Drenching his body with oil, she massaged him all over, except for his genitals. She didn't want a mouthful of grease slipping down her throat when she sucked him up like an oyster.

Holding the vibrating cock ring in one hand, she stroked his miniature penis. Up and down she maneuvered, trying to give him an erection. She cupped her wet mouth over his dick. With each strong stroke she vacuumed him hard and deep into her mouth. His erection eventually began to grow—slow, skinny, but steady.

Storm glanced up at the camera, smiled, then resumed bobbing her head. Editing the tape later would make the footage flawless. "Yes, Randy this is nice," she moaned. "Randall, you taste so good. I'm so glad you asked me to give you a blowjob. I know you're going to win the race. And when you do, I'll give you another blowjob, baby."

When his cock was almost standing tall on its own, she slid the ring over his head and down his shaft. Storm pressed the remote, leaving the vibrator at mid-speed. That should be enough stimulation to make him hard enough to ejaculate.

She continued easing his dick in and out of her mouth. Removing a dildo from her bag of toys, she squeezed lubrication onto the black silicone, then gently slid the head of the dildo into Randall's ass. His body twitched. As if he were having a prostrate exam, his cum instantly shot into the air. She soaked up his sperm with her bikini.

Her work was almost done.

She washed his body with shower gel to remove the oil then hosed him off. Patting his body and the lounge chair dry, Storm redressed Randy, dragged him back to the chair he'd sat in earlier, propped a pillow behind him, placed his cap on his head, and left him there.

Now her job was done. Well done. She'd let him sleep off the sedative; his contributors would have to tee off without him. And no matter how much money he received from them or anyone else, Randall Wallace's race to become governor was now headed down a dead-end street.

CHAPTER 10

Morgan

This Saturday's meeting was special because they would be celebrating how smoothly Morgan's plan was going. Five weeks had gone by since Brooks had agreed to run for governor and another five weeks remained before the announcement of her campaign.

The first thing Morgan did before today's meeting was call her husband.

"What now, Morgan?" he answered.

"Damn. I'm just checking to see if you need anything from the house."

"Not a thing, babe," he said. "When have I ever needed anything from the house on the weekend in the last three years?"

Damn, her husband could've said, "You." But that was cool. She wasn't trying to give him a reason to come home. "Not a change of clothes?"

"I said nothing. Go on, have your lil' political meeting. I told you she's not going to win. You're wasting your time, but at least you're helping Anthony Dennison win. Whatever you do, do not take money from our investments to fund this. Bye."

Guess he's trying a different approach, Morgan thought.

Magnum's relentless requests that Brooks not run had repeatedly fallen upon Morgan's deaf ears. Talking down to her was out of character for him—he was definitely making his position clear that he was strongly opposed to her idea, but Morgan wasn't about to let his selfish, chauvinistic attitude ruin her plan.

She didn't want him to come home. What she really didn't want was for him to overhear talk about her obligation to sex Goodman or to catch her sexing another person in their house. She prayed her inquiries wouldn't make her husband decide to show up after he'd promised not to.

The DVD player and large flat screen television were powered up and ready so they could view Storm and Hope's footage. The mimosas and Bloody Mary bar were fully stocked for the girls. Bo had put out fresh mangos, pineapples, and pitted cherries, along with caviar and organic wheat crackers on silver platters. He'd placed them in the center of the conference table and left the clubroom immediately. Now he was back in the kitchen preparing the hot side of the menu for their brunch, and would only return upon her request. Morgan couldn't risk having anyone outside of the group discover their secrets, especially a man.

On her way to the foyer, she stopped in the kitchen. "Smells delicious in here, Bo," she said with a wide smile.

Bo smiled back. "I always aim to please you, Mrs. Childs. Anything I can do to be a pleasure to you is why I'm here."

The way he said, "pleasure," made her moist. Her eyes lingered longer than they should have below his waist. The bulge there showed her how endowed he was under his white pants. Since Magnum seemed to be rationing out his dick lately, she might have to do her chef until her husband resumed sexing her four days a week.

"I might need you to stay a little late today."

Bo smiled then started chopping garlic cloves. "Anything you need or want, Mrs. Childs, don't hesitate." The rhythm in the movement of his wrist let her know dicing wasn't all he was good at.

Imagining him teasing her clit, she stared at his dick, then said, "Yeah, in fact. I do need you."

He nodded. "I'll be here."

"When you're done, take a shower and relax in one of my guest bedrooms. I'll come and get you when I'm ready."

Exhaling, she continued her journey, making her way to the front door. Her timing—or should she say *their* timing—was impeccable. Morgan was elated to see all the girls walking up the stairs.

"Well, this is the first time in a while that everyone is on time," she said, closing the door after they'd entered. "Let's go. Everything is set up in the clubroom and I can't wait to see the juicy stuff Storm and Hope captured."

"Mine first," Hope said, "because I know I'm not going to top Mz. Girlie here."

"You know it," Storm agreed, handing Morgan, Brooks, and Hope a copy of her DVD. "Keep those duplicates in a *safe* place. 'Safe' being the operative word. I have the masters from all three cameras at home."

"Here's mine," Hope said to the group. "Ditto. Except I copied footage from one camera. But that's all you guys need to see," she said, then laughed.

Morgan realized then that as part of the plan she should've told them that she was the only one that would hold onto copies of all the videos and the masters. "I need both of you to give me the originals and those copies you just handed out. The more copies that are out there, the greater the risk."

"Too late," Storm said. "I'm keeping mine."

Morgan would have to find another way to convince them. Finding a secret place that Magnum didn't have access to was easy. But for the first time, she'd have a reason to lock the vault in the clubroom and have a door installed at the entrance to the West Wing. Controlling what happened to the other videos was impossible unless the girls agreed to turn over everything to her.

During the stroll through the corridors and into the clubroom Morgan noticed that Brooks was unusually quiet, seemingly deep into her own thoughts. Brooks walked straight to the bar, poured herself a Bloody Mary, then sat alone on her chaise. She stirred the liquid inside the crystal glass with a celery stalk pinched between her fingers her eyes fixed on her drink.

Morgan thought back to the first time she'd met Brooks— eight years ago at the women's club in Beverly Hills. It was at their orientation with the organization. At that time, Morgan had been twenty-nine, Brooks thirty-seven. Brooks was the most striking woman in the room, and Morgan had quickly gravitated toward her.

Over the years of getting to know one another, eight had become their lucky number. Brooks was eight years older than she was. They lived eight miles apart, loved competing for the eight ball when shooting pool, and of the members in the Rich Girls' Club, they'd known one another the longest—those eight years.

Storm snapped her fingers in Brooks's direction. "Hey, girl. You, okay? This is our most exciting meeting yet and you seem so down. Take a few big swigs of your drink. Maybe that'll help pep you up." Storm went to the bar, grabbed the vodka and poured an extra shot into Brooks's Bloody Mary.

Brooks shook her head. Smiled, halfway. "I'm good. It's just that trying to keep up with all the background information on each opponent is overwhelming. I can't shut my brain off." She stood, joining them at the conference table. "Right now Randy's voting record for the last decade is scrolling across my mind like it's on a teleprompter."

"Well, we're about to lighten your mental load because when you see my video, honey, you will never view Randall Wallace the same way. Girl, you are going to strut down easy street. I can't believe how simple these guys are," Storm said.

"Before we roll the footage, let me have the food brought in," Morgan said. She lowered the electronic shades, dimmed the track lights, then waited for Bo to arrive. As soon as he did, he set up the warm dishes.

"Thanks, Bo." What Morgan hoped Bo would agree to do to Brooks later would help take Brooks's mind off of all her opponents.

Once Bo was out of sight, Morgan suggested the girls prepare their plates. When everyone was once again seated at the table, she pressed play on the remote.

Hope's high-definition video was so crystal clear it almost appeared as 3D. Her neatly arched dark brows, long lashes, vibrant red lips, and silky brunette hair showed beautifully in the opening scene. A soft hint of blush made her face glow.

"How did you get your camera to zoom in on your face like that?" Brooks asked. "Mine doesn't do that."

"I'm sure it does," Storm answered. "All cameras these days have zoom."

"I'll turn you on to my tech guy. He's the biggest geek I've ever met. I keep him around," Hope said, watching herself in action, "because he's very in tune with the latest technology. He's the best and I keep him a secret from Stanley."

"That's why I need all the DVDs. We can't afford to have this geek or Stanley leaking this to the press...oh, oh," Morgan said. "The ol' spill-the-drink-to-get-him-out-of-his-underwear routine. Nice move but...damn."

Storm commented, "The look in his eyes says he wants your pussy in his mouth right away girl. Damn...look at that nice big dick. Who would've thought he was packing all that? If this goes public, Mr. Waters will have a line of women eager to ride that. Trust me. I know a champion when I see one."

Brooks laughed. "No, you are not breast feeding him like your nipples are pacifiers. This doesn't look staged at all. You should get an award for your performance."

Morgan was happy that in the middle of watching Hope's video, Brooks smiled. And the awards idea was a good one. After the election Morgan might put together the best clips, create categories, and give trophies to the girls just for fun.

Laughing out loud at the video, Brooks seemed closer to being her usual jovial self.

The Rich Girls had never watched one another sexing anyone. Focusing on the screen, they could see that Hope's body was gorgeous in motion. Fluid. Flexible. Seeing their friend nude was more exciting than watching her fuck Johnathon. Morgan wondered if the camera would love her naked body as much as it complimented Hope's. A few minutes later, in the middle of her thoughts, the screen faded to black.

"That's it! Johnathon's ass is done!" Storm said, downing her glass of champagne.

"Not bad at all," Hope said, patting herself on the back.

"I'll second that," Morgan said with a smile. "Girl, seeing the way you roll your pussy is so orgasmic I swore I was watching a porn star in action. And those twins are simply to die for. Storm is right. Poor Johnathon doesn't stand a chance."

Brooks's smile turned upside down. *What now?* Morgan thought but refused to ask. Watching her friend flash these highs and lows, Morgan prayed Brooks wasn't becoming bi-polar.

Storm's footage was next. Morgan pressed play. If she paused to babysit Brooks, the enthusiasm of the group would vanish.

"We are some clever bitches," Hope said. "Storm, you're putting that pussy right in his face while he's asleep. Or did you hypnotize his ass? By the way, love the swimsuit."

Hope was loosening up in a way Morgan hadn't witnessed before. Morgan wondered if it was Hope's videotape that made her more vocal. Was this her first time seeing herself sex a man? Morgan had so many tapes of herself she kept them in storage so Magnum wouldn't find them. Husband or no husband, no man wanted to see his wife fucking another man.

"Hypnotize my ass. I did not want to waste time seducing that man. I added a few sleeping pills in the OJ and knocked him out. Wasn't my fault he gulped nearly two glasses in fifteen minutes. He passed out immediately and I fucked him right away." Storm danced around her chair. "Don't miss the good part," she said, sitting on the edge of her seat. "Watch the screen, not me."

Brooks asked, "What did you tell him when he woke up?"

"I wrote a note. Told him he fell asleep and I couldn't wake him. Lied about having an appointment and for him to let himself out," Storm explained. "He's still trying to figure that shit out."

Morgan frowned. "What the hell. I know that's a cock ring but what's that black ball on top of his tiny nuts?"

Storm cleared her throat. "First off, that's a10-Speed Vibrating Cock Ring. It's a nice, wide, jelly ring that stretches over his dick. The vibrating egg fits inside this lil' cocoon and has soft stimulating ticklers to massage his balls and the woman's clit. I chose to give him an awesome blowjob while setting the speed on cruise control. I could've rode that little ass dick but the vibration would've had to make both of us cum. The most important thing to remember, ladies, is," Storm said, holding up a small device, "never relinquish your remote."

"Shit, I need one of those for Magnum," Morgan said. "Damn, I'm about to have an orgasm just thinking about how the vibration would stimulate both of . . . damn Storm! Where do you get all of this from?" Morgan's eyes grew wide. Shaking her head and looking at the screen she said, "Please tell me that is not what I think it is."

Storm laughed. "You know it is. That's my trademark now. When I say 'fuck 'em' I mean it."

Randall was going to lose it when he saw that big black dildo inside his ass, making his dick shoot cum in the air like a fountain.

Hope chimed in. "That's blackmail for your ass right there."

Morgan frowned then laughed at Hope. "Well, now that we have two home runs, ladies, whose head is on the chopping board next?" Morgan asked, staring at Brooks.

Brooks was back to being unusually quiet. Morgan shared a look with Storm.

Hope chimed in. "Let's see . . . Anthony Dennison and Laura Littleton. Storm has got Anthony and Laura is all mine. Haven't figured out a way to blackmail her. I don't do chicks but if that'll make her fold her hand, I'm sure I can come up with something."

Morgan replied, "No, she's a lesbian but even if she weren't, the media and society do not care about two women having an adulterous relationship—"

"Or if a woman cheats on her husband," Storm added.

Staring at each of the girls, Morgan said, "Mine better not ever cheat on me."

Brooks stated, "Maybe Laura had a baby that she gave up for adoption when she was a teenager. Or had an abortion. Or she's hired illegal aliens to work for her. There's got to be something scandalous we can uncover."

Morgan raised her brows. "You're right. What if she kicked her dog? You know Californians will stand up for animals and hug trees before they vote against the death penalty."

Hope interjected, "Speaking of the death penalty, that's what we need to eradicate. California is spending billions of dollars keeping inmates on death row. I'll research the details and see if it's a cause worthy of Brooks's support."

"Brooks can't support that," Morgan said. "It's too risky."

"Back to Laura. She's a tough one. We can switch if you'd like, Hope," Storm suggested.

"I've got it. I'm loving the challenge. Trust me, come Election Day, her name might be on the ballot but I guarantee you girls, Laura will not win."

Brooks was silent again.

"Well, let's toast," Morgan said, handing each of them a glass of champagne. "Storm, do not spill yours, okay?"

"Especially not on me," Hope commented, then laughed.

"We haven't received an investment report in a few weeks. When should we expect the next one?" Brooks asked.

Of all the things she could've mentioned, she would bring that shit up. Morgan laughed in spite of her unease. "I've been so busy with the plan I haven't had time. I'll have it ready for our next meeting. Storm, why don't you make the toast."

"My pleasure." Holding her glass high in the air, Storm confidently said, "Ladies, pussy is best served...ice cold. We are going to bury these men alive."

"I'll drink to that," Hope said.

"I second," Morgan agreed.

Brooks nodded.

That was okay. Morgan knew exactly what Brooks needed to relax, and to keep her mouth shut.

CHAPTER 11

Brooks

Relieved that the meeting had finally ended, Brooks exhaled, stood, picked up her purse, then walked ahead of Hope, Storm, and Morgan toward the foyer. "Great job, ladies. Thanks. Now it's back to reading more documents for me and more sex for you guys. Anybody want to trade places? Anybody?" she asked jokingly, just to hear what they'd say.

"Brooks, don't start asking questions you already know the answer to, honey," Storm replied. "We know you don't have a man, but actually that's a good thing because we need for you to stay focused. Take it from me: men are a distraction. After you win the election, I promise I'll personally hand pick a good eligible bachelor for you."

Did any female politicians have healthy sex lives? Now that Brooks thought about it, she couldn't think of a single super sexy woman elected to or running for a political position. If the females didn't look masculine and wore pantsuits all the time, they were clothed up to their necks and down to their knees. Brooks was a lady and she intended to continue dressing like one.

"See you guys next week," she said, heading out the door.

After watching the videos, Brooks was beginning to believe she'd signed up for the wrong part of the plan. Why had Morgan selected her? Morgan was married. Her background wasn't squeaky clean but it was solid enough for her to win. The one secret that could destroy Morgan, if revealed, was the same one that could destroy Brooks. Brooks prayed that Morgan wouldn't pry into her personal life.

Behind her, Storm said, "Can't wait. I'm enjoying the hell out of this ride. Anything a man can do, the Rich Girls can master."

Brooks stopped at the bottom of the stairs, turned around.

"I second that," Hope agreed. "In fact, I'm getting ready to go to Stanley's, fuck him hard, get my pussy satisfied, and keep it moving. He's been asking too many questions about what I'm doing and getting way too serious regarding our future. Nothing I can't handle, though. Bye, ladies." Hope waved as she by-passed Brooks. The wings of her sleek onyx Mercedes Benz SLR McLaren swung above the roof. Hope sat behind the wheel of her million-dollar purchase, and the doors lowered as she eased on her dark sunglasses.

Morgan stood on the porch. "Brooks, wait; come here for a moment. I forgot. We need to go over one more thing before you leave."

"Bye," Storm said, getting in her Porsche.

Reluctantly re-entering the house, Brooks sighed heavily. She wanted to go home, soak in her tub, get in her bed, and read more documents until her secret lover arrived to service her.

"It won't take long, I promise." Morgan closed the front door and led the way to her bedroom. "Make yourself comfortable, sweetie. I'll be right back."

Brooks dropped her purse on the chaise, kicked off her

shoes, stretched her legs on the sofa, and reclined into the plush pillows. Closing her eyes, she let the weight of her body seep into the cushion like melted butter on hot sourdough. The muscles in her shoulders, back, and neck started to ache.

Wishing she'd kept moving, Brooks sleepily opened her eyes and scanned Morgan's décor. The new winter white drapes complimented the turquoise accent wall. A hint of rosemary fragrance filled the room. She stared at Morgan's bed, imagining herself in it. At this moment she didn't care. *What the hell. Why not?*

Brooks removed her clothes then sprawled atop Morgan's comforter. *Damn, I'm mentally and physically exhausted*, she thought, burying her face in a pillow.

Morgan entered the room laughing. "You deserve a few hours off and that's all you can have, so don't get up, girl, but don't get too comfortable either. I promise I'll have you camera-ready on announcement day. If the public sees you looking beat, you won't have a chance of winning." Morgan said this as she set three glasses and a bottle of chilled champagne on the nightstand.

"I wanted you to have a drink with me but I see you need the rest. I'll do the drinking and talking; you make the decisions."

She could do that if she didn't pass out first, but Brooks wasn't too tired to notice the third flute. "Okay. What do I need to decide?"

Oil drizzled down her spine, seeping between her butt cheeks, soiling her satin panties. "Oh, no." This wasn't the direction she wanted to go in. She did desperately need a massage, but not from Morgan, or the other person's hands she felt gliding across her skin.

Thick fingers and wide palms kneaded her lower back. In

spite of her reservations, she said, "Oh, my, gosh. That feels so good." And it did. She couldn't deny the incredible feeling, but she wished they were Goodman's hands instead. He would be at her house in a few hours. "You'd better hurry up and tell me what I have to consider before I doze off," Brooks said, looking over her shoulder. She gasped. "Are you serious?"

"Headquarters. Where do you want me to setup your headquarters?" Morgan asked, pressing Brooks's head back into the pillow. "Relax. He's not going to do anything you don't want. Now, how many campaign offices do you need and where do you want them? I have a list of suggestions."

Had Morgan intentionally left this topic out of today's discussion? Hope and Storm's opinions mattered to Brooks.

"Since you have the list, let's consult with the group next week. Is this man the reason you asked me to stay?"

Suddenly there were four hands on Brooks's back. This was not like one of the professional, synchronized massages she'd had at Angel's. Having a man on each side of the table, rubbing her up and down in unison, was heavenly. The feel of Morgan's hands sliding up one side of her back, over her shoulder blades, and up to her neck was okay, but Brooks was annoyed that this man she barely knew was touching her in the same way.

Other than seeing Bo in his familiar chef uniform, he was technically a stranger to her. Could he be trusted? Brooks buried her face in the comforter. Morgan massaged her shoulders; Bo continued massaging her lower back. Brooks had herself to blame. She shouldn't have given in to Morgan's sexcapades when they'd first met.

Now Morgan was taking things too far, but she'd also piqued Brooks's curiosity. Brooks never had a ménage à trois... and she'd seen enough to know that Bo was packing. Maybe her friend thought she needed to get some dick. But sexing Bo would be like eating forbidden fruit.

"I don't need help," Morgan said.

Did she mean with selecting the locations or the fact that Bo was rubbing Brooks's neck? Bo hadn't said a word, and Brooks thought that was smart on his behalf. His hands continued roaming.

"I can select the locations but you know how you are. The minute I decide, you'll have a long list of questions, so it's best we do it together," Morgan climbed into the bed. "After we're done with this we can enjoy that."

Lifting her head to look up at Bo, Brooks said, "Why don't we deal with that now? I can't do him." Brooks scooted beside Morgan.

Morgan caressed one of Brooks's breasts and motioned for Bo to do the same to the other.

Brooks pleaded, "Please don't. I need dick badly but I'm not letting your chef fuck me. I just remembered I have to go home."

Morgan forced her back onto the bed, continuing to touch and tease her nipples. Bo gently covered her areola with his mouth. Brooks realized that the only thing missing from the masculine side of Morgan's personality was a real dick.

Looking at both of them Brooks wondered, who was more confident in the bedroom? Men like Bo who might have a comfortable cushion in their bank account? Or multi-millionaire women? When things went wrong, a man could be a bastard but a woman could be a bitch. What if Bo could be both?

Morgan removed her clothes, stretched Brooks's legs along the mattress, then straddled her thigh. She positioned her pussy atop Brooks's clit and started tribbing. Her hips rolled back forth, and each time she moved she ground her engorged shaft against Brooks's clit. Bo's hands were caressing both Morgan's and Brooks's breasts. His twirled Brooks's nipple to a rhythm that made her cum quickly.

Moaning, Brooks stared at her friend. "We really shouldn't be doing this in your bed. What would Magnum think if he walked in?"

The mild orgasm took the edge off. Her release was an energy she wanted to save for Goodman, not release to Bo.

～～

Sex was how her friendship with Morgan had begun. Could a woman have a one-night stand with another woman? Even so, Brooks had known when her initial one-on-one with Morgan happened it was destined to be more. Love for each other was how their relationship had grown.

After meeting at the women's club in Beverly Hills, Morgan had come to her coffee shop late that night. There were about twenty customers; a few, like Morgan, sat alone with only their computers and cell phones for company. Morgan started a casual conversation that led to their discovering they shared similar views on success, money, politics, and sex, with the exception that Brooks had never been with a woman.

～～

Morgan looked down at Brooks, leaned toward her, then grabbed her hips. "Shut up and give him my pussy."

Brooks's body was hot from the constant gyration. The inside of her vagina felt like it was on fire and ready to combust. "I'm not sexing him and I mean that." Morgan may have been on top but she wasn't in control.

Brooks's opposition represented so many things. She never should've let Morgan talk her into running for governor. Since she'd agreed she had to think smart, and letting Bo put his dick inside her was everything except. What if Morgan had a hidden camera recording them and Magnum found it?

Two months ago Brooks's life had been perfect. Normal, sort of. In five weeks the deadline to enter the race would be here and her privacy and the privacy of those around her might become public.

But maybe she should take advantage of this opportunity with this fine man. If Morgan trusted him, why shouldn't she? Except it wasn't as though Brooks didn't have a man. She actually had two.

The men in her life might eventually be exposed and Bo, if things went well, could replace them. Her ex-husband could become media-worthy for all the wrong reasons. And the woman that loved her more than anyone else, might end up hating her. And only God knew what this Bo guy was really up to.

"Ah, yes, that's it. Fuck me harder," Morgan moaned. Leaning her head forward she kissed Brooks's breast.

Consumed with her thoughts, Brooks hadn't realized that Bo was fucking Morgan doggie-style until Morgan's hips were thrusting fast. He banged Morgan so hard Brooks heard his balls slapping against Morgan's skin.

Brooks stared at them, imagined she had a dick. Imagined that she was deep inside of Morgan the way Magnum was deep inside of her when they made love.

Brooks slid her hand between Morgan's thighs and massaged her friend's clit.

"That's right. Get it. Both of y'all do me. You know exactly how to please me, don't you?" Morgan stared down at her. "Keep stroking my pussy, Brooks, I'm about to cum for you," Morgan said, sliding her finger inside of Brooks.

Brooks wondered if Morgan's marriage would be in jeopardy if Magnum walked in right now, or would he join the party without asking any questions? Would a man really leave his woman or his wife for infidelity if the person she was cheating with was another woman? Or what about a man he'd heard about but had never met, like Bo? Brooks hated that in the moment all she should've focused on was going home, but she couldn't turn off the endorphins in her brain.

"I've got to taste you," Morgan said. "I want your pussy in my mouth."

Brooks had been on the giving end of performing cunnilingus. Morgan was her first and only. "When a woman knows what she likes, that's a good place to start," Morgan had told her. And she was right.

She positioned herself closer to the headboard, tilted her ass upward, spread her thighs wide. Bo kneeled behind Morgan, started licking from her clit to her asshole. Were women better lovers for women and men for men? Did one's ability to deliver intense pleasure to the same sex make cumming more fun? Brooks stared at Bo as Morgan's mouth cupped her pussy.

"Go slower," Brooks said, gripping Morgan's platinum blond hair. She didn't want to come too fast.

She brushed Morgan's hair away from her face so she could see her gorgeous grey eyes. Brooks wondered what Storm and Hope would think if they knew, and whether Morgan was fantasizing about Hope's bodacious boobs or voluptuous butt. She couldn't blame Morgan if she were. Hope's body was undeniably beautiful.

Closing her eyes, Brooks pretended Hope's double-Es were rubbing against her nipples right now. If Storm were there, too... Brooks didn't want to visualize what Storm might do to Bo.

She held Hope's breasts in her mind and twirled her nipples until they became erect. Then she whispered to Morgan, "Lick me the way Bo is licking you."

The complexities of sexuality and life wouldn't be so complicated if all her fantasies had stayed in her head.

"Um, yes." Morgan moaned, then inserted her middle finger deep into Brooks's vagina.

Strumming softly against her G-Spot, Morgan suctioned the tip of Brooks's clit into her mouth. Gradually the rhythm of her fingers kept pace with the flick of her tongue. Her tongue began to flutter. Her finger flickered faster until...

"Oh, my gosh, Mag... gan," Brooks screamed, grabbing Morgan's hair. "Morgan, baby! Morgan." Brooks kept repeating Morgan's name. Fluids gushed from her urethra, showering Morgan's face.

Brooks continued, "Baby, baby. Oh, my gosh, I love you so much." The near hiccup bothered her. She'd never done that in eight years. Why now? Maybe it was because in her mind she'd replaced Bo with Magnum.

Morgan slapped Brooks's ass hard.

"Ow, that hurts!"

Morgan pushed Bo backward. "Leave now."

Quietly he gathered his clothes, exiting the same as he'd arrived.

"What hurts is your lying there while I'm eating your pussy

and you almost called out my husband's name. What the fuck is going on in your head? What was that about? And don't you dare lie to me."

Brooks shook her head. The sheet beneath her ass was soaked. Her explosive orgasm was about to blow up in her face. "No, I didn't."

"Yes, you did. I know what I heard. Were you fantasizing about Magnum while I was eating your pussy?"

Brooks stared Morgan in the eyes, kissed her, then said, "No, I wasn't fantasizing about your husband. The thought of that is absurd. You're my lover."

And that was half the truth.

CHAPTER 12

Hope

Sacramento, California was like most state capitals. Outside of politics one couldn't find an abundance of exciting or entertaining things to do here, especially after dark. Sac was contrary to LA, with its stars and wannabe celebrities looking and acting alike. Men, women, and children competed for the spotlight on Venice Beach, hoping to be discovered. Whatever God didn't bless people with in Los Angeles, a plastic surgeon could. And having so many functions and parties happening in the City of Angels, there were plenty of moments for the struggling folks to shine and party as though they were rich.

The Streets of Sacramento would never make it to Hollywood as a movie or reality show. Filmmakers didn't care enough about small towns, or the people that resided in them unless those people were famous before moving there, like Arnold Schwarzenegger had been. Living in Sac could be a good thing if one wanted peace and enjoyment in their day-to-day activities, and depending on what neighborhood one chose.

Hope was sure today's face-to-face with Laura Littleton would prove uneventful. No blackmail cameras. No hotel suite. No hidden voice recorders. This was the beginning of a business relationship with an end in mind. By every means she could think of, Hope would eventually find a way to make sure Laura lost to Brooks. Men usually screwed themselves because they underestimated women. But with only four weeks left before Brooks's announcement, Hope wasn't taking the chance that Mrs. Littleton would somehow sabotage her own campaign.

Laura had chosen Lucca, one of Sacramento's top ten restaurants nestled between midtown and downtown, for their meeting. Hope arrived twenty minutes early, hoping to watch Laura walk through the doors. A person's walk and body language were their first forms of communication.

If Laura slouched, she was just that. Slouchers were procrastinators and underachievers. If Laura stood tall, exhibiting confidence in her stance, her character was possibly the same, but not necessarily: People who exercised regularly generally had good posture. But being poised didn't equate to having intelligence. Hope had met enough great-looking men to know that looks and brains weren't always equal partners. Hope would draw her conclusions only after Laura opened her mouth.

Approaching the host, Hope said, "Reservation for Lau—"

"Hey, Hope. I got us a booth away from the door. I'm so glad to meet you!" Laura said, rushing in her direction. Extending her hand, Laura's shake was firm and tight, her rhythm stiff like the black crinoline pantsuit she wore.

Damn, girl. Relax. Laura almost cut off her circulation. "My pleasure," Hope lied, stretching out her fingers. Laura never noticed.

"You know what they say: if you're on time you're late." Laura's high-pitched laugh sounded like she was a hyena gasping for air. Patrons' heads snapped in their direction. Laura never noticed.

"Follow me, Hope. I just adore this place. Have you eaten here before?" she asked, sliding into the booth. Her back and shoulders flushed against the vinyl. There wasn't much up top to thrust forward. The smile on her face almost appeared permanent, like something painted on the face of a porcelain doll, except that Laura's manly persona was not so adorable. Her hair was short, blond, tapered on the sides and higher on top, just like Johnathon's. She wore no makeup.

"No, can't say that I have," Hope said, picking up the menu, raising it to cover her face. She exhaled, rolled her eyes to the side, composed herself, then lowered the menu.

The restaurant's red-brick wall décor reminded her of New Orleans. The ambiance was warm, inviting, and the staff appeared happy. The place was spacious but not so spread out that Hope couldn't see the faces of other diners across the room.

"You're going to love the food here. I'll order for you," Laura said, leaning across the table and taking the menu out of Hope's hand.

If Laura wins by a fluke, she'll need someone to taste her food first just to make sure the person in the kitchen or at the table isn't trying to shut her up. Was she for real? Hope took the menu.

"Just like I'm capable of giving you a check for a million dollars—which by the way may I remind you, you haven't gotten yet—I can and will order for myself."

Mentioning the check reminded her she needed to have a conversation with Morgan. There was still that undisclosed reason why they weren't using resources from the Rich Girls' Fund, and Hope was determined to find out what was going on. The fact that Hope's father was wealthy and that she earned her own millions was no reason she should have to invest more of her money to trap Brooks's opponents. When the campaign was over, Morgan was going to reimburse her.

Laura gasped. "Oh, my. I didn't mean any harm. It's just that I'm so used to taking charge and I thought rich people like yourself loved having others do things for them. I figured I was doing *you* a favor." Fanning her hand in a downward position, she continued, "Take your time. I already know what I'm having."

Laura's contrived smile never vanished. "You're beautiful, Hope. I'm surprised you can afford such a generous donation. I like you already."

Stay in your lane, Missy. Hope was sure Laura's wife wouldn't appreciate the comment, which accompanied Laura's lustful stare at her cleavage. But if licking Laura's pussy on top of the table right now would end their luncheon and give Brooks a slam-dunk win, Hope would do it without hesitation.

If nothing else could lose Laura votes, her fake personality was a guarantee. Hope was beginning to believe Laura's entering the race would split the Republican vote. Maybe Goodman, a Democrat, had orchestrated having Laura run. Hmm, perhaps helping Laura to get more votes was an even better strategy than buying her out.

Maybe the Rich Girls could create an in-house competition and let the Republicans fight amongst themselves. Truly, Laura couldn't be serious about being in charge of California. But then again, Sarah Palin did run for Vice President after having been elected governor of Alaska.

Hope shook her head. She hadn't selected a single item on the menu. Her purpose overruled her hunger for food. "Let's see." Maybe if she spoke a few words aloud she could decide what she wanted to eat. That was, if she didn't lose her appetite first. Truth was, she didn't want to break bread with Laura. She wanted to regurgitate.

The waitress approached their booth, no pen or pad in hand. "May I start you ladies with something to drink?"

"Yes, we'll have two waters, no ice, with lemon. Hope, what else would you like?" Laura asked.

To, leave. Now. Hope looked at the waitress. "I'll have a strawberry lemonade with ice and I'd like ice in my water, no lemon. And I'll have the Myzithra Cheese Bread with the red lentil hummus, green olive pesto, and mixed olives to start." *And end her meal.*

Laura's smile widened. "That's exactly what I was going to order for you! I'll have the same but I'd like a regular lemonade, no ice."

The waitress walked away, and Hope desperately wanted to follow her wherever she was going.

"So is your dad like a real Indian Chief? How much money do his casinos make? You know, taxing the revenue made from casinos on Indian reservations would really help boost California's economy."

Oh no she didn't. Had any lobbyist groups given this woman money to support their agenda? Obviously, Laura didn't understand how large campaign contributions worked. Hope wanted to hit Laura in the head but feared even that wouldn't knock sense into her.

Hope stood, then lied. "I just remembered. I have another candidate to meet with."

"Wait, you're not leaving, are you? What about the million dollars you promised me?" Laura pleaded.

For the first time, Hope saw the smile on Laura's face disappear. Laura's ignorance was unbelievable. Hope refused to financially aid her campaign.

"Like I said, I've got to go." And Hope strutted out of the restaurant. If she stayed, the story of her beating up Laura would definitely be breaking news.

Hope had met with Laura intent on giving her the money in order to gain access to inside information. She glanced at her watch. Fifteen minutes of digesting ignorance was fourteen minutes too long.

There had to be a better way.

CHAPTER 13

∽

Storm

I love you, Storm."

Love represented a wide array of meanings that dwelled in a person, not in the person's words. Chancelor's eyes softened as his finger trailed under her jaw to her chin. His thumb brushed across Storm's lips. Gently she held then kissed his hand.

She knew what Chancelor's *words* meant but what did he mean? What was his heart saying to her in the moment? Had he given considerable thought to what he said? Was this the kind of love that made a man want to propose? Was he responding to her financing his past, present, and possibly his future? Or was his confession based on how amazing she made him feel sexually?

Storm placed her feet on the bar underneath his stool, put her hands on his firm thighs, then searched his eyes for answers to her questions. This was her opportunity to let go, to trust that he'd catch her if she admitted she was falling in love with him.

Frowning, he squeezed her hands. "What's taking you so long

to say something? You don't believe me? Or you don't feel the same way I do?"

Why did he have to do this at Trader Vic's? He should've waited until they were at his or her house. He could've told her before they got out of the car. Was the liquor talking for him? They sat at the end of the bar. The nearest person to them was the mixologist, who was laughing with a couple of females at the opposite end. Storm motioned for him to come over.

"Another round of our original Mai Tai?" the bartender asked, smiling happily.

Storm nodded. She was enjoying the fruitful Pacific Island, Indo-Chinese, Japanese, and Creole flavors of her drink more than her conversation with Chancelor, but this was her last one. She had to drop him off and meet Tony at her house in a few hours.

"I do believe you, and please don't lead my response. You know how much I hate it when you do that."

"Well."

"Well what?" she said, sighing heavily.

"Am I annoying you?"

Storm's voice rose. "Chancelor, stop it!"

The bartender switched their empty glasses for the new round of drinks, then quickly headed back toward the lively, giggling females.

Chancelor released her hands, folded his arms high across his chest.

"Excuse, me. Bartender. Close us out," Storm said, slapping her credit card on the counter.

"I am annoying you. Sorry," Chancelor said, turning his back to the bar.

She hated when her man acted like a child. Chancelor's moping was solely for sympathy and she refused to pacify him. Refused to tell him what he wanted to hear.

What did love mean to a twenty-one-year-old? Had he lived long enough to understand what he'd said? Dated enough women to figure out if she was truly the one? Maybe he'd have more in common with those girls across the bar. They were definitely closer to his age.

Storm exhaled. What did love mean to her, a thirty-year-old who never felt the depths of caring for a man so much that she could say, "I love you," or "I love you, too," and mean it... until now.

"Let's go," were the words that escaped her mouth instead, as she signed off on the bill.

The drive to his condo took forty minutes. The silence was equally as long. When she parked in front of his building, Chancelor exited her car, slamming the door. Storm drove off. She had more important things to tend to. In transit to her house, her cell phone rang non-stop. What did Chancelor have to say now that he wouldn't say while they were together? She ignored each of his calls.

Disgusted, Storm arrived home and immediately turned on her iPod. Music played throughout her entire house. The list containing her favorite slow jams didn't help her to forget about Chancelor but it did put her in the mood to have sex with Tony.

Standing in the shower, Storm let the hot water pulsate against her body. Why was it so difficult to have an intellectual conversation about love with Chancelor? She wasn't opposed to answering his question, but love for her wasn't some casual acknowledgement that he should've made at a bar over drinks.

"Whatever," she said, massaging anti-aging cream on her face and body.

Storm slipped into what she called her indoor/outdoor attire. Dancing barefoot around her bedroom, she draped her body in a sheer green, blue, brown, and white printed dress. The hem clung mid-thigh, the sleeves flared over her wrists. She flung her arms wide, twirled like a ballerina. Brown beads lined the plunging V-collar that dipped below her cleavage, slightly exposing a hint of her areolas.

The black boy-cut Rodeo-H briefs were her new way to strapon. No harness. No straps around her waist and thighs. All she had to do when he was ready was attach the dildo to the front opening. The briefs would allow her to get close like a man, while fucking a man.

Three-inch black sandals exposed her succulent onyx-and-diamonds pedicure. She was ready for Anthony and he was right on time.

Opening the door, Storm smiled. "Hi, come in."

"Well, I'm glad we were able to get on the same page before I got here," Anthony said, strolling into the foyer like he'd been to her house before. Immediately he removed his shoes and socks.

Storm extended her hand. "Pleased to finally meet you."

"Aw, with your generosity more than a handshake is in order," he said, raising his brows twice. "We don't have to be that formal behind closed doors. I want to hear more about your riding techniques," Tony said, giving her an affectionate slow rub down her spine.

The things men agreed to do for money or sex were astonishing. Their freakish fantasies were jaw-dropping. If anyone had seen Tony walk through her front door, based on his Calvin Klein, charcoal, slim-fit suit they might assume he was the CEO of a Fortune 500 company. Nails impeccably manicured and pedicured. Tapered afro, just enough to pinch, not grab. The sexy skinny goatee that showed he was edgy, different. Unlike the other opponents, he wasn't afraid to grow a little facial hair.

He navigated his way to the first stop in her home, the bar. The living area was off to one side, entertainment room to the other. "Wow, this would make the perfect bachelor pad." Reaching for a bottle on the top shelf, Tony helped himself to a hefty glass of scotch. "So you live in this mansion by yourself?"

If he thought her place was a mansion, what would he think of Morgan's, Brooks's, and Hope's homes? There was one thing he was right about: every man that had stepped foot in her spot drooled.

"Only when I don't have company," Storm replied with a smile. She set an empty glass on the bar in front of him.

"Oh; how rude of me." He laughed, poured her a triple shot, refilled his glass.

Well, Anthony Dennison wasn't short on being a self-centered asshole. If she didn't need the footage, she would've put him out, then thrown his shoes and socks after him. Storm left the glass of scotch untouched, opened a bottle of chilled champagne, poured herself a drink, then hurried to catch up to Tony.

"I hope you don't mind me giving myself a tour. I need to buy my wife a house like this."

What he really meant was he wished her house was his. "You do plan on winning the election, don't you? Otherwise, I can invest my money in Randall Wallace."

He downed the remainder of his drink, plopped the glass on her nightstand, removed his clothes. "Don't be silly. That's enough small talk. Let's do this."

Damn, she had enticed him over the phone but this man seemed to have zero reservations. Maybe he subscribed to the Rich Girls' motto: Never fuck anyone who had nothing to lose.

Storm wondered why some men just wanted to get off with lit-tle or no conversation. Maybe Tony had fucked so many women without getting caught that taking off his clothes was automatic.

Inspecting his body, Storm determined that Tony's best asset wasn't his ass. It was his creamy chocolate lips that exposed per-fectly aligned teeth. His smile alone was worth a million dollars. Maybe that's what had gotten him in the race.

Cocktails, the promise of a check, and a candid conversation about sex had landed Anthony Dennison in Storm's bed. When some men thought no one was watching, or there was no way anyone would find out, and they believed that the woman they could act out their fantasy with was naïve, their pants quickly came off.

Not every man wanted to sex the woman they were with. Some desired spankings, others flogging. Some wanted to mu-tually masturbate or have the woman jerk them off. Others, like Tony, claimed, "I just want to role-play with you, Storm. I've never had a real jockey mount me. Ride me, baby."

Storm exhaled, eased pink lace panties over Anthony's feet then pulled them up to his hips. The head of his dick nearly touched his navel. His balls hung out of the bottom of the boy shorts. His lower shaft was snug inside the elastic.

His colossal dick was long and hard, just like the rest of his body. Storm's pussy wanted him inside her. She wanted to pull her harness underwear aside and let him fuck her, but Tony had made it clear that pussy wasn't on his agenda.

"Those shorts are hot on you, Tony. How long have you been into cross-dressing?" Fastening the back of the pink lace bra, Storm trailed kisses from the nape of Tony's neck down to his sweet ass.

Storm had to find a way to convince him to fuck her, or else she was going to have to text Chancelor to come over and take the edge off for both of them. That wasn't a bad idea. Makeup sex would be the perfect apology for not answering his calls and his question.

"You have to promise to keep this between us," Tony said, smearing on strawberry lip gloss. "I've been secretly doing this since I was a little boy, playing dress-up with my mother's wardrobe."

"And your mom never caught you?"

"Never. Parents don't give kids enough credit for knowing right from wrong. Whenever she noticed her panties were missing, I blamed my sister."

"What about your wife. Doesn't she know?"

"Are you serious? Hell, no. The worst thing a man can do is confide in his spouse. Telling my deepest secret or fantasy to my wife is a divorce wish. If she doesn't leave my ass the first time I make a mistake, she'll publicly embarrass me or throw it in my face, like a feeding a pig slop."

"So are you into men at all?" Storm asked, glancing up at her hidden cameras then back to him.

"You're hot, Storm, but if I wanted pussy, I'd fuck my wife."

"If I were a man I'd want to fuck you in the ass, Tony. You're, like, irresistible."

Tony laughed. "It's like a straight guy knows he shouldn't do a dude, but if no one was watching, he'd definitely bang another straight guy like me. Turn around, babe. Look at me."

"Keep it real. Have you ever had sex with a man? If you did, I sure hope you weren't on top," Storm said, sliding her hand along his firm dick.

Anthony shook his head, then nodded. "That's the thing about my liking to cross-dress. It's not about fucking men. But I can't lie. I've been on the top and the bottom with a man. Once. I prefer having a woman penetrate me. Life is short, you know. No matter who I fuck at the end of the day, it's my decision and it's my dick." He shook his head. "Why am I telling you all of this? You have a pair of heels and wig I can put on? And since you've got me all hard and shit, go on and strap on for me like you said you would."

She'd gotten everything in his size to fulfill his desires: shoes, lingerie, and wig. The makeup on the nightstand was fresh, plentiful, and colorful. If he asked, she'd create a work of art, from making up his face to polishing his toes.

Tony sucked in his lips, raised his brows, strutted back and forth in his stilettos, then tilted his head down toward her. He was totally dressed in drag but he wasn't a drag.

"It'll be my pleasure," Storm said, easing her dress over her head. Her titties were perky and her nipples hard. She licked the silicone dick then snapped her dildo into the opening of her harness underwear.

Storm peeled back the pink boy shorts clinging to his hard round ass, squirted lube inside, then massaged his asshole with the lace. She pulled his underwear to one side then said, "How would you like this dick? Gentle? Or rough?"

"Start off easy, then fuck the shit out of me. And don't you hold back, bitch," he said, looking over his shoulder.

Bitch? That's cool. "Bend over. On your knees," she commanded, shoving him forward. She kicked his knees farther apart.

Storm eased the head up and down the crack of his ass, slowly put the head in then pulled out. In and out. She went a little deeper, gently squeezed his balls. Holding his nuts in her hand, she glided all the way in.

"Uh, yeah!" he grunted. "That feels amazing. You sure know how to ride."

With the millions of dollars she had, if Storm had a dick, what kind of man would she be? Nice and considerate? Careless, reckless...getting women pregnant then dogging them out? Would she be the marrying kind? Or would she be like Anthony, with a dick in her ass?

"Yes. That's it! Now fuck me like you mean it," Tony grunted. "Give it to me like an F5 tornado. Swirl then rip me apart!" Anthony braced himself on the edge of her bed, tilted his ass higher in her direction.

Whack! Storm slapped his ass.

Riding him like he was her champion thoroughbred, she stroked his dick until she couldn't take it anymore.

Damn! She thought about him ejaculating and had to feel that dick deep inside of her before he came. In one fluid motion, Storm tore open a condom, covered Tony's dick, pulled the dildo out of his butt, flipped him onto his back, turned her dildo in the opposite direction, sat on his dick, then slid the dildo back in his ass.

"Aw, shit!" Tony screamed like the bitch he'd soon become.

Perfect, she thought.

Tony invited himself into her shower, put on his clothes, then collected his million dollar check. "Thanks," he said, staggering to the left, then right. Speechless, he shook his head. "I'll see myself out."

CHAPTER 14

Morgan

Their silence seemed different tonight. Perhaps it was all in her head.

From the day they'd met, even when they didn't speak the energy between them was uplifting and comforting. Even without touching, their love was always present. Not tonight. For the first time, she suspected he knew her silence was about more than the fact that something was on her mind. She felt he detected she'd let another man penetrate her.

Unless they were spooning, Morgan had never turned her back on her husband. The space between them now was wide enough for Brooks and Bo to slip in without touching either of them.

Glancing in his direction, Morgan saw that Magnum was on the edge of the bed facing the wall. He looked over his shoulder. She turned away.

Brooks's announcement was three weeks away.

"You want to talk about what's bothering you?" he asked. His tone was flat, as though his inquiry was a mere courtesy.

No, she didn't. What if she accused him of cheating and she

was wrong? Was her infidelity to blame for her distrust? Sexing Brooks in their bed had been a bad decision but letting Bo fuck her...what had she been thinking? Watching Storm and Hope's videos had aroused her. Made her feel adventurous. Morgan wished she'd exercised control. The orgasms definitely weren't worth putting her marriage at risk. But her indiscretions were irreversible.

"Hah, what's bothering me?" she asked, trying to conceal the quaver in her voice. "What you mean is, am I ready to tell Brooks I'm not announcing her candidacy? That she can't enter the race? Or do you want to tell me something else that I should know regarding Brooks before we go public? You know everything about her past will be revealed."

The distance between them was wider than the space in their bed and about something bigger than the politics of Brooks's candidacy. For the first time, she sensed Brooks's energy oozing from her husband's pores. Why hadn't she noticed before?

Morgan stuck her finger in her ear then rattled her head. Maybe the situation was all a figment of her imagination. Perhaps only her slutty conscience had heard Brooks call out Magnum's name while she was making love to Brooks.

Morgan wondered if Magnum had sexed Brooks in their bed. The thought made her heart pound against her breast. Her breathing became shallow. She knew her husband was handsome. Knew many of the women that visited the spa flirted with him each time they came in for services. Some came for treatments just to have a reason to see her husband. But he wouldn't fuck her best friend. Would he? If so, why?

She could deal with all of those other women with undeserving pussies. What she couldn't approve of was her husband fucking *her* woman.

"Baby, I'm not psychic," he said, facing her. "Come here. Let me hold you." He moved to the center of their bed, where Brooks had been sprawled not long ago, then opened his arms. "I love you. And no matter what you do, I will always love you."

Did that mean regardless of what she'd done, he'd never leave her?

Morgan's frustrations were to blame for her not embracing her husband. On the edge wasn't where she wanted to be, but it certainly was where she'd ended up. The wrong words could cause her to crash and explode. Best if she stayed where she was.

Facing the nightstand, Morgan sat up, placed her feet on the floor, turned on the light. "This won't last forever. We've never had this kind of tension between us and I pray it will end soon. It's just that I need to process what I think is happening between you and Brooks."

Magnum sat beside her, held her, then looked into her eyes. "Baby, did I hear you correctly? Me and Brooks? What made you say that? I don't know what you're talking about. Stop procrastinating and give it to me straight so I can give you a direct answer."

There was no use in confronting Magnum. Morgan stood, paced the floor. He blocked her path. When it came to cheating, she believed he'd die with the scent of Brooks's pussy on his lips before he'd admit, "Yes, I did fuck Brooks and baby, I'm sorry. It won't happen again."

She stood before him, folded her arms. Magnum got back in bed, slid his hands behind his head. "I give up."

Realistically she was dying to ask him again. Should she? Was she prepared to hear his truth? Maybe she should rethink her approach and listen to her own truth first. Wasn't as though she had proof. If she questioned him about her suspicions, he'd probably just change his routine.

Men were like that. The more their women confronted them, the smarter they became. If her husband were screwing Brooks because he'd grown bored with their sex life, he'd find another bed to bury his skeletons in.

"It's silly," Morgan finally said. "Go back to sleep."

"It is silly," he agreed. "Come here. Suck my dick. You'll feel better."

For the first time this morning, she laughed, crawled back into bed. She kneeled over him. When she held his shaft, it stiffened then pointed up at her. Indeed she craved his chocolate magic wand. No matter how upset she was, Morgan couldn't deny how much her husband excited her.

The energy stirring inside her made her playfully dive toward him, open her mouth wide and suck him in. She kept taking him in until his head hit her tonsils. Opening wider she pressed deeper, held his head to the back of her throat. Her body shivered.

"That's right, baby. Get yours, too," Magnum said, oozing precum in her mouth.

Morgan swallowed, sucked him until he ejaculated and his dick stopped pulsating. When her husband's dick stopped throbbing, the pounding in her temples started. She was not going to be able to drown her problems no matter how many orgasms they shared. Sooner or later, the truth was going to surface.

"Damn, Morgan. What now?" he asked. "Never mind. Don't answer. I'm outta here."

Morgan slid under the covers and closed her eyes. Letting her husband go now was best for both of them.

Magnum wasn't the only reason she had a headache. Hope's demands to see the investment reports had become more frequent after the million dollar checks given to the candidates were paid directly from Storm's father's account. But the reimbursements had had to come from Storm and Hope. With all of their questions unanswered, the girls had decided not to contribute any additional money to the Rich Girls' Club fund.

She knew Magnum had told her not to touch their household investments for Brooks's campaign, but he hadn't said she couldn't donate money to another candidate. The funds could be transferred from her and her husband's account to that of the Rich Girls' Club, then be given to Bailey Goodman. But it was still only a matter of time before she would have to explain to Magnum and the girls how she'd lost twenty million dollars.

Morgan would give herself time to think about what was best.

CHAPTER 15

Brooks

The research was becoming time-consuming, tedious, and monotonous.

Never in her life had she read more words than she'd had to do now, but her degrees from UCLA and Stanford, and completing her dissertation had prepared her for this task. There had been times in her life that she'd wondered why she so aggressively pursued higher education and hadn't stopped until she had her Ph.D. She insisted her closest friends call her Brooks, but there were a few patrons and associates at the women's club in Beverly Hills that knew to address her as Dr. Kennedy.

One of her favorite quotes was by Steve Jobs: "You can't connect the dots looking forward; you can only connect them looking backwards. So you have to trust that the dots will somehow connect in your future. You have to trust in something—your gut, destiny, life, karma, whatever. This approach has never let me down, and it has made all the difference in my life." Instead of her dots connecting in a good way, Brooks was worried that her bad decisions, that had seemed harmless at the time she'd made them, would snowball into her future, roll downhill, and crash into a brick wall.

Seeing her number one guy tonight was a welcome diversion. Brooks organized the documents on her desk into seven piles. Each stack represented one of her opponents. Laura had the shortest, Goodman the tallest. She'd lined up the candidates' background information as Morgan had outlined in the plan. From ascending to descending order, they were ranked accordingly from what she considered the most to the least challenging to her own campaign.

Brooks closed the door to her office. *I'm so glad I didn't let Bo penetrate me.* She wondered how that episode was playing out in Morgan's world. What was Morgan thinking?

The linen on her bed was fresh. She hadn't grown accustomed to doing her own laundry and cleaning, didn't think she ever would, but for now it was necessary and perhaps best not to have staff in her private space. Sneaking in a maid or two a few days a week would be helpful but not worth the risk if they found any of the scandalous videos still in her possession.

The water in the enclosed backyard Jacuzzi was heated to a hundred and four degrees, the way he liked it. Brooks placed a bottle of his favorite merlot beside the tub with two wine goblets. She'd ordered a tray of the finest cheese, caviar, and crackers. Tonight, she was considering telling her longtime lover what he might already know.

The chiming throughout her house meant he was at the front door. They'd known each another long enough for her to bypass the hours of prepping and primping before his arrival. Wasn't as though he were *her* husband.

The moment she looked into his expressionless face she knew he knew something, but she wasn't sure what.

"So, how are you?" he asked, entering her house. He walked past her—no hug, no kiss—and sat on the sofa. "You got a minute? We need to talk."

"You can stay there as long as you'd like. I'll be outside in the Jacuzzi." Brooks meant what she said. He was the man in her house, not of her house. No man was, not even her ex when he'd been her husband. "We can talk there."

If Brooks was going to acquire the political power bestowed upon men, she had to start thinking and acting like a man. Removing her robe, she settled her naked body deep into the bubbling water, until her entire body was submerged up to her neck.

"Oh, this feels so good," she moaned, watching him walk toward her.

She inhaled the fresh mild scent of chlorine bursting through the tiny bubbles splashing on her nose. Above her, as far as she could see, the sky was lit with almost a thousand stars. If her estimate was accurate, she'd read about the same number of documents today.

Sliding one of her lounge chairs near the tub, Magnum sat on the edge. "So are you telling me you won't take a moment to hear what I need to say?"

Brooks stared at Magnum. "I never said I wouldn't listen to you."

The intensity of her projection matched his. Stern. Cold. Unwavering. "We can discuss it after you take off your clothes and get in the tub. I have a lot on my plate right now and I don't need you adding any mental or emotional stress to my already heavy load. Get in and fuck me or go to the spa where you're supposed to be."

His eyes bulged; he cleared his throat. "What the hell has gotten into you?"

Yes, there was a first time for everything and he'd heard her correctly. She wasn't repeating herself or responding to his "What..."

Brooks filled a glass of merlot nearly to the rim. If he wanted a drink he could help himself. If he wanted her pussy, he could help himself to that, too, but neither the wine nor the cheese would go to waste. She prayed the same was true for her orgasms.

Sipping her merlot, she resumed gazing at the stars. The ambiance and the wine began to relax her. Fifteen minutes went by. Magnum was still seated on the edge of the lounge chair.

Were the stars in alignment? If the stars connected the dots from her past, would they form a volcano on the verge of erupting, an atomic bomb, or a tunnel that led to brighter days? Was there a proper order to all elements of nature, including human behavior? Were men supposed to lead and women to follow, even when women didn't want to?

Brooks had always preferred to show her softer side by wearing dresses but from now on, underneath her dress would be a pair of those Rodeo-H underwear Storm had told her about. Even though she'd never used a strap-on, knowing that she was prepared would make her feel manlier than any man, including Magnum. A woman fucking a man represented a woman's highest sexual power.

Not being born with the ability to do something that one could later conquer represented the ultimate achievement. Any man with a dick could fuck without engaging his brain. But a woman with a dick could fuck things up for anybody.

Yeah, she was definitely in control and she sensed Magnum hated her for that.

Quietly he removed his clothes, tossed them on the lounge

chair, then joined her in the Jacuzzi. He sat across from her, starring at her. "Brooks, why?" he asked, looking as though he'd just lost his best friend.

Brooks wasn't confused. She was best friends with both Magnum and Morgan, though Morgan had no idea about the connection she and Magnum had built.

Every woman needed a male friend they could confide in, laugh with, cum with, and stay together with through the toughest of times. But successful women didn't need to fuck insecure men. Magnum had always seemed confident, until now. Another first for them. He was entitled to his feelings but he'd have to deal with his unspoken issues, not she.

The obvious response would've been, "Why, what?"

Instead of engaging him in conversation, Brooks waded to Magnum and began kissing him passionately. Her tongue slid into his mouth, suctioning his tongue. She held the sides of his face the way he liked as she continued their exchange of saliva.

Magnum pulled back. She refused to allow him to break their connection. Her hand slipped under the water in search of his dick. Ah, there it was. Nice and hard, the way she wanted it inside her pussy.

Positioning her vagina atop his head she slid down on his shaft. Men were so predictable when it came to pussy, or so she'd thought until he pushed her off of him.

He severed all physical contact with her then said, "We—"

She swallowed his tongue and whatever he was going to say next. No need to talk. His words were not what she wanted. Grinding her clit against his pubic hairs as she squatted onto his dick again, Brooks felt his head damn near pressing against her stomach.

She took control of his dick. Rotating her hips into his, she grabbed the back of his head, sucked his tongue deeper, until the walls of her cheeks caved in. He moaned for a moment, then grunted when she bounced nice and slow. She wasn't trying to audition for a music video. Mature women knew exactly what to do to please a man and themselves at the same time.

When she raised up, she paused. He was the one to grab her hips then, lower her onto his lap. Now he was kissing her, grabbing the back of head, following her lead. Brooks knew he thought he was in charge but he wasn't.

"Whose dick is this?" Brooks whispered, fucking him harder.

"Morgan's. You know that."

Right answer. She just wanted to make certain he wasn't confused. Brooks never wanted Magnum to love her more than he loved his wife.

"When you're done fucking me, we're going to have my conversation," he said, thrusting harder.

Her body felt amazing all over. She'd listen to what he had to say if she didn't fall asleep first. "Oh my god, Magnum, I'm cumming so hard ba—" At the peak of her climax Brooks froze. "What was that?"

"What was what?" he asked.

She placed her finger over his lip. It was too dark to see but she'd heard something on the other side of the fence outside. She waited. He remained silent.

"I'm uncomfortable. I know heard something unusual. Let's go inside."

"It's probably a raccoon or a deer. Relax."

"You relax if you want to. I'm going inside," Brooks insisted. Getting out of the tub, she grabbed a towel and tossed him one.

Magnum powered off the Jacuzzi, followed her to the bedroom. Drying himself he asked, "Brooks, why are you running for governor?"

Before she could answer he said, "Don't do this to us. Don't let the public do this to us, to my wife. They'll find out about our affair. Trust me; it's going to become public and when it does, you'll lose. I'll lose. We'll all lose."

"I can't drop out," Brooks said. "End of conversation."

"I'm not asking you," Magnum said, sliding under the covers. "I'm telling you."

Being exposed more than she already was was a risk that Brooks was taking with or without Magnum's blessings.

"What part of 'end of conversation' didn't you get? Good night, Magnum."

CHAPTER 16

Hope

N o. I'm not reconsidering my offer. Please, ... I said no.
Stop calling me!"

"But this is the other Mrs. Littleton and my wife extends her
sincere apology if she offended you in any—"

If? Hope ended the call, placed her cell phone on the dining
table. "Damn! Only a fool could talk themselves out of a million
dollars." She sprang from her seat, picked up her and Stanley's
plates.

That had been the fifth person to call on Laura's behalf, begging for the donation. But Hope didn't care if Laura's mama
called. What part of "no" didn't they understand? Maybe the
next time Laura would engage her brain before opening her
mouth. The woman was a loser. What Laura's wife should
do was tell Laura the truth. Laura wasn't attractive, smart, or
charming, and all her stupid grin did was to make other people
frown.

"So now she needs my money? Her campaign funds must be
extremely low..." Hope paused, placed the plates on the gran-
ite countertop.

"What are you talking about? Never mind," Stanley said, cutting himself off. "This is ridiculous. You know that. I feel like a silent partner that's been trapped into something illegal. I shouldn't be subjected to this. Why your sudden interest in politics? And why are you considering giving her that much money? I hope you're not smuggling drugs for your dad or something." Then he mumbled, "Stranger things have happened."

Hope sat on the stool, covered her eyes for a moment then stared at the floor, thinking out loud. "Hmm. How can I convince others not to contribute to Laura's fund? That woman couldn't run her household, let alone a state. She seriously believed that having her wife call would make me change my mind. Okay. Marinate on this for a moment, Hope. This may be the simplest and best way to handicap Laura's campaign. Low funds equate to little or no advertising. If I can create negative propaganda about Laura, Laura will have to invest her financial resources to clean up her reputation. Whatever that is."

Brooks's announcement was two weeks away. Hope brushed her hair away from her face and smiled at her man.

Stanley pushed back his chair, snatched his keys off the kitchen's island. "Thanks for lunch. I'm out. You don't need me for the conversation going on in your head. In fact, you need to make up your mind. Either tell me what's going on, or I'm moving on. I can't afford to lose my job. If you're transporting drugs, do it without me."

"Stop trying to wedge yourself into something that doesn't concern you. Nobody is transporting anything."

She knew she was the catch in their relationship, not him. Replacing Stanley could happen with the press of a button. One phone call would do it if that were what Hope wanted. But she'd invested three years in training him to sex her the way she liked, and finding another man as trustworthy as Stanley would probably cost her more than the amount she was unwilling to give Laura. Starting over a new relationship would be a complete waste of time when she already had the right man in front of her.

Hope dated Stanley because he didn't compete with her like the millionaire men she'd gone out with. He hadn't asked to drive any of her luxury cars. Wasn't trying to move into her house. Didn't take advantage of her generosity, like the guy who'd asked her to open a joint bank account. That fool thought he'd hit the jackpot when he'd met her. Just as fast as he'd appeared, Hope had made his broke ass disappear.

Stanley was transparent. He didn't have a hidden agenda for being her man. That was her dick and he wasn't going anywhere except back to bed to fuck her again.

"Baby, you're right. Sit down and let me explain," she said, taking his keys.

He backed away. She stepped closer, lowered her eyes then glanced up at him. "Please."

Sighing heavily, he conceded. "If I didn't love your ass I would've been gone. Now if I'm staying you need to tell your man: what's up with you?"

Now she was the one sighing. Hope began clearing the serving dishes from the table so Stanley couldn't see the shiftiness in her eyes. Turning on the water she rinsed the dishes, then loaded the dishwasher. "If I tell you the truth, you have to swear you won't tell anyone. Not even your mama. Especially not your mama."

"Keep my mom out of this. You haven't even met her."

True. A woman with lots of money didn't care much about

meeting a man's mother, unless she was sure he was the one she'd stand beside at the altar. "Promise me."

"You've got it," he said, picking up the dirty glasses. "We've never had secrets, baby, and I don't want us to start being dishonest with each other. I tell you everything. I deserve the same respect."

She'd had enough of his telling her what he'd already told her. She slowly kissed his lips, shutting him up, trying to conjure a believable lie. "My dad is considering running for governor." Where in the hell did *that* come from? She would've been better off not saying anything. *Damn, Hope.*

"Of what?" he asked, placing the glasses on the top rack. "His tribe?"

"Tribes don't have governors. California, silly."

"He can't do that . . . can he? Can Indians hold office and own casinos? Seems like a conflict to me."

"Please tell me you're not serious," Hope said, drying her hands on his shirt.

"I guess I never thought about that, but I am serious. Besides, why would you give his potential opponent a million dollars?" he asked, looking in her eyes. "Why in the hell are you doing this? You're still fucking lying to me. I'm out."

Then why was he still standing in front of her?

"I don't want you to leave here upset. Let's relax outside in the Jacuzzi and have a drink."

Stanley sighed. His lips and forehead tightened.

"Please," she pleaded with sad eyes.

"Don't look at me like that," he said. A tiny smile emerged and his eyes widened a little.

The power women possessed to enhance their relationship was persuasive when they weren't combative. "I need you.

Come on." Hope didn't wait for a response. She kissed him softly, picked up her iPad, then turned away.

"I'll get the vodka, cranberry, and ice and meet you outside," he said, slapping her ass.

Reclining on the patio chaise, she thumbed through the catalog of new car models she'd left there to see what she'd purchase next. "Come see, babe. Look at this."

Stanley made two drinks, held on to his, placed hers on the nearby table, then sat beside her. "Damn, that's the shit! Are you going to get it?"

"Just decided. I'm buying four."

"Four?"

Hope knew online car shopping would distract Stanley from revisiting what she didn't want to discuss. One lie would only beget another and another and there was no way she was telling her man the truth, or letting him go.

"One each for Brooks, Morgan, Storm, and myself," she said, showing him the three-hundred-sixty-degree tour of the Mercedes SLS AMG.

"Baby, I'm going to customize mine. The exterior is going to be bubblegum pink with twenty-inch, five-spoke alloy wheels. Bubblegum interior with aluminum trimmings. And of course they'll all have to come fully loaded."

"Damn! That's going to be the sexiest girl car on the road."

Instead of giving the money to Laura, with the press of a button, Hope spent a total of 1.2 million on gifts for her girls and herself. She'd have the cars delivered to Morgan's house during their next meeting and surprise them.

Placing her computer on the table, Hope exchanged it for a drink and relocated to the Jacuzzi with Stanley.

CHAPTER 17

Storm

Morning was her favorite but any time of the day was great to hold her man.

The rising sun cast a ray through the skylight in her bedroom that warmed her soul. Feathering her fingers over his hair a bright idea shined in her mind, and a wide smile beamed across her face.

Storm peeled back the covers. Chancelor's erection spiked. Her libido would've followed pursuit but she was already hot for him. Careful not to awaken the rest of him she eased out of bed, escaped into her lingerie closet, and closed the door.

Scanning left to right, her outfits hung first according to color, next by fabric. From lace to satin to the silkiest silk, with accents of rubies, diamonds, and pearls on garters, bras, and thongs. The animal prints had a section of their own and they were organized by feline—cheetah, jaguar, leopard, tiger. Life for her was never about black and white, so there wasn't a single zebra print or stripe in her collection, filled with pieces by Agent Provocateur, Argento Vivo of Italy, Chantelle, or her favorite, Lise Charmel of France.

Since the cheetah was the fastest of them all and she wasn't feeling as dominating as the leopard, she selected a pair of red platform stilettos to go with a silky cheetah cami set. The panties gently hugged her hips while barely covering her pubic area. The spaghetti-strap top caressed her breasts and torso.

Standing over her man, softly she sang his name. "Chancelor."

His eyes fluttered open. He blinked, sat up. "Damn." A wide smile stretched across his cheeks. "Come here," he said, pulling her on top of him. He kissed away her red lip gloss, slid his hand inside her panties, and cupped her ass.

Moving his hand, Storm said, "I'll do whatever you like... but you have to give me five minutes. I'm going to hide and you have to come and get it. And don't cheat," she said, tiptoeing out the bedroom.

She couldn't have initiated such a game with the mayor. He was too lazy and wanted the pussy brought to him each time. That was boring. She wasn't sure what had prompted her to expose her secret space this morning but she didn't question her spontaneity.

Storm remained in her attic for fifteen minutes, hoping Chancelor would find her soon. He'd never been in her attic but surely he'd think to look up as he searched her house. She'd left the opening ajar. The last boyfriend she'd invited to join her up there had wanted to fuck in the attic every time she invited him over.

Chancelor called out, "Storm. Where are you? I can't find you."

She couldn't blame that ex for wanting to live out his fantasies in her love nest. The ceiling was high, the floor space was wide, covered with wall-to-wall black carpet. She'd had a shower, a vanity, and a toilet installed. The onyx free-standing tub with its platinum fixtures and feet was in the center of it all.

Any woman with an imagination bold enough to reserve a room in her place designed with "everything" sex in mind had an environment that would make most men fall in love at first sight, not to mention jealous. In a man's mind, her space might be seen as a place that should be his. But it wasn't his, so a man might create as many opportunities as possible to revisit her love nest.

The ones lucky enough to have such an experience were likely sure to share with all their friends and lovers the most intimate details over and over and over. And when her men weren't reliving the fantasy with others, she thought they were probably rewinding and replaying the highlights in their minds while masturbating.

Sounded like Chancelor's voice was echoing from the kitchen. Storm lowered the attic's ladder, sat on the top step, and opened her legs. She remained quiet, fingered her straight black hair, then repositioned her titties to slightly expose her nipples.

"Damn! So that's where you went," Chancelor said when he found her, and he climbed the stairs. "What's up with all the hidden cameras? You've been recording us without telling me?"

Shit! She hadn't thought about him noticing the cameras. "Security. A woman can't take her safety for granted," she said, drawing the stairs up to close.

Her attic wasn't ordinary. She'd decorated it with a sex lounger, Tantra chair, sex swing, and massage table. A blow up doll sat on a stool. Toys galore were generously on display, powered with batteries, ready for use. A refrigerator, a wine rack, and a fully stocked wet bar were in one corner. "Would you like to make a sex tape with me, baby?" she asked, passionately kissing him. There was a camera set up in the attic just in case she'd decided to invite Randy or Tony to her love nest. But she hadn't.

"Sure." He followed her to the bar. "Wow! And why haven't I seen this before now? I've only been your man for what? Three years."

She hadn't believed their relationship would last beyond three months. Each man that she'd invited into her attic later questioned her about what other men had been up there. Storm wondered if she'd made the wrong decision.

"Your talking is spoiling the mood. Here," she said mixing then handing him a drink.

"You think we'll ever get married?" Chancelor asked, tasting his dirty martini.

Tuning into one of her favorite Pandora stations, she welcomed the sound of smooth Jazz floating throughout the attic. Her plan was for them to enjoy a romantic morning with a couple of martinis. Relax on the sex chair with his back against one side, hers against the other, with her legs over his shoulders. They had all morning to enjoy each another. Longer, if he didn't mess up the mood.

Finishing her drink in a continuous flow, she told him, "Take off your clothes and don't ask me any more relationship questions. If you do, we're done."

Chancelor exhaled, stared at a painting on the wall of a naked couple.

"And lose the attitude or you can go home right now."

"I'm cool," he said.

Storm filled the tub with warm water and bubble bath. "Get in and don't say a word."

She sponged her man all over, twice between his legs, then

stroked his dick one time before getting in. She lay her head on his chest, and he returned the favor and bathed her.

Chancelor kissed the nape of neck. "I love you, Storm."

There were those words again. She didn't want to think. She just wanted to let their energy resonate in harmony. Between the vodka and Chancelor's erection pressing along her spine, her pussy was percolating.

Storm stepped out of the tub, dried herself, then her man. She positioned him on the S-shaped, armless chair. Two feet high, two feet wide, the chair's firm cushion was the perfect length for Chancelor's body. The perfect width for her to straddle him and squat onto his erection in the reverse cowgirl position.

Gently he massaged her back. Featherlike strokes moved from her shoulders, down her sides to her ass, back up to her shoulders. Again his hand traced the strokes. The love in his touch overwhelmed her.

"I'm not sure if you noticed, but I had my accountant deposit two hundred and fifty thousand into your bank account yesterday," she told him.

Storm closed her eyes. The heaviness in her body gave way to his touch. He slid his hand between her thighs. Grazing her clit he moved toward her knees, barely making contact with her clit, then squeezed her inner thighs.

She felt like she was going to explode from the inside out. His love consumed her. She'd hoped her mention of the money would distract him. But it didn't.

"Thanks. I appreciate you," he whispered. "This is why I want to share my life with you. You care about me unconditionally. Your word is bond. No one has ever shown me this kind of love. I can't repay you with money but I will always love you, Storm."

Holding her chin, he turned her face sideways toward his. His lips pressed against hers and she came hard as he held her in his arms.

"I love you, too, Chancelor," was what she wanted to say. But she didn't. She couldn't.

She cherished the way he ended their lovemaking sessions with what she thought of as a cool down period. Light touches streamed all over her body. Her eyelids became heavier. She led him to the queen-sized bed. Her body nestled into the mattress. The more time she shared with Chancelor, Storm knew it was only a matter of time before she told him what was in her heart. She'd become emotionally attached to him. But that wasn't supposed to happen.

Her parents wouldn't approve.

The truth was they were perfect for one another. She knew that. But what about five, ten, fifteen, twenty years from now? Would he feel the same? Would she care? Knowing that she left Chancelor better off than when he'd met her at least made Storm feel good about sponsoring his education.

If he used the money wisely, in four years he could begin making his own millions. She didn't want Chancelor to do what she thought was best for him. If a man were to become a man, he had to make his own decisions. Find his own way.

"I'm going to take a quick nap, then I have some other business to tend to," Storm mumbled.

"I'll just watch television," he said. "If you need me, call me. I'll be downstairs in the entertainment room." Chancelor kissed her cheek, tucked her in.

Oh, shit! Storm's eyes sprang open. Did he say the entertainment room?

Her feet hit the floor. She hurried down the ladder, rushed to the other side of her home, stood in the doorway. *Damn!*

The video of her fucking Tony was playing on the flat screen. But Chancelor wasn't there. That meant he'd probably seen the previous footage of her sexing Randy. Chancelor was young, but she was about to find out whether or not he was naïve. That was if she could find him.

"Chancelor!" she called out.

Her voice echoed. She hurried to the garage. His car was gone. Whatever part of his heart was broken, she prayed she could mend.

It was time for Storm to tell Chancelor how she truly felt or risk losing him for good.

CHAPTER 18

Morgan

Morgan drove slowly along Interstate 405. A ten o'clock traffic jam was unexpected for a Saturday night. Morgan hardly noticed. The nerves in the pit of her stomach felt like she'd swallowed a baseball.

"How could she fuck my husband?" she asked herself, gripping the wheel tight. She felt the edges of her nails digging into her palms but she didn't care. The pain didn't compare to what was in her heart.

Going down on Brooks after another one of their meetings earlier today had been a big mistake. One she immediately regretted afterward. Brooks didn't taste the same, didn't feel the same, and Morgan was suffering from nausea. The sickness was so horrible it felt like a bad case of food poisoning.

Have it your way, Brooks. Three can play this game but just like the election there can only be one winner, bitch.

The rubber-soled shoes, black slacks, shirt, and ski mask she'd worn Friday night were buried in the bottom of Morgan's garbage can the same day. Trespassing on her so-called friend's property wasn't ladylike but suspicions of infidelity made people do strange things. That noise Brooks had heard while in the hot tub with Magnum hadn't been in Brooks's imagination.

Desperately struggling to suppress the roiling in her stomach, Morgan was losing the battle not to vomit. She heaved, then closed her mouth tight. *Oh, my, god.* She parked in the emergency lane, turned on her flashers. Searching for something, anything, to throw up in, but all she had was her purse. *No way.* She covered her mouth, heaved again. Vomit oozed between her fingers. She caught what she could with her other hand. *Shit.* Morgan flung open her door, leaned her head over the concrete, then opened wide. Her stomach contracted several times until all that was coming up was air.

Spitting on the ground, she yelled, "How could she walk into my house, sit in the club room, drink my liquor, eat my food, stare me in my face!" Morgan slammed her door closed.

She retrieved a package of wet wipes from the glove compartment, cleaned her hands, face, and clothes as best as she could, and tossed the soiled wipes out the window before merging back into traffic.

"Fuck!" She barely avoided hitting the car in front of her. She rubbed her aching head.

"That's what you get," she told herself.

Why had Morgan had to confirm her suspicions? Now that she knew the truth, she wished she didn't know at all. "Call off the plan. File for a divorce. And start a new life without both of them."

Magnum was to blame. "He did this shit hoping I'd find out and Brooks wouldn't enter the race. He's fucking both of us," she said to herself, lowering her window. The stench of puke disgusted her. The fresh air instantly made her feel better.

What about Storm's and Hope's investments? Time? Money?

This situation was bigger than she was. But bailing out was not the smart thing to do. "I swear on my mother's grave Brooks and Magnum are going to pay for betraying me."

"He had the audacity to stick his dick in my woman...and he thinks he's going to bring his dick to me, stick it in my face, and expect me to suck it!" She slammed on her brakes again. "Fuck!"

She had no business being on the road, or heading to her spa to get back at her husband. Magnum's transgression made her having fucked Bo easier for her to accept. Now, instead of sexing Bailey in Sacramento, Morgan had invited him to their spa.

Shaking her head side-to-side, she said, "And I don't give a damn if my cheating-ass husband walks in on me sucking the governor's dick and tea-bagging his balls. That'll serve his ass right." Her husband would have a better chance of fucking Bailey than feeling the inside of her pussy again anytime soon.

⌒

There was no documented record of Bailey's appointment but earlier in the day she'd installed a few hidden cameras in their deluxe massage room. Nothing over the top, high-tech like Storm had, but as long as she had the governor on tape, her job was done.

How long had her husband been fucking her woman? "It doesn't matter, bitch; stop tripping."

Things were bad. She was cursing herself. But even if he'd only done it one time that was one time too many. "They're both going to live long enough to regret their damn affair...fuck! I can't believe this shit. Not again! Where in the hell is everybody going? Why does that bitch keep hitting her brakes? Doesn't she know how to go with the flow?"

Thinking of flow, Morgan realized she still hadn't figured out how she was going to get back the Rich Girls' twenty million dollars. She'd promised to show them the statement at today's meeting but again she couldn't produce what she didn't have. Her life was a mess.

"Thank God." Her exit was next. Morgan drove a few blocks, parked at the spa. Her car was where her husband's car was normally. She did something she seldom did, called his cell phone.

"Hey, where are you?" he asked, sounding concerned.

Morgan was not the one that needed to provide answers. "Where are you?"

"At, home. I left the hotel. We need to talk about something important. When are you coming home?" he asked.

Wanting to say, "When I feel like it," she lied instead and said, "I'm on my way." Ending the call, she unlocked the spa from the street entrance, hoping no one would notice her. She navigated her way to the couples massage room, turned on the light and waited for her guest. Hopefully he'd show up on time.

Things were working to her advantage. Best if Magnum didn't walk in on her fucking Bailey Goodman. She didn't want to give her husband any leverage.

She showered, put on a robe. Bailey wouldn't be there long enough to soak in her amazing rose petal bath with the scent of fresh flowers floating abundantly under his nose, but she would. Dropping cinnamon oil onto a heated lamp, Morgan smiled. The scent of cinnamon in the air brought out the animal in men.

Governor Goodman was going to be the beneficiary of all her frustrations. His call was timely.

"Hi, Governor. You're here?"

"I'm outside in my car," he said.

"Wait exactly two minutes, then walk to the door. Let yourself in. I'll be waiting for you. I'm not turning on the lights because I don't want anyone to see you."

"I can do that," he said.

Exactly as timed, he was standing in the spa in front of her. "Give me your hand, follow me."

Morgan locked the door then led the way to the room where she'd get revenge on Magnum. She locked the door to the lighted room.

The Governor looked around. "Wow, nice spa. From what I can see. I'll have to come here more often."

"And when you're re-elected you can stay here as my guest. Complimentary."

"There are still kindhearted, generous people in the world, Morgan, but everybody wants something for something. What is it that you truly need for giving me a generous donation?"

"I just want to see you continue the excellent work you've been doing. I'm sure you could use a massage before you leave." Morgan tightened her robe.

His eyes caught a glimpse of the tip of her red lace. "Whoa," he said, "I'm glad you closed that up."

"If you don't want a full body massage, I'll just treat your neck and shoulders. All you need to remove is your shirt, but of course you'll be more comfortable if you take off everything and get under the covers," she said, turning her back to him. She smiled but he couldn't see her excitement. "Let me know when you're ready."

The rustling of clothes told her he'd removed his jacket, tie, and shirt. When she heard the unbuckling of his belt and the removal of his shoes, she smiled again.

"I'm ready," he said.

"Are you on your stomach, face nestled in the headrest, and covered up?"

"I sure am."

What she would do next would make history. Morgan removed her robe, placed it on a hook on the wall beside her. She decided to keep on her red lace bra and panties. Since the nerves in the feet were connected to every part of the body, she started with his toes, balls of the feet, arches, and heels.

"Ah, that feels so good," Bailey moaned. "I need this so much. I'm always on my feet, you know."

"Just relax, don't talk."

Morgan's hands traveled up his calves to the back of his knees. She took her time kneading the small of his back, then worked her way up to his shoulders and neck, giving a little extra attention to his erogenous zones.

The governor grunted then exhaled.

Gently she touched his bicep. "I want you to turn over slowly for me and slide down until your head is on the table." She held the sheet up shielding his naked body. "We'll be done here in a few," she lied again.

Saturating her hands with more oil, she started with his hands and worked her way up his arms. Standing at the head of the table she massaged his neck, shoulders, and chest. Morgan paused, teasing his nipples, then stood by the side of the table. She slid her hands over his stomach in a circular motion.

The last movement would be her best. Morgan stood at the foot of the table. This time her hands glided slowly up from his feet, up his legs to his inner thighs. She swept his genitals, continuing her flow down to his feet and back up again.

"Oh, I'm so embarrassed," he said, seeing his manhood rise.

Morgan peeled away the cover and began streaming light flutters up his shaft with her fingertips. Gently she kissed his engorged head, watching him grow larger. "Relax, and let go," she whispered.

She continued strumming him until the Governor's sperm squirted in her hands. She squatted beside the table, smeared his semen inside her panties, all over her pussy, then stood. That would be enough evidence to wreak havoc on his campaign.

"Is there a place I can shower?" he asked. "I really didn't mean for this to happen. The massage was wonderful but I apologize for letting myself go."

"No apology needed. The shower is straight through that door. Here's your check." Morgan handed him the million dollars as promised, but she'd written the check against revenue earned from the hotel.

It would've been easier to fuck Goodman and not give him the money than to explain the contribution to Magnum. Either way, her work was done and she'd kept her commitment to the Rich Girls.

CHAPTER 19

Brooks

Why did love pass through her like water?

Essential to sustain life, like the water she consumed, her love was recycled. One day she loved her husband. The next day her husband loved another woman. Friday Brooks had sexed Magnum. Saturday, Morgan. But the sex with both was different. Neither of their orgasms had been filled with passion. Domination took over Morgan's energy. Frustration had consumed Magnum.

Taking control of Magnum felt liberating. Struggling not to submit to Morgan had been a battle of the same sexes that neither of them had won. The only thing missing after both fights were the tears.

Morgan's actions cut deep. She had forced Brooks's legs open, yanking at her unnecessarily, spitting on her pussy, then finger-fucked her like she was trying to push her uterus through her navel. "Stop, it," Brooks had had to say.

If she was going to get fucked as if by a man, she would've let Bo stick his dick inside of her. Brooks knew something was bothering Morgan, but she never said what was on her mind and Brooks couldn't bring herself to ask. She prayed Morgan wasn't plotting something evil and that the upcoming announcement one week from now wasn't a setup.

Brooks's guilty conscience sensed her friend wanted to revisit her slipup, when she'd almost called out Magnum's name, but if she was going to run the state, she couldn't go running her mouth, confessing what could prove harmful. Best to act like a man and take her secrets to her grave. What good would it do for her to win the election yet lose her best friends?

In some ways, Brooks felt helpless. It was as if she craved human connection, stimulation, gratification, and sex, but she was temporarily emotionally detached from those who'd given her orgasmic pleasure. Like eating a prime Grade A steak and not caring how the cow was slaughtered; she had that same kind of simultaneous satisfaction and distance from her lovers. Her husband leaving her for another woman had pissed her off. But it was the principle, that he hadn't honored his vows, that had made Brooks bitter. Not the extramarital pussy.

Being in the moment of cumming felt amazing but after the excitement was over, she realized she didn't need or want the person she was with in her space. She enjoyed having someone to hold at night but when it was time for them to go she was ready for them to leave.

New partners were okay for some. For Brooks, familiarity was better, but wrapped up in her selfish desires she'd become oblivious to Morgan's feelings.

Love was essential to Brooks; being in love was not. She couldn't deny she had to have some elements of love to sustain her happiness. But was she so insensitive to Morgan's feelings that she no longer cared about her best friend? And now that he knew she was running for governor, Magnum acted as though she'd put a knife in his back. How could she regain Morgan's and Magnum's trust?

Was it best to minimize her interaction with Morgan (until after the election) and stop sexing Magnum forever? If one relationship had to end, undoubtedly it was her affair with Magnum. Brooks had to keep Morgan's friendship in order to remain a member of the Rich Girls' Club. But Magnum was a better friend.

For the first time in years, Brooks couldn't get out of bed. Pulling back the sheet, she stared at her feet to make sure they were still there. Her legs were numb. Mentally she tried to get up but physically her body declined. She felt paralyzed.

She heard footsteps headed her way. "Who's there?" she called out, knowing only two people had access to her home. Morgan. And Goodman.

The tall, silver-haired sexy white man she should've married stood in the doorway grinning like a little boy. "I had the best massage of my life last night!" Bailey exclaimed. Entering the room, he stood over her.

"Don't tell me I've got to get you going again? Why are you in the bed this time of day? Get up. I'm feeling frisky," he said, wiggling his fingers and shuffling his feet.

"Give me a minute. Seems like I need one of those massages."

"Oh, no. This was one of those male massages with a very happy ending, if you know what I mean." Bailey patted his zipper. "And to top it off, she gave me a million-dollar donation for my campaign fund. What do you say about that?"

Should Brooks be jealous? Not about the money. She knew Morgan had given him the check. It was all a part of the plan Bailey knew nothing about.

Brooks looked at Bailey. He seemed more excited about whatever Morgan had done to him than he had all the times she'd sexed him. Well, if she was going to top Morgan's performance and double-blackmail Bailey, she might as well stay in bed.

She could burst his bubble and tell him she was entering the race but that wouldn't benefit either of them right now. Instead she said, "Come here. Let's keep this party in your pants going."

"That's what I'm talking about," he said, eagerly taking off his clothes. Standing there grinning, Bailey didn't realize his orgasm would end in tragedy.

CHAPTER 20

Hope

E very woman's pussy had platinum potential. Hope's was double platinum.

A text message registered on her phone from Johnathon. "Available for dinner tomorrow night? At your place? Best for us to keep our interest low profile."

After chuckling to herself, Hope thought, "Men are clueless."

First, Hope was not responding to his text. Next, he was not coming to her house or cumming inside of her. Johnathon wanted more of what he would've never gotten if she didn't have to blackmail him.

To have the best pussy, a woman had to treat her punany like royalty. Hope's daily pampering and monthly Brazilian investment commanded a return not many men could refuse, if they were fortunate enough to get close to her with her clothes off in the first place. Laying on the spa table at Angel's, she placed the bottom of her feet together, then spread her knees wide apart.

"I'm going to apply the wax. Let me know if it's too hot," her esthetician said.

"Oh, you know I'll tell you and if you leave any marks I'll file a claim with Lloyd's of London. My pussy is fully insured."

The esthetician laughed. "Hope, stop exaggerating."

Hope shifted her eyes, tightened her lips, then said, "Honey, I'm serious. I don't play when it comes to taking care of her. So, what have you been up to lately?" Hope had a few questions about the upcoming election but didn't want to start the conversation talking about politics.

Another text registered: *Did you get my text?*

Less than five minutes had passed. A desperate man was a dangerous man. Good pussy made men irrational. He'd probably planned the trip to Los Angeles assuming he'd fuck her again. That wasn't happening.

"I'm focusing on finishing up the semester at USC. Working here part-time to help pay my bills. But I'm almost done with college. I get my degree next summer," she said, ripping away the first strip of wax.

Hope was accustomed to the pain. It didn't hurt nearly as much as when she'd gotten her very first Brazilian. Over the years her hair had grown back more slowly with each treatment but if she waited more than six weeks, a full bush would cover her pubic area like a Chia Pet. Whenever her hairs were too long, the esthetician trimmed them before waxing.

"Congratulations. I'm proud of you. Just think, when you first became my esthetician you were starting your first semester. Now you're almost done. That's . . . Aw, hell no! Now's he's calling me."

Hope ignored the call, sending it directly to voicemail. Was he in his right mind? "I'm sorry. Men. Some of them just don't get it. I was saying that's commendable."

"All men aren't bad. I've got a good one that's proud of me," she said, ripping another strip of wax, this time from Hope's inner vaginal lip. Then she applied wax to the inside of the other lip.

The hot sensation calmed Hope. The young girl had an innocence that was definitely worth holding on to. "Would you vote for a politician if you knew he cheated on his wife? I'm asking because young college students view relationships differently."

"No, we do not. I expect my boyfriend to stay faithful to me like I am to him. I'd never knowingly vote for a cheating man to make decisions that affect me. I mean, every politician deserves an objective analysis of what they've done and what they have the potential to do. Goodman could do better but he's not so bad. Unless one of the other candidates changes my mind, right now he's got my vote," she said, snatching off another strip. "Okay, assume the position. On your side, spread 'em. Lift your cheek in the air so I can remove the hairs between your butt."

Hope's phone rang again. She exhaled, ignoring his call again, then snapped her pink jewel phone case shut. Johnathon had best be glad his check had cleared or she would've stopped payment on it by now.

"You know, a lot of women would love to have your problem. I get tired of hearing clients complain about how they can't find a good man. Maybe if they didn't complain about everything, they'd have a man. I don't argue with my boo."

But this session was not about her love life.

The esthetician asked, "What did you do to that man to make him keep calling you? Is he possessive or mad at you?"

That was a question not worth answering and none of her business. "Stay focused."

Hope was confident her esthetician and lots of other voters would change their mind about Goodman once Brooks made her announcement. The wax ripped from her cheek. "Oh, yeah. Make sure you get every single strand," Hope said. Nothing was worse after a fresh wax than discovering a missed hair.

Her phone rang again. This time Hope pressed the button on her Bluetooth. "No, I can't have dinner with you tomorrow. No, I don't want to fuck you again. And if you call me again, I want my money back," Hope yelled, resting on her elbows. Her ass was still in the air.

Opening her phone she checked the caller I.D. It was Stanley. "Hey, what's up?"

"You tell me what's up. So you're fucking another man. That's why you couldn't go with me to Paris? Well, he can have you!"

"It's not what you think. This guy somehow got my number and he's been playing on my phone. I think it's one of those ballers. Look, I'm in the middle of getting your pussy waxed. Meet me at my house in an hour. Bye, babe."

Stanley's timing was the worst but the hot wax had increased her libido. There wasn't a situation she couldn't talk herself into or out of.

"I want to be like you one day," her esthetician said. "I mean, you have men eating out of your hands. You can go shower. We're done."

A woman that didn't know how to breast-feed a man would starve. It wasn't difficult. "Men like smart women but nine times out of ten they'll choose beauty over brains because men are always in fifth gear, fuck mode. So no matter how many degrees you earn, lady, stay sexy and never be afraid to speak your mind."

Overall, Hope was what men considered the total package. She realized that the next man was always waiting to be her man.

Hope slipped on her robe. Her esthetician opened the door.

"Never forget this," Hope said. "Beautiful women always, always get a bitch pass."

Praying the young girl didn't misunderstand the importance of never letting herself go, another text popped up on her phone. She read it then laughed. How stupid can he be? There was no denying that she was looking at a nude photo of Johnathon's genitals. Hadn't he learned anything from that Weiner guy? "Wow."

She secured her purse in a locker, turned on the showerheads. At thirty-three, Hope looked better than some girls half her age. She stepped under the dome, shampooed then conditioned her hair.

Irrespective of size, not every woman was beautiful. Some had ugly ways, others from their head to their feet wore the wrong shades of makeup or clothing that didn't compliment their skin tone or figure. Being attractive required effort and awareness. Being intelligent required education. Being a bitch—well, that came natural for Hope.

Good girls seldom got the man they desired.

CHAPTER 21

Storm

Valet parking her platinum Bentley Continental GT, Storm placed the keys in the attendant's hand. "Leave it here. I won't be long."

She retrieved her phone from her purse and checked for missed messages. There were no missed calls from Chancelor. No texts or e-mails from him, either. Never imagining a twenty-one year old would give her the silent treatment, Storm dropped the phone back into her purse.

Several days had passed since she'd last seen or heard from him, but it felt like months. She'd called him three times, and that was her maximum. To reach out to him again would make her appear desperate.

Having an explosive conversation with Chancelor about the videos would still be better than him ending all communication with her. Was he unable to sleep at night? Had he met a female closer to his age? Older than she was? Was he planning on talking to the press about the videos? *Damn, why didn't I listen to Morgan? If I'd left the footage at her house he wouldn't have seen it.*

Now she not only had to pray her man forgave her, but also

the Rich Girls. Storm didn't weigh much but had lost a few pounds stressing over all that had happened.

She didn't buy them matching cars because she had to; she wanted to. His platinum Bentley Continental GT was being delivered to his place in a few minutes. At the end of her life she couldn't take a single material possession with her but what she could afford to do was purchase items that would make and keep her man quiet and happy. There was faith that he was still hers. He deserved to have time to sort things out for himself.

Men, like women, enjoyed being taken care of. Every person had their price and anyone that claimed they couldn't be bought was a liar. That or they didn't think big enough.

Storm strutted into the Four Seasons hotel on Wilshire Boulevard near Rodeo Drive. She'd reserved a luxury suite, hoping Chancelor would meet her later. Hopefully he'd test drive his new ride and not disappoint her as she'd done him.

But for now, it wasn't about Chancelor. It was time for her to handle business.

The lobby was absolutely breathtaking. The most amazing crystal chandelier welcomed all guests into the foyer. If she could give the five-star hotel endless stars, she wouldn't hesitate. There was an unforgettable ambiance even when she only visited the bar. Today she wouldn't be there long.

Balancing her ass on the edge of a plush emerald sofa in the Blvd Lounge, she thrust her breasts forward, adjusted her hemline upward to expose her perfectly waxed legs. She crossed her feet at the ankles and waited for him.

"What can I get for you?" the tall and sexy bartender asked, placing a napkin on the end table closest to her.

You. Naked. Right here, right now, on your back, she thought, staring at his abs. Her peripheral vision honed in on his dick.

He could relieve her sexual tension but that would complicate her already strained relationship with Chancelor.

"I'll have a slow screw and a bottle of your finest champagne. Two glasses, please. And charge everything to Storm Dangerfield's room," she said, removing her iPad from her purse.

"I'll get that for you right away," he said, offering her a menu.

"I won't be needing that. I'm not staying here long," she said, retrieving her phone from her purse. No messages registered.

Storm should've had Hope deliver the car to Chancelor but she didn't want to risk appearing foolish in front of the girls. Powering on her computer, she opened the video she'd saved of the soon-to-be ex-candidate, Randall Wallace. At lease he had more dignity and sense than Johnathon Waters.

He had no idea that what he was about to see would change his life forever. Make his wife, kids, and the political world, rallying for him, view him differently.

Meeting in an upscale public place was best when a woman faced the threat of a potentially volatile confrontation. Witnesses made affluent men behave rationally even when they wanted to be barbaric.

Storm's initial thought had been to hire a driver but she wanted to showcase her new Bentley. Being behind the wheel of an automobile that commanded others' attention made her feel more powerful than the men who stared with envy.

Jovially, Randy entered the restaurant with his shirt opened two buttons down. He sat beside her on the sofa, touched her knee.

"Hey, how are you?" he asked quickly, moving his hand. "Oh, I see you have the latest iPad. I've been thinking about getting one of those. I should buy one after I'm elected. No, that wouldn't be a good idea. The taxpayers will hold it against me and swear I spent their dollars on a computer when I should've funded health care or education."

He laughed. She didn't.

"That's the way politics go. Better wait until I win this thing and let it be someone else's idea."

Or he could stop being so damn cheap and just buy the computer himself. Storm remained silent, letting Randy continue his monologue.

"Things are going great, but I'm not ahead of Goodman yet so I have to stay focused, you know what I mean? A few more dollars wouldn't hurt. Especially since you made me miss my golfing session."

Again, he laughed. She didn't.

The bartender placed her orange juice and vodka cocktail on the napkin, set the champagne on the table, filled both flutes, then asked, "What can I get you, Randy?"

Randy's naturally ruby lips parted like the Red Sea. His tongue ejected from his mouth like a kid who'd just scored the winning goal for his soccer team. "Ah, you know me by my nickname, man. I sure hope I've got your vote."

"You can count on it." The bartender probably quoted the same to all the candidates he'd met.

"In that case, I'll have an Arnold Palmer with lots of ice man. I'm going to skip the bubbly." Randy stared at her. "Cancel the Arnold Palmer. I'm good. Don't want to pass out in public." He returned his attention to the bartender. "It's an inside joke. Never know who's watching me." Pointing his finger at the bartender in a playful manner, he stuck his tongue out again, then added a wink.

When the bartender left, he told her, "As much as I appreciate your money, I still can't believe I passed out at your house."

No need to delay the inevitable. Storm awakened the sleeping screen. The only file on her computer was his video. She sipped her slow screw. "Here's another check," she said.

She couldn't believe it was possible but Randy's smile widened as he snatched the check. "Wow, you sure are generous. I should have you working on my campaign. You have friends with money, too." His tongue darted from his mouth again. He gawked at the million dollars not realizing he'd been bought and paid-in-full.

"You can't afford me. It's a reality check. Come closer. I have something to show you," Storm said as the bartender set a glass of iced water in front of Randy. Storm arched her back, angled the computer in front of them, continued sitting on the edge of the green sofa.

"Technology is great! I'm building my following on Facebook, Twitter, all that. I've got to follow in the President's footsteps if I'm going to beat an old head like Goodman. Borrow shamelessly." He laughed, rubbed his hands together, shoved the check in his jacket pocket. "Let it roll!"

Randall Wallace's mannerisms matched that of a gambler on a winning streak at the craps table. Little did he know when his video rolled he'd discover that his luck had run out.

Storm tapped the play button. Randy's jaw dropped immediately but there was no ejection of his tongue or laughter. There he was, naked on her lounge chair with a black dildo stuck up his ass. Now that was funny to her.

"What the hell is this shit?" he yelled. His head snapped in every direction as if the few people in the lounge could see what he saw.

"Your resignation," Storm said, standing, straightening her dress.

"I'll sue you for this, b—" He swallowed the *itch*.

"Just for almost calling me a bitch, the check I gave you won't clear." Storm whispered in Randy's ear, "Pussy is best served ice cold. Remember that when you go home and fuck your wife."

Storm walked away, leaving the computer in his hands. If he had any doubts, by the time he watched the entire tape, he'd realize he was already defeated.

CHAPTER 22

Morgan

It was the end of March and the week they'd all been waiting for had finally arrived. January was two and a half months behind them. Today marked another milestone in Morgan's big plan and the start of their eight-month journey to Election Day in November.

Waiting in her car in front of Brooks's home, Morgan thought about how men could fuck the same woman, talk about it like that idiot politician who didn't realize his microphone was on, laugh at a female behind her back, sexually assault and degrade the woman to her face, and never let their encounters interfere with their careers. Business first. Bitches came last, if they were lucky enough to come at all, in the boardroom and in the bedroom. But some female dogs came all the time, namely the one getting into her car.

Brooks cheerfully said, "Good morning," as she climbed into the passenger seat.

Morgan drove off.

She'd never tarnish Brooks's image but she hated Brooks for lying to her. To Morgan, not telling the truth was the same as lying. This election was no longer about Brooks. Morgan had to prove to herself her plan would work and find a way to recoup the twenty million. Once the money was paid out, and the election was over, she would decide what to do next.

"You okay?" Brooks asked, staring at the iPad in her lap.

Sarcastically, Morgan replied, "Why wouldn't I be okay?"

"I asked because you've been unusually quiet since you picked me up."

"Well, my unusual is becoming the norm. Get used to it."

Storm's name registered on Morgan's car's display and Morgan smiled, happy for the distraction. She perked up hoping that Storm wouldn't sense the tension in her voice. She didn't want her girl to worry.

"Hey, honey! We're almost there. Are you there yet?"

"I'm in transit but I just had to pull over." Storm's voice trembled.

"What? You got pulled over?" Morgan said, focusing more on the road than on the conversation.

"No, she had to pull over," Brooks said.

Was that Brooks's way of trying to break their silence? It wasn't happening.

Storm cried, "I'm not sure if it's a good idea for me to be there today."

"I need for you to stop crying and tell me what's happened. I'm behind the wheel. This is not the time for me to be emotional." Morgan had enough non-political issues clouding her thoughts.

"It's Randall. He called and threatened to kill me. If he sees me with Brooks he'll figure out that we set him up and he might kill all of us." Her sobs turned to sniffles.

"Honey, please. Is that all?" Morgan said with a laugh. "Have you ever heard of a politician killing anyone for blackmail? Now, if he was an athlete, I'd worry."

Storm laughed.

"Good, girl," Morgan said. "We'll meet you there in a few. Bye."

Morgan didn't take Randall Wallace's threat to kill Storm lightly but she didn't want Storm to fear what would probably never happen. She'd have a private security person follow Randall. If Randy made a single attempt to harm Storm, he'd suffer a few more hiccups and he might end up missing.

Parking the car, Morgan walked side by side with Brooks. They represented the ethnicities of the majority of the female voting population in California. Comforting as that was, each step beside her so-called confidant was painful.

Being hurt and being afraid were two different things. Morgan didn't fear anything, not losing her husband or her best friend. But both of them had wounded her like she'd never been injured before.

The sensation of having someone stab her in the back with a knife, leave the blade there, and watch her slowly bleed to death was how she felt as she stood at the podium beside Brooks with camera crews from each major station zooming in on them.

Two powerful, attractive women, one black, one white, stood side-by-side for a common cause. Makeup flawless, dark power suits impeccable. Morgan in pants. Brooks in a skirt. Morgan took two steps back. It was Brooks's time to shine but her time would come soon.

Morgan had schooled Brooks to never publicly say anything secretive even when she thought the microphones were off. That was how Jesse Jackson had politically slit his own throat.

Smile when appropriate but not too much. She didn't want

Brooks to appear phony to others. Compliment often but not so much that she'd appear an ass kisser. Use real people and businesses for examples when etching a point into the minds of voters.

Brooks would now have to tour California and Morgan, like today, would be right by her side. Everything was temporary and eventually her heart would stop aching. She hoped. If not, after Brooks won—and she would win—their friendship would transition into a business relationship. Despite the downturn in their personal affairs, Morgan was confident that a woman could run the state better than any man that had preceded Brooks.

"Today, I am announcing that I, Brooks Kennedy, am entering the race for governor of the state of California. I know many of you are wondering what qualifies me to represent this gorgeous state. Don't judge me prematurely. I encourage you to not only listen carefully to my campaign commercials but please watch my debates against my opponents. Thank you."

Job well done. Saying less was more when it came to politics. Brooks's announcement was short and direct, the way Hope had written it. Morgan smiled on the inside as she stood behind Brooks and looked out into the audience at Hope and Storm. Brooks not showing her hand too soon was key to the girls not having to expose all of the other candidates.

"Ms. Kennedy," one reporter began, "how do you plan to eradicate the huge deficit in the state of California's budget and keep cities from going bankrupt?"

"Wendy Campbell, your question is one every citizen of this great state is awaiting a response to. Not only do I have the answers but I also have viable solutions. Be in the audience for my debates...next."

Brooks pointed to the slim white gentleman in the back with his hand raised high. "Yes. Thomas Wiley, what's your question?"

Damn, Brooks really had been studying. Morgan's heart stopped bleeding for a moment. Brooks had taken the time to learn not only the first but also the last names of all the news reporters. Thomas was new and the station he worked for, a Public Broadcasting Station, was struggling to stay on-air.

"Ms. Kennedy, the lottery was supposed to help fund education in the state of California. Why are our public schools severely underfunded. Students are not receiving the textbooks that are being stored in warehouses, the student-to-teacher ratio is forty-to-one. Why aren't we hiring more teachers? Why are the schools cutting sports programs? What will you do to make sure the children of California have a competitive chance in the global economy?"

Thomas was new. No reporter asked four questions at one time.

"Great questions. I do believe the children are our future."

Oh, no. Morgan prayed Brooks wouldn't break out into a song the way Chris Tucker had done in *Rush Hour* when he'd recited the lyrics to Barry White's *My First My Last My Everything*.

"There is a solution to this ongoing problem and when I'm elected education will be one of my top priorities...next." Brooks pointed at the Asian reporter up front.

Each answer was the same. Firm yet indirect.

"I thank each of you for your support. Please tune into my debates. Remember: no matter how difficult the journey, Californians navigate with faith."

Brooks had done an excellent job. If Morgan weren't married to Magnum and pissed off with them both, she'd have her best friend back.

The ride to Brooks's took forty minutes because of all the traffic. Morgan parked in the driveway.

"You want to come in for a celebration toast?" Brooks asked.

"Congratulations. Your announcement was excellent but it's best I go home. Magnum and I are having a few marital concerns." Staring into Brooks's eyes, Morgan continued, "I think he's cheating on me."

Brooks went silent. Her gaze shifted toward the passenger door before returning to Morgan's. "Well, if you confront him, ask. The worst thing a person can do is accuse someone of something they have no proof of. Besides, your relationship with your husband is strong. Don't let anyone come between that."

Did that include her? Why wouldn't Brooks admit the truth?

"Thanks. And you know what they say, 'What's done in the dark will always come to light.' I love Magnum but if I find out he's having an affair, I'll kill both of them."

"If you go looking for something, you're sure to find it. Let it go. Channel your energy elsewhere. Why don't you focus on getting us that investment report for the next meeting?" Brooks asked, closing the car door.

Morgan wanted to run Brooks's lying ass over, but prison was not where she wanted to spend the next twenty years of her life.

CHAPTER 23

Brooks

Milestones were accomplished once the announcement of her entering the race had been made. Her friendship with Morgan wasn't going as well. Her heart pleaded with her head to tell her friend she'd been sexing her husband regularly but the timing was off. She'd done the best thing by ending their conversation and getting out of Morgan's car.

How much longer am I going to have to look her in those beautiful jade eyes and lie?

. Brooks removed her clothes then sprawled across the bed. Now that Magnum and Goodman both knew she was in the running, Brooks had to get used to masturbating again. She got out of bed, opened her vibrating rabbit. For the first time in years she'd have to fuck herself. Vibrators felt better when Morgan or Magnum used them on her.

Crawling back into bed, she powered on her television for background noise. Bailey Goodman was ahead in the most recent polls. None of the opponents, including Brooks, ranked close to his percentages. But in less than a day analysts projected she'd rank ahead of Laura in the next poll.

Great. We're the only two women running and we're competing for last place.

Commentary aired from an anchorman. "Does Brooks Kennedy have what it takes to decrease unemployment and pull California out of the recession, or is she just hopeful that her last name will beat Goodman's? Will she keep billion-dollar contracts for building bridges from going to companies in China? Is California ready for a female governor? Soon the voters will have to decide. ..."

"What in the world? I just entered the race, people!" Brooks powered on her cordless companion.

She decreased the volume; the comments weren't worth her divided attention. Storm had reassured her, "Just like with my award-winning thoroughbreds, when your momentum kicks in, the others will eat your dust, honey, and the Rich Girls will control this state."

Lubrication wasn't necessary. As soon as the head pulsated against her clit, Brooks's secretions saturated the vibrator enough to slide an inch inside of her. Motioning in and out, she kept maneuvering until it was all the way in.

Thanks to Morgan's courageous effort, Storm was back to being her usual self. Morgan had hired an anonymous person to accost Randall Wallace. The guy was six feet eleven inches and weighed three hundred-thirty pounds. His only job was to tell Randy, "If you or anyone affiliated with you contacts Storm Dangerfield by phone, mail, text, e-mail, or in person,—show up at her house, follow her, harm or threaten her—you'll have to deal with me. The choice is yours."

The rotating pearls massaged her G-spot while the rabbit ears stimulated her inner lips, shaft, and clitoris.

"Oh, my, god," she said, replaying the moments when Bailey

had played with her pussy while she was in the tub. "Yes," Brooks moaned, thinking about the last time she'd felt Magnum's dick inside her. "Ahh," she called out to an empty home, wondering how long she'd have to rely upon past memories to aid in her orgasms.

As she came hard her upper body rose from the bed, tensed, then collapsed onto the mattress. *I've got to find a man to do this for me even if fucking me is all he does.*

But who would discretely replace her lovers now that she'd become a public figure? The orgasm didn't linger beyond the five minutes it took her to get out of bed. She showered, put on a robe.

Brooks sat in her office reading a few more documents. Her potential placement was a testament to the male-dominated politics surrounding the governor's seat. The only experienced woman that had run against Goodman in the last election had invested millions of her own dollars but she'd lost before she ever even announced her candidacy. Not many people had liked her or her politics, and truth be told she was a horrible liar and that made her even more unattractive. Her hair stylist had tried to pretty her up by smearing on lipstick and highlighting her hair but there was nothing they could do about her bald-faced lies. When her skeletons had been revealed, she looked hard, mean, like she was lying before she parted her polished lips. Someone should've told her to invest, instead of waste, her millions elsewhere and stay out of the race. Brooks prayed that she wouldn't suffer the same fate.

There were months to go and a lot more work to be done before the pendulum would swing in Brooks's direction. Even with the videotapes in her favor, she had so many skeletons of her own that there was no room for comfort.

Unable to concentrate, Brooks closed her office door, went to the bathroom, and filled the spa tub with hot water. Since the incident on the deck with Magnum, Brooks hadn't felt safe being in the Jacuzzi outdoors.

The water was so hot she saw steam hovering, creating a white blanket. Turning on the wall-mounted flat-screen television, she powered on the jets before settling into the tub. Flipping through channels, she saw her announcement for candidacy was still airing on every major station.

Muting the sound, Brooks opted out of reliving the moment. She wanted to call Morgan but thought it was best to wait and see her friend at the next meeting. Confessing was no longer necessary, but ending her affair with Magnum was.

For the past eight years, at the end of the day Brooks had been sexing somebody's husband, wife, or sleeping alone in her bed. There was no man to claim as her own. Being governor meant she had to seriously consider getting married again and never having another affair.

Maybe she could find a new lover that was single and keep their relationship a secret. Although men labeled women conniving, men were more naïve than women. By now Goodman knew that.

Bam! Bam! Bam! Ring! Ring! Ring! Bam! Bam!

"What the hell?" Brooks stepped out of the tub, grabbed a towel and covered her body before trailing water to the front door.

Ring! Ring! Ring! "Open the door, Brooks! I heard you walk up."

The voice was a familiar one. She'd known he'd show up at her front door but she didn't think he'd drop everything, leave Sacramento and come to confront her tonight. Wasn't he concerned now that she was in the race, that the media and paparazzi were keeping watch over her every move?

Brooks cracked her door open enough to see his angry face. The rage in his eyes indicated she'd be foolish to let him in.

Both of his hands slammed against her door, knocking her to the floor.

Slamming the door, he yelled, "I should stomp your lying ass into the floor like the conniving bitch you are! What in the fuck are you doing?" His hand rose high above his head.

Brooks slid her back against the foyer's wall. "It wasn't my idea," she pleaded, praying he wouldn't strike her. The entrance table, with its three-foot floral vase filled with real gardenias and water, was closer to Goodman.

His eyes trailed hers to the vase then shifted back to her. "But it was your decision! You bitch! You screw me then stab me in the back. I trusted you. I should kill you right now!" His eyes went from white to blood red in seconds.

Right now was immediate. If he'd meant it, she would already be flat on the floor fighting for her life, not sitting up staring at him. *Your balls are bigger than his,* she reminded herself. That was why he was in her house. Why was he outraged with her for indiscretions? She was surprised yet pleased that he hadn't struck her. Did he honestly hate her? Had she underestimated him? She should've changed her gate code before making the announcement.

Brooks stood. "Get the fuck out of my house before I call the police." She entered her living room, picked up the cordless phone she seldom used, pretended to dial 9-1-1. Then she went to her bedroom, opened her nightstand drawer, got her gun, and returned to the foyer.

Bailey was standing in the same place.

Shouting into the speaker, Brooks said, "Don't make me shoot you . . . Yes, please send the police immediately . . . Yes, I do know the name of the person threatening me."

Goodman stared at her, nodded. His look acknowledged she'd won this round but their fight wasn't over.

Brooks aimed her pistol barely above his head then pulled the trigger. The bullet blazed through the open door. "Don't ever bring your arrogant ass back to my house again!" She was prepared to shoot him if she had to, but that would instantly ruin both their careers.

Bailey Goodman darted out the door, got in his car, and drove off.

Brooks regretted losing him as a lover more so than as a friend. She had female friends, of course. But next to Magnum, Bailey was the best bed partner she'd ever had. She locked the door before returning the phone to its usual place. She then stored her gun in the safe inside her closet.

Brooks knew she needed to let Magnum go, too, but now wasn't a good time. Who would protect her if Goodman was foolish enough to return?

CHAPTER 24

Hope

L et me get this right. You want me to show up at Brooks's house unannounced and go through the files on her opponents? Am I hearing you correctly? You want me to search Brooks's *personal* records too?" Hope asked.

A month had passed since the beginning of Brooks's campaign. With seven months left, Hope wanted to make sure Brooks was properly prepared for her upcoming debates. She didn't want her stuttering or prolonging her responses to any questions. She also didn't want any more surprises since Brooks was now apparently keeping secrets. But she was uncomfortable sneaking into Brooks's home.

Morgan emphatically replied, "That's exactly what I want you to do, sweetie."

The Rich Girls had always had an unspoken pact of honesty amongst themselves. They were the most powerful women Hope knew. Their trust and openness with one another was what set their relationships apart from the members of the women's group in Beverly Hills and in other organizations. In addition to being wealthy, the Rich Girls were comfortable with their sexuality, and not afraid to dominate men. No topics were taboo. There were no secrets or deception amongst them. That was what Hope loved most about being one of the girls. But now...

"Why me?" .

"Because she'll trust you."

"And she wouldn't trust you?"

Morgan sat across from Hope in the office at Brooks's coffee shop. It was seven o'clock in the morning and the place was standing room only. Actors waiting for calls from their agents frequented Brooks's place during the week. Retired people started their days with a cup of hot java and warm conversation with friends. Business people stopped by en route to work. No matter the reason, customers craved BK Brew's coffee.

The windows were covered at eye level with Brooks's vibrant campaign posters. Hope glanced at the security monitor. They could see the customers but the patrons couldn't see them.

"Aren't you concerned that we're being recorded? Why did you choose to meet here without inviting Brooks? What's really going on?"

Morgan stared at her. Hope remained silent. Morgan scribbled on a piece of paper then handed it to her.

"Okay, look. First, she doesn't review her surveillance tapes. Next, we have to make sure there are no surprises down the road. Hopefully Brooks is telling us everything but... there may be something major that she considers insignificant. She could be too close to a potentially volatile situation for her own good. Best for us to find the flaws before any of her opponents do. I don't want us to end up having to do unnecessary damage control. In case she doesn't respond when you arrive, this is the access code for her gate. Here's the key to her house. If you must, let yourself in."

Somehow Hope felt the damage Morgan was speaking of was already done, and now her job was to get proof. But what was the harm of Hope sincerely trying to help Brooks? They'd convinced Brooks to run but neither of them had physically been by Brooks's side as promised.

The agreed-upon timing for her to reveal the blackmail tape to Johnathon was still months away. Laura Littleton was steadily proving to be her own worst enemy. And actually, Hope needed to stay occupied between sexing Stanley and delivering cars.

"I understand the purpose of my going but why shouldn't she know I'm coming over before I get there?"

Morgan stared at the monitor, exhaled as though the question was rhetorical, then answered. "Because that'll give her time to hide what she doesn't want us to know."

Hope stood. "Fine, I'll go now. I'll call you later."

The drive to Brooks's took over an hour. Hope entered the code. It didn't work. She called Morgan. "Hey, you gave me the wrong code."

"No, I didn't." Morgan told her the code verbatim from what was on the piece of paper in her hand.

"That's what I entered—twice—and it's not working. Maybe she changed it."

"Hold on. Let me call her on three-way."

Although her gut instinct told her she was doing the wrong thing, Hope patiently waited. She hadn't driven for over an hour just to go back to downtown Los Angeles. Morgan conferenced her on three-way.

Brooks sleepily answered, "Hey, Morgan. What's up?"

"Hey, are you okay?"

"I will be. And I don't need any food deliveries from Bo or any other caterer. Bo is—"

"You know I know you almost better than you know yourself. Your voice sounds strange," Morgan said. "What's wrong? Too much to drink?"

Brooks sounded unusually different. Not as though she was recovering from a hangover, but as if something was disturbing her.

Hope continued to listen, wondering when Morgan was going to ask for the code.

"Look, sweetie. Now that your announcement is made, you need to up your security and change the code on your gate."

"I've already changed the code. I meant to tell you yesterday but forgot. It's seven, two, three, nine, zero. I see Hope's Maserati GranCabrio at my gate. You must be sending her to spy on me. I would feel better if you were here to lick my pussy the way—"

Morgan coughed, interrupting Brooks's statement. "Wrong arena, my friend. I thought you had that base covered. Look, sweetie, you really are tired."

"Am I on three-way? I know you don't have Hope on the phone. Hope, are you there?"

Hope remained silent.

"It doesn't matter. The girls were going to find out about us eventually. I'll let her in."

Hope's mouth fell open along with the gate. She remained silent as she drove onto the circular driveway in front of Brooks's house. She sat in her car waiting for Morgan to end the call. Had she heard Brooks correctly? They were fucking each other? Hope frowned. But there hadn't been any signs of that between the two women, had there? Maybe Brooks had pictures that Morgan needed Hope to find so they wouldn't leak to the public.

"Hope wants to come over and assist you in any way that she can. That's all, sweetie," Morgan said. "You'll thank us later."

If "help" meant licking Brooks's pussy, *That was a damn lie*, Hope thought.

"Look, I need to call my husband. I'll check on you later. Bye."

The call ended and Hope walked to Brooks's front door. Was Magnum in on this deal, too? Bo? Were all of them sex buddies? Brooks opened the door.

"Dang, girl. You look a hot mess," Hope said.

"Well, you look fabulous and I'm happy to see you, too. If you'd come over as promised, you'd see that this is my new indoor attire, since all I do all day is read anything I can find on my opponents and watch them on television."

"Well, you've been doing a kick-ass job. I'm here to see if there's anything I can do to help you be more efficient."

Brooks led the way to her office. There was a maze of papers stacked against the wall and in the center of the floor.

"Poor thing. I had no idea you were this consumed. You should've said something. Why are you printing all of this stuff out when you have a computer? I want you to take the rest of the day off. Relax. Leave the house if you have to do errands. I'll scan these documents and upload them to your iPad. That way you can take them wherever you go, because pretty soon you'll be on tour campaigning and you cannot take this with you. I'll backup your info up on my computer too and help you stay abreast of new developments."

"It's like studying my business plan. I retain information better when I read it on paper, so don't toss out my printed versions."

"If you insist. I'll organize those, too."

"Girl, you should've been over sooner. Thanks, Hope. You have no idea how much this means."

"I was supposed to be by your side from the beginning. I'm here now . . . go on out."

⌒

After hours of scanning documents, Hope was only a fraction of the way through. She somehow knew whatever Morgan wanted her to search for would not be in any of the piles on the floor. She peeked in Brooks's bedroom. Brooks was sleeping there, snoring, naked atop the cover.

Hope returned to the office, opened Brooks's personal filing cabinet. Immediately she began thumbing through the folders. Opening the last folder in the drawer, Hope couldn't believe what she saw. "Damn." Quickly she stuffed the file in her purse and resumed scanning documents.

The contents of the file would make for the hottest discussion the Rich Girls had ever had.

CHAPTER 25

Storm

"I t's my dick and I want it now," the mayor begged. "Give me my dick." The mayor waddled in her bed like a toddler having a temper tantrum.

Storm understood why some men were paranoid about anal penetration. It wasn't that they were afraid of being considered gay. Most men who protested having a finger or dick in their ass were afraid they'd like it.

Sexuality was complicated. Gay sexuality was misunderstood. Every gay man wasn't penetrated. Just like sexing a woman, a hole was a hole was a hole even if it was an asshole. Being gay was an emotional and physical attraction to the same sex. The mayor was definitely not gay. If he were, anal penetration would have been reserved for a real dick, not to some chick strapping on.

This time Storm was wearing a tan leather harness thong. She latched on her four-inch dildo then generously lubed the mayor's asshole. "How do you want this dick?" she asked, kneeling beside him.

"Get on top of me. Make love to me like I'm a woman," he

said, spreading his thighs. "I want to know what missionary to a woman feels like."

For him, experiencing the vaginal sensation would be impossible. The anal and emotional pleasures were only attainable if his imagination plunged into the depth of his deepest desires.

Perhaps she was incorrect in her assessment of him. Perhaps he was bisexual, but Storm didn't judge him. There were times when she wished she had a real dick. Wished her genitals were external. Wished she had balls the size of plums. But if she had to choose between being a woman or a man, her choice would be to be what she was, because women ruled the world.

The way the mayor tilted his ass upward, grabbed his ankles, shoved his knees toward his shoulders, and howled, "Come and get it," then submitted to her, indicated this wasn't his first time in this position.

What was it about men that wanted to feel like a woman? Was it that behind closed doors they desired domination? Was it the absence of being raised by their father? No, she knew too many straight men that had been reared by single mothers. How many straight men were bi-curious but never acted upon their curiosity? The psychology of it all was terribly confusing and obviously there were no simple explanations.

As soon as she put the head in, the mayor grabbed his dick, held it tight, then grunted, "Aww. Go deeper." Stroking his erection, he moaned while sucking her nipple.

She'd done as requested. Grinding her hips with passion, she moved her thong to the side, rubbed her clit against his balls, then held her other breast. She didn't know whether she should ask, "Whose pussy is this?" or "Whose dick is this?", so she focused on responding to his body language. The mayor wasn't on their blackmail list but this was another great video moment she'd have to share with the girls this upcoming Saturday.

"I've been a bad boy. A really bad boy." Tears escaped his eyes as he began crying.

Storm was very familiar with the rules of a dominatrix. Safe words were necessary for lightening up the pressure or stopping. But this was new. She wasn't dominating him in the traditional way. They didn't have a safe word so direct communication would have to continue. She penetrated him harder, praying he wasn't on the verge of an emotional meltdown.

"I love you, Storm."

His words made her think of Chancelor. His brand new platinum Bentley Continental GT was sitting in her garage. He'd refused to accept it. Still hadn't communicated with her.

Six weeks had gone by. She should be focused on the remaining six and a half months left for Brooks's campaign, but all she could think about was Chancelor. If only she knew how much longer her heart would ache she could count down the days.

Why did men so carelessly use the word "love"? What kind of love was the mayor referring to?

Men weren't always as strong as they appeared. Maybe the mayor needed to release frustration. Perhaps Chancelor was crying over her, too. The ringtone of her cell was a welcome time out.

"Let's take a break," she said. Not waiting for his response, she pulled out.

Instantly his tears stopped flowing. He touched his asshole as if he couldn't tell the dildo wasn't there, then he grabbed her. Tried to reconnect. "I was almost there. Don't take that call.

Whoever it is, they can wait a few minutes. I need you to make me cum right now."

Honestly, for Storm the thrill was gone. Once again she was exhausting herself trying to please him. She wondered if during intercourse, men grew tired of trying to please women. At some point the excitement wore off and what was initially pleasurable gradually became more of a chore, a borderline bore. Was boredom the reason men needed new adventures? New pussy?

Leaning over him, she picked up her phone and answered, "Hey, girl, what's up?"

Hope rattled on for two minutes straight, seemingly without exhaling.

Storm rolled off of the mayor and onto her bedroom floor. "Shut the hell up!" Was Hope serious or delirious? "Please tell me you're lying, girlfriend."

"I wish I were."

The mayor pointed at his erection. Hunched his shoulders.

Shaking her head, Storm got up, tossed him his clothes. It was time for his lazy ass to go, anyway. Usually, Chancelor would arrive at her front door in about an hour to fuck her the way the mayor couldn't even if he'd tried. The mayor didn't possess the stamina and Chancelor was her biggest challenge.

Damn, she missed the way her man felt inside her pussy. Storm stroked her clit in memory of Chancelor's dick. Maybe she'd masturbate when she got off the phone with Hope.

Staring at the mayor, Storm wondered if she could find a way for Randy to become mayor of his city. San Diego would love his upbeat personality and innovative ideas and if he were interested, he could run for governor again when the Rich Girls decided. No man would become governor for quite some time unless women chose to let them back in.

"Are you going to finish me?" he asked, interrupting her thoughts. His eyes, shoulders, and dick drooped.

Muting her conversation, Storm told the mayor, "I'm in the middle of an important call. I'm sure you understand. It's business." Storm unmuted the call and tried to give Hope her undivided attention.

"Business this time of morning? What could possibly be more important than us finishing what we started? Please, tell whoever it is you'll call them back in fifteen minutes. It won't take long."

His clothes were in his hand and if he didn't put them on his ass soon he'd be standing outside naked.

"What the hell are you doing to that poor man this time?" Hope asked, laughing. "You still meeting with Randy today? If so, have the bodyguard Morgan hired go with you. I mean, you did say Randy threatened to kill you."

"Damn." Storm had planned to give Chancelor a surprise visit, hoping his seeing her would allow them to reconnect. Even with her thoughts of Randy moments ago, she'd forgotten about her meeting with him to discuss his exit strategy.

Hope reminded her, "How we finish is more important than how we start. This is not the time to drop the ball. You have to meet with Randy today."

Better to emasculate than to castrate. That was another part of the Rich Girls' motto.

The mayor put on his clothes and left without saying another word. He'd be back next Wednesday. Where else would he find a safe place to act out his newfound fantasy? Storm watched him on her monitor as he drove off of her property.

"Girl I can handle Randall Wallace by myself. We're meeting in a public place."

"I know where you're meeting and I'm calling Morgan to make sure the bodyguard is there. At least if Randy sees you're not alone, he won't try to harm you."

"Okay, fine. You're right. Now back to what you just said. Morgan and Brooks are doing what?"

CHAPTER 26

Morgan

The first set of commercials for Brooks's campaign were ready for the Rich Girls to preview at today's meeting. There were fifteen-, thirty-, and sixty-second spots slated to air on every major network between seven a.m. and ten p.m. The champagne was on ice to celebrate their overall accomplishments to date.

Morgan left the clubroom and stood in the foyer. She stared up at the painting of her standing by her husband's side at the altar. *Do you take this man to be your lawfully wedded husband...* she still did. Regardless of what Magnum had done, she couldn't all of a sudden stop loving the man she'd married. Her heart never wanted to stop loving him. But he'd definitely made the biggest mistake of their relationship. Magnum was at the spa, where he'd stayed for the past week.

Magnum was disgusted with Brooks entering the race but there wasn't a damn thing he could do about that. Obviously he wasn't fed up enough to stop fucking Brooks but if he knew his wife had almost had sexual intercourse with Bailey Goodman at the spa, he'd probably quit working for her and file for divorce the same day.

Men were like that. Accepting of their own infidelity, minimizing or denying the significance of their cheating as though it were natural behavior. But most men were unforgiving if they discovered their woman was guilty of even thinking about fucking another man.

Exhaling, she shook her head. He had been exceptionally handsome on their wedding day. The artist was so talented he'd captured everything, not just Magnum dressed in his custom-made black tuxedo, crisp white shirt, and bowtie, but even the love in her husband's eyes. Morgan gazed into them trying to rekindle the love, and relive the moment.

I needed this reminder. I ain't fooling nobody, not even myself. I love that man.

Undressing him with her imagination, she craved to have his dark chocolate flesh inside her. She shook her head again, exhaled, suppressed her rising libido. *Stay focused.*

The things he could control, like sticking his dick inside another woman, was what she needed to address. But how could she? Morgan was pissed off that Magnum wouldn't admit he was fucking Brooks.

Determined not to fail at what was her brainchild, Morgan would remain professional and be on her best behavior when Brooks arrived. Brooks would win the election. Morgan would run the state of California from a backseat. There'd be no asking her friend to stay afterward to take the edge off. If she sexed Brooks today, Brooks would have the upper hand. When the meeting was over, Brooks was being escorted out the front door, along with Storm and Hope.

Hope had called a few days ago, saying she'd found something significant, and insisted on revealing her findings to the group. Whatever it was about, Morgan was sure it couldn't compare to Brooks having an affair with Magnum. And that little hiccup of Hope finding out that Morgan and Brooks were lovers was insignificant in the grand scheme of things.

Morgan went to the kitchen. "Bo, it sure smells good in here. You can set up the food now. Thanks."

"Will you be needing my *services* after the meeting?" he asked.

"It's too soon to tell. I'll let you know," Morgan said, walking away. Her sexing Bo later depended on her energy and attitude after the meeting.

Morgan opened her front door before the bell chimed. "Come in, ladies. Hello, Hope. Hey, Storm. Brooks."

She didn't intend to give Brooks more than a lukewarm greeting. She'd thought she could conceal her emotions. Pretend that what had happened didn't matter. Obviously it did. But she'd have to try to push through it or else one of the other girls would have to accompany Brooks in public. No. Morgan couldn't allow that. She had to stay closest to her enemy/friend, in that order.

"I need somebody new to do," Storm said. "Because the mayor is becoming boring since we've implemented our plan."

"You can have Laura," Hope said. "She'll annoy the hell out of you because there is nothing, I mean nothing, exciting about that woman. I just don't know what to do with her."

Morgan chimed in, "She's her own opponent. If she were the only one running, she'd still lose. Let's start with an update from Storm on Randall, then the videos, then we'll give Hope the floor, and last, I have a surprise announcement."

Brooks stared at Morgan. Her eyes widened before she said,

"Hope was a tremendous help. I now have all of my documents on this," she patted her iPad. "Thanks again, Hope."

"No problem, honey. That's what I'm here for. To assist you."

Brooks tossed her computer on a chaise, then headed to the mimosa and Bloody Mary bar. She poured champagne, drank the entire glass, then refilled before walking away.

"Girl, we need to start with what's on your mind," Storm said.

Brooks's eyes slightly rolled upward. "I'm good. Let's get started. I have to tend to my coffee shop for a few hours today."

"Well, my meeting with Randall went well for me. He's pissed but now he realizes how bad he fucked up and there's nothing he can do about it," Storm said, smiling.

"Let's not underestimate him," Hope advised. "Believe me, he's plotting something. They'll all seek revenge and we have to stay prepared until every male opponent is caught with their dick in their hands."

Morgan pressed play on the remote. The first commercial ran fifteen seconds.

California needs a governor that will run this state like a successful business, balance the budget . . . tax those who can afford it, and give tax credits to those who need it. I'm that person. Vote for me. Brooks Kennedy for governor.

The emphasis in Brooks's name was always on Kennedy. A name that people could not only easily remember but also associate with "good." Brooks's crisp, clean look—flawless toasty skin, full attractive lips, large white teeth, wide trusting smile, and sparkling brown eyes appeared genuine. And in politics, for the undecided, image won votes, and every vote counted.

"I like this one," Storm said. "You look perfect. Sound great. Not contrived. Very natural."

The next two commercials ran uninterrupted. Morgan powered off the television. "Now that we've got that part covered, Hope, you've got the floor."

Brooks interrupted. "No discussion about the commercials? No replay?"

Morgan firmly said, "We can recap at the end. Hope, what do you have to share?"

"I'll get right to the point," Hope said, handing each of them a piece of paper. "Brooks, I came across this license while organizing your files. You need to explain . . . in detail."

CHAPTER 27

Brooks

S ix months to Election Day and she had to explain what? Hope didn't just happen to come across the document in Storm's, Morgan's, and her hands. Was this a conspiracy? Couldn't be. Not with her girls. What would be the purpose of them launching her political career then slandering her name? Surely Morgan wouldn't do this over some dick, would she? If Brooks became defensive, her reaction would be counterproductive.

Brooks stared at her friends. Her lips tightened, then shifted to one side. She focused on Morgan's expressionless face, realizing her so-called BFF had sent Hope to her house with the intention of invading her privacy.

"Brooks, drop the childish attitude and the piercing looks. We're all grown-ass women and no one here is intimidated by you," Morgan said, staring back. "I know what you're thinking."

"No, you don't. You have no idea what's on my mind."

"Regardless," Hope said. "This is not a pissing match. We're all on the same team. Morgan doesn't mean any harm. Best for us to dig up whatever skeletons you have now. At least then we can do damage control."

Hope was wrong. Dead wrong. But to see what the girls were trying to prove, Brooks went along. "You're right. Sooner or later the truth would come out. It's better for me to explain to y'all than to justify in front of millions of voters why those divorce papers aren't signed." Explaining her marital status to the public would be easier than trying to defend a double affair.

"That cheating bastard was a horrible husband," Brooks said. She looked at Morgan, thought about Magnum, then said, "And . . . I'll leave it at that."

Morgan calmly commented, "Your husband was horrible so you slept with mine?"

"What the hell?" Storm gasped.

Brooks hadn't been expecting that one. But if she was going to win the race she had to beat every opponent, and if that included Morgan, too . . . well, bring it on. "Whose team are you on, Morgan? You send Hope to my house to spy on me, now you're making accusations. You shouldn't speak of things you know nothing about."

"And you shouldn't be so assured that you know what I know. But what I know for sure is . . . no thanks to you, I'm pregnant."

Storm leapt from her seat. Brooks prayed Morgan's last comment was another test to see if she'd break. Neither Storm nor Hope knew what Brooks wasn't supposed to know, either, but she did. Magnum had had a vasectomy years ago.

"Aw, hell no! Y'all gon' stop this foolishness right now!" Hope, the one that usually remained silent, spoke with disgust. "Wait one minute. Let's put ev-ve-ry-thing and I mean everything, the truth and nothing but, on the damn table. For the rest of this meeting, I'm asking the questions." Hope looked at Brooks. "Are you fucking Morgan and Magnum and you're married?"

"Shut the hell up," Storm said in disbelief, sitting on the edge of her seat. Her eyes were fixed on Brooks.

Brooks had the floor, but it was quickly collapsing underneath her. She stood. Could've answered, "Yes, yes, and yes," but instead replied, "No, no, and what difference does it make." Now that response obviously didn't set well with Morgan, especially since she knew they were lovers. But as far as Brooks knew, Morgan had no proof about her sexing Magnum and she intended to keep it that way.

Storm stood facing Morgan. "Why would you say something like that? Why would you accuse Brooks of having an affair with your husband? Listen to me. No dick will ever divide the Rich Girls even if it's attached to one of our men. Got that? And I think I speak for us all when I say that I'm happy about your pregnancy. But you could've picked a better time to tell us."

Morgan replied to the group. "You're right, but Brooks has to be prepared to expect the unexpected. Goodman, Wallace, Littleton, and Dennison are going to come gunning for her from all angles. We have to throw Brooks every curve imaginable."

Morgan's words were sensible on the surface. Underneath, her intentions were like a stick of dynamite waiting to explode in Brooks's face. This wasn't about Brooks. It was about Morgan wanting to maintain control even if it meant humiliating her in front of the other girls.

"I don't get what's happening between Morgan and Brooks, as long as whatever you're doing stops right now and stays right here. I also agree with Storm. No dick will ever divide us. And Morgan, I suggest you have an abortion because we all know Magnum had himself fixed."

Storm stood again. "Aw, hell no! How do you know that, Hope?"

"Doesn't matter. Moving on. Let's figure out what to do about this," Hope said, waving Brooks's unsigned divorce decree in the air. "This is what's most important."

"I can help with that," Storm said. "I'll call in a favor from Mr. Mayor, have him pay the right people to back date the papers, forge Brooks's husband's signature and clear this up. Brooks. all you need to do is sign your copy for me."

"And," Hope added, "I can locate this ex-husband of yours, Brooks, and pay him off to keep his mouth shut."

"It's a little shady, ladies, but I love it," Morgan said. "Hope that works. And I'm not pregnant so no worries. I should've used a better prank."

Bitch. Brooks couldn't gauge Morgan's underlying intentions. She was throwing daggers all over the place. The other girls seemed united and that was all that mattered in the moment.

"For the record, I am legally divorced," Brooks said. "If you want to know something about me, just ask."

Morgan shook her head. Brooks ignored her.

Just like that, the pieces to Brooks's life were starting to fit again. All except one, Bailey Goodman. None of the girls knew about her affair with him. He'd been quiet since she'd shot at him. Brooks would have to prepare for his unexpected resurgence. Surely Bailey would return for revenge and try to mutilate her campaign the same way he wanted to do her.

Brooks prayed Magnum and the girls would not only support but also protect her. Brooks wanted to question Morgan about the investment but she'd rather forfeit her five million to the group than to deal with another issue today.

"We can resolve these matters throughout the week. I have

the perfect surprise to adjourn this meeting. Follow me, ladies," Hope said, handing each of them a small box with their name on it. "And don't think we've forgotten about the statement, Morgan."

Happy to get the hell out of Morgan's house, Brooks grabbed her purse and trailed two steps behind Hope. When Hope opened the door, they all gasped, ripped open their boxes, and screamed.

"I thought we could use a little more unity, girls, so I bought each of us a Mercedes SLS AMG...and I've already arranged to have the cars you drove here delivered to your homes."

Everyone gave Hope a group hug as they jumped up and down.

"Damn, look at the rims," Storm said. "I'm out!"

"This is really generous of you Hope. Thanks." Morgan went inside, closed her door.

"I love the pink and chrome exterior," Brooks said. "Catch me if you can, baby!"

And that was exactly what Morgan would have to do for whatever she was trying to prove.

CHAPTER 28

Hope

Friendships were priceless.

Hope was not willing to bail out of making sure Brooks won the election even if Brooks had been fucking Magnum and Morgan at the same time. That was their kinky business. Morgan was no saint even if she had been betrayed. When adults shared their body parts with one another, they were well within their rights even if they were wrong.

The expectations of exclusivity should be left at the altar. People knew when their partners were unfaithful before they said, "I do." Yet they stood before each another exchanging lies instead of truths.

It was time for Morgan to stop the madness. Obviously her prank, proclaiming she was pregnant after her husband had been snipped, and confronting Brooks, were cover-ups for what she'd done with the investment fund.

Though they were having marital problems, Hope believed Morgan and Magnum loved each another. That was more than what she had with Stanley. No marriage was trouble-free and all friendships over time encountered situations that would test the bond. In Morgan's case, Hope felt all would be good after Brooks won the election, because despite Morgan's disillusionment and disappointment, her heart was good.

Flipping through TV channels, Hope stopped on CNN. Stanley was reclining on the sofa next to her while he read something on his iPad. It was like he was joined at the hip with his computer whenever he wasn't sexing her. She couldn't complain; her cell phone was in her hand and her computer was within reach.

"Baby, what do want to do this morning? You want to eat in? Or you want to eat out?" she asked.

"Both," he said.

"I'm serious, Stanley."

"Me too. First I'm going to eat your pussy. Then you're going to do me and I'm going to give you every inch of this," he said, stroking his dick. "We're going to do it until we work up an appetite. And then I'm going to take you to breakfast," he slid his finger across his screen like there was a picture slide of what he'd just described.

A man's mind was always on sex. At least Stanley had no reservations about what he wanted. She didn't mind him talking about having sex but at times the overkill diminished her enthusiasm.

"Sounds good. Just so you know, I have to deliver a car this afternoon."

Stanley looked at her, exhaled. "First we couldn't go to Paris. Now this. I took off from work to spend time with you. Today was supposed to be our work-free day."

The thought of doing nothing all day was driving her insane. She switched to the ten o'clock morning news. Until they made it to France, he'd complain about their not going every opportunity he could.

"It was supposed to be my day off, baby, but my client texted me and he wants his half-million dollar purchase today. I won't be long and it's not until later."

"I'll go with you."

"No, you can't."

"Then show me the text."

She shook her head. "Why don't I stop by your house when I'm done? I have to leave at two and I'll be done by six."

Truth was, Brooks hadn't produced a copy of her divorce decree. Hope couldn't locate it. She'd arranged to get a copy from a contact Storm had. If that person didn't find the alleged decree, they'd falsify one. Hope wasn't sure how long that would take. Factoring in time for delays was wise.

Stanley resumed focusing on his computer. Hope increased the volume on her television when it was announced that news about the governor's election was coming up next.

Hope believed in communication, and as long as a person expressed their true feelings, that was sufficient. Whether or not they kept their word was often but not always a reflection of their character. If Stanley didn't move off the sofa until two, that was okay. She understood that sometimes a man's ego had a change of heart. An innocent statement had changed Stanley's mood from hot to cold.

An update on the California governor race was coming on after Brooks's commercial. Hope smiled and turned up the volume a little more. "That's my girl."

Hope would never marry Stanley. They weren't close to being equally yoked. They were sexually compatible, but good dick wasn't enough of a reason for her to make a lifelong commitment.

If Hope's mom ever divorced her dad, her mom would get twenty-five percent of the business and their mutually shared assets. That was what her mom had negotiated when she'd exchanged vows with her father. A deal was brilliant when both partners had some bargaining power. The problem Hope saw was that most people didn't see marriage as a business arrangement or as an investment.

"Baby, you look so sexy," Stanley said, interrupting her thoughts. "I'm not going to ask what you're thinking. Give me a kiss." His hand traveled between her thighs, fingered her clit.

Guess his dick had changed its mind. His ego seemed to decline commenting on Brooks's commercial. Hope touched his face, then kissed him softly.

"Let's go out dancing tonight when I'm done dropping off my client's car. I want to rub these," she grabbed her breasts, "all over you in public until my nipples get really hard, then we can come back here and you can have your way with me. Oh, and if we go, I'm not wearing any panties or a bra."

Stanley slapped her ass. "This is why I can't resist you." The sting immediately excited her, making her pussy wet.

Hope squeezed his hand, but the television screen caught her eye. "Wait a minute."

Laura Littleton stood in front of a podium with several reporters in the background. "With regret, I'm going to have to withdraw from the governor's race due to insufficient funding. I simply do not have enough donations to travel and campaign effectively. I want to thank all of you who contributed and supported me. All the volunteers . . ."

Hope sprang from the sofa, screamed with laughter, and started dancing in the middle of the floor. "Yes! I did the right thing by not giving her that check! I'm so happy she's gone."

Her phone rang. "Yes, girl, I'm watching. We have to toast; one down! You talked to Morgan?" she asked Brooks.

"Not, yet. I'm going to call her now. You're still picking up my divorce papers, right?"

"Of course, sweetie. Don't you worry about that. Now call Morgan. Bye."

Hope dropped to her knees. "This calls for a celebration. This here dick in my hands is going down."

She removed his pajama pants, spread his legs. Hope opened her mouth as wide as she could. She wanted to suck Stanley's dick nice and slow, but she was so excited she slid his entire shaft as far as it would go until his head hit the back of her throat.

"Damn, hearing that made you hot like this," he said, running his fingers through her hair. "Aw, shit. Slow down before you make me cum. I want to enjoy this."

Providing fantastic fellatio was a woman's best weapon. Hope wasn't Superhead but she gave superb head. By the time Hope finished doing Stanley, he'd cook breakfast, happily leave at two, and eagerly wait to find out what she'd plan for their evening.

CHAPTER 29

Storm

*C*urve ball my ass.

It was clear as the blue summer sky blanketing her home that Brooks and Morgan were undercover fucking. What wasn't clear was whether Brooks was sexing Magnum or if Morgan was truly pregnant. Whatever was going on was their business. Storm was committed to fully executing her part of the plan but the day Brooks won would be Storm's last day of doing the mayor. She'd no longer need his connections; he'd need hers.

Men could avoid so many problems if they just kept their dicks in their pants, or their hand. Man had no best friend. Not a dog. Not their dicks. Man was his own enemy, not women, and definitely not pussy.

Storm brushed her hair back on the sides and top, gathered the shoulder-length strands into a ponytail. She brushed her teeth, washed her face, then applied her tinted moisturizer that also provided her the perfect foundation.

Red lipstick completed her flawless look. There was power in words but the confident color on her lips would reinforce what she had to tell Anthony Dennison today. Releasing the ponytail, she let her hair flow straight. She tucked the sides behind her ears, neatly combing her bang to her brows.

She stepped into a red long-sleeved dress, then zipped up the back. The flat collar circled her neck. The hem, high enough to be sexy yet long enough to be conservative, was four inches above her knees. The silk gently clung to her breasts, waist, and butt. The closed-toe, platform, three-inch pumps were comfortable enough for sprinting if necessary.

Storm gathered her purse and the iPad she'd give to Anthony, then headed to Nobu on North La Cienega Boulevard. In between the lunch and dinner crowds, the restaurant was fairly quiet. No need for a table. According to the plan, Storm wouldn't be there long. Meet the opponent. Deliver the information. Leave immediately. Then toast to the girls' victory. She waited for Anthony at the bar, crossed her legs, ordered a bottle of their best champagne.

Believing the surprise she promised was another healthy donation, he'd agreed to meet her on his stopover while he was in transit to campaign in San Diego. In a few minutes, Tony would be devastated as much as Randall had been. But would Tony wait to threaten her over the phone? Or would he strike in an angry moment? Storm wasn't taking any chances on potentially being attacked. Her bodyguard was seated at a table nearby.

Tony entered the bar. His dark suit was crisp, goatee immaculate. She wondered whether he wore boxer briefs or pink lace panties under his slacks.

His smooth chocolate lips parted. "I don't have much time. My plane was late getting in. Traffic on the 405 is ridiculous, as usual. My driver is outside waiting for me. I've got to be back at LAX in less than two hours for my next flight."

Just like an "all about me" man. Tony hadn't even bothered with saying "hello." His ass was on the edge of the stool. He poured himself a glass of champagne. Gulped it down.

"I have something special for you," Storm said, reaching into her purse.

His eyes widened like a kid's on Christmas morning. "You shouldn't have...but I could certainly use the money. You see, Laura dropped out because she didn't have enough funds. That can't—make that won't—happen to me thanks to contributors like—" he paused. Stared at the computer in her hand then continued. "What's this?"

"Let's just consider this an investment," Storm said, handing the iPad to him. "Watch the video on your way to the airport. Have a safe flight." Softly she kissed his cheek, leaving a red lip-print stain behind.

"You mean I came here for this? I thought you were giving me another check," he lamented, standing beside his seat.

Storm looked over her shoulder. Her six-foot-nine protector moved closer, stood beside her, clamped his hands in front of his zipper, then spread his feet apart. He didn't have to speak a word as he stared at Tony.

"You'd better hurry. You don't want to miss your flight." Dropping three one-hundred-dollar bills on the bar, she told the bartender "Keep the change," walked to her car—the pink jewel Hope had given her—that was parked out front, and drove off.

If Tony thought he was upset when she'd left him holding a computer, wait until he saw the footage.

CHAPTER 30

Morgan

Five months down and five more to go before Election Day.

Burying the hatchet was impossible when you knew what your best friends wouldn't confess. Morgan willed herself to make one last attempt with both of them.

Sitting alone by the pool at her spa, first she called her husband. His voicemail spoke to her. She redialed using her speed dial.

"Hey, baby. Sorry about that. I accidentally hit 'decline.' Where are you?" To Morgan, the tone of his voice when he asked sounded like someone had just given him the best blow-job of his life. "I woke up and you were gone."

"I'm trying to sort things out." He'd better not be in their bed sexing someone. "Magnum, I need to know the truth. It's tearing me up inside. I feel like I'm losing my husband, my friend. I can handle whatever the answer is. Please tell me. Have you been having sex with Brooks?" Morgan pleaded. "Is this your way of trying to hurt me and ruin Brooks's political career?"

One of them had to reveal what they'd hidden. She'd already

seen proof. She just had to hear her husband admit his infidelity. But why? What difference would it make if he told her? At least she'd feel she could rebuild their trust from there. Maybe.

"I've got to go, Morgan. Don't call me back if that's all you have to say."

"No, wait!" she cried. "Please don't hang up on me. Why can't you give me a simple yes or no, Magnum? I'm your wife!" Her voice echoed through the empty spa. Today was the day the spa was closed for business. She hated the politics, lies, and games her husband was playing.

"Bye, Morgan."

The phone went silent. *Bye, Morgan?*

Morgan set the phone beside the lounge chair and stared at the blue chlorinated water. Tears streamed down her cheeks. She was strong but she was also a woman deeply in love with her husband. A woman on the verge of having a nervous breakdown. Sliding on her sunglasses, she sighed heavily.

Again, Magnum's curt response made it easier for what she would do when Bo arrived at the spa in an hour. Drying her eyes, she made her next attempt at satisfaction.

"Hey, Morgan. I was just about to call you," Brooks said, sounding like she'd just had the finest yoni tongue massage of her life.

Morgan texted Magnum. "Where are you?" Just because he'd said he woke up and she was gone didn't mean he was really at home.

Perhaps Morgan's blues were sparked by what she'd seen that night. And if one of them didn't tell her the truth both might end up...dead. What was killing her might ultimately kill them.

"You go first since you were about to call me. What's the good news?" Morgan asked, staring up at the glass ceiling. A few clouds hung over her head, like the secrets her best friends kept.

"Haven't you heard the latest? My commercials are a huge hit. I'm finally ahead of Randall in the polls! Now all I have to do is pass Tony and catch up to Goodman. You, my friend, are a genius. I'm coming to pick you up for lunch."

"I'm in Sacramento," Morgan lied. "I have to meet with Goodman to give him the blackmail video." The sex acts she'd done for Brooks, Brooks had probably done to her husband. *Dammit! Tell me the truth!*

"Oh, I thought that was next week. Be careful. No telling what he's capable of."

Like you keep forgetting to say, "Morgan I fucked your husband. I apologize." Morgan was silent. At this point there was no telling what she was capable of.

Brooks became quiet, too.

"Congratulations," Morgan finally said, then ended their call. She knew what she had to do to Bo, Bailey, Brooks, and Magnum.

No reply text from her husband. Brooks had gotten too comfortable with the success that Morgan had generated. Maybe Morgan would hold off on giving Goodman the tape and give him another contribution instead. She could make Brooks fail without being viewed as the culprit.

Her heart ached with anger and disappointment. She had never imagined her husband would hurt her like this. Why?

A text finally came . . . from Bo: *I'm outside.*

Approach the spa from the street. I'll meet you by the entrance, she texted back.

Locking the door behind Bo like she'd done with Bailey, Morgan led the way to the pool. "Take off your clothes," she said.

"Is this another one of those don't say anything sessions?" he asked, smiling. He removed his shoes, pants, T-shirt, and underwear. His manhood stood at attention, making her pussy throb.

Morgan dove head first into the deep end. Bo jumped in feet first, making a huge splash. She swam to the five feet marker. He followed her.

"You can say whatever you like," Morgan told him.

Holding the back of her neck, his tongue darted into her mouth then suctioned her tongue against his.

"Mmm," Morgan moaned, stroking his dick. She wrapped her legs around his waist.

Bo braced her back against the side of the pool, and penetrated her until his head was all the way inside her. "I'ma pull out before I cum," he said.

She knew he was thinking with the right head but Bo had no idea she was already pregnant with his child. There was no point in him pulling out. She'd wanted to tell the girls what she'd said was true but instead she withdrew her confession after Hope told everyone about Magnum's vasectomy.

The thrust of Bo's firm ass was exactly what she needed. Sometimes a woman just had to get fucked real good by a man that could satisfy her without becoming emotionally attached.

Would Bo want her on a full-time basis if her marriage ended? Would she want him in their child's life?

Morgan didn't want to think. She just wanted to enjoy Bo's every stroke. He gave her the dick just the way she loved it, and the feeling of her breasts sliding against his chest excited her further.

"I'm about to cum, baby. What do you want me to do?" he asked, slowing his pace.

"Don't pull out."

"You sure?"

"Positive," Morgan said, hugging his neck.

Bo thrust his shaft deeper. She felt his hard dick pulsating. Morgan tightened her vaginal muscles and exploded with him.

"Aw, yes. I feel you," he said.

"I feel you too."

Bo's legs shivered. "I have got to be the luckiest man in the world," he said.

Clap. Clap. Clap. Clap. "No, I am," Magnum said, entering the pool area.

CHAPTER 31

Brooks

Ablack Lincoln Town Car stopped at her gate. Brooks watched the security monitor intently. The gate opened, the car cruised along her driveway. Brooks's heart raced. "Couldn't be." She'd changed her code. There was no way for him to have access to her home.

She opened then shut the front door, ran to the living room, grabbed the phone. Peering through the keyhole, she watched as the car parked in front of her house. Brooks's breathing became heavy. She ran to her bedroom, got her gun, pressed her eye against the hole again.

The driver opened the back door. Black stilettos with beige trim rested on the cement, and Morgan emerged wearing dark sunglasses. Her blond hair was slicked back. Her black pantsuit made her look elegant and powerful.

"Thank you, Jesus." Brooks placed her firearm and cordless on the coffee table in the living room, grabbed her computer, purse, and keys, then opened the door.

"Why didn't you tell me you were coming? I thought you were a trespasser."

Firmly Morgan said, "We have unfinished business. Let's go."

"Um, I was on my way out. I have somewhere to be," Brooks lied.

"Get in the car. I'll take you wherever you need to go when we're done with what I have planned," Morgan said, standing aside.

"I'm headed to my coffee shop, then Hope is meeting me at—"

"I know your schedule. I'm the one who made it. Get in the damn car."

"What's gotten into you?" Brooks asked, sitting on the backseat. The driver closed the door, escorted Morgan to the opposite side of the car, closed her door, then got in and drove off.

"You mind telling me what this is all about?" Brooks asked.

"This is your permanent driver and I'm now your full-time manager. I don't want you going anywhere without me. I don't want you driving yourself anywhere. Your driver is available to you twenty-four-seven and so am I."

"This really isn't necessary," Brooks commented.

Morgan instructed the driver, "BK Brew is our first stop," then told Brooks, "At least if you're with me, you can't fuck my husband behind my back."

Brooks felt it was best not to respond. What if the driver told the media of Morgan's accusations? She wondered if Morgan's pregnancy was to blame for her friend's erratic behavior. How could an intelligent married woman have made such a careless decision to have unprotected sex?

The driver parked in front of BK Brew then opened her door.

"I'll wait here for you," Morgan said.

Walking into her coffee shop, Brooks inhaled the fresh smell of roasted java. Her nostrils flared for two reasons. One was because of Morgan. There was no way she'd be joined at the hip with her every minute of the day. Two, the place smelled of French roast.

Patrons gathered up posters from the stack near the entrance, expressed their excitement about supporting her, and requested her autograph. Brooks smiled, shook hands, and kissed babies while thanking her customers and signing her name. No need to prolong their next stop, wherever that was.

"Free coffee for everyone for the next hour," Brooks said on her way out. The driver opened her door.

"Hey, Brooks Kennedy. You've got my vote!" a man shouted from the passenger window of a car driving by.

"Mine too." This voice was seductive, flirtatious. Made her stop.

Brooks turned to face a twentysomething eyeing her up and down like she could be his breakfast. *Wow!* He was the most beautiful man she'd seen in years.

Hollywood was full of aspiring actors, people that looked like their full-time job was working out, but this man's physique was perfect. He appeared to be about six feet, four inches. Smooth caramel skin that glistened under the sunshine complimented his smile. His brown T-shirt wasn't too baggy or too tight.

She glanced at his flat abs, scanned up to his eyes, then said, "Thanks."

"You need help with gettin' it, Ms. Kennedy? I can do whatever you like. Manage your online campaign. Work you over and work you out. Mount...posters." He licked his lips. Stared at hers. "But what I'd really like to do is protect you. Let me be your bodyguard, ma'am."

Brooks's head snapped to the left, to the right, then inside the car. All she could see were Morgan's pants leg and shoes. Could anyone else hear what the young man was saying? She tried to remain cool but she felt heat rising up her thighs to her clit. "What's your name, young man?"

"Jason. But you can call me Big D or Daddy. Because if you give me the opportunity to take care of your needs, that's what you'll be screaming in my ear as I whisper in yours, 'Get it, mama. Big D has got you.'"

Whew! "Have a good day, Jason," Brooks said, leaving the young man standing in front of her coffee shop. Jason's lines probably worked for a lot of women. And if she hadn't been running for governor, she may have given him her number and invited him to her house after dark.

"Wait. Here's my info," he said, handing her a basic white business card.

"Thanks." Glancing at the card, she laughed as she read, CEO OF JASON'S PERSONAL FITNESS, IN-HOME TRAINING AND MASSAGES AVAILABLE. There was a phone number and an e-mail listed.

"I can train you any time," he said, flexing his chest and fluttering his brows at the same time.

"Have a good day, Jason." Brooks tucked the card in her purse and got into the car.

"Make that your last time lingering when we have appointments. You've destroyed enough. Next time, keep things moving," Morgan said.

"Driver, take me back to my house," Brooks insisted. "Now."

"I said you have an—"

"Shut the fuck up, Morgan! I'll drive myself there. If you want out of the plan, get out. But I will not allow you to subject me to your madness."

"If I want out?"

"Perhaps you missed the part when I said, 'shut the fuck up, Morgan!'"

En route to her house, Brooks thought about how she could win the election without Morgan's help. She probably couldn't, but she'd take that risk before she kissed Morgan's ass ever again. Hell, life wouldn't be bad going back to her coffee shop. Business had increased seven hundred percent since she'd announced her candidacy. People dropped in at all hours of the day and night hoping to see her, and ended up loving the coffee.

Morgan grabbed her bicep. "Brooks, wait. If you value our friendship, tell me the truth. Did you have sex with my husband?"

"You're asking the wrong person. Get your hand off of me," Brooks said. Letting herself out of the Towne Car, Brooks slammed the door. She didn't need Morgan questioning her. Brooks needed a stiff drink and a stiff dick.

Jason. Could she have a boy toy to service her womanly needs like Storm had with Chancelor? She definitely wouldn't buy him a car. Maybe she could lie and say he was the handyman. A massage was what she needed. He could be her therapist. A few hours a week would help keep her stress free. Then she thought, *What if Bailey paid Jason in order to get back at me?*

Morgan had ruined her good attitude, but Jason had stirred up her libido. How long had it been since Brooks had had sex? Suppressing her sexual energy was the source of her frustrations. Maybe Magnum wasn't fucking Morgan either, and that had made Morgan angry with her. Great sex with Jason could take the edge off in several ways.

Thinking of great sex, Goodman crossed her mind again. He

205

was still quiet. Magnum claimed he was disappointed in her for entering the race. Said she should've discussed it with him first. Demanded she withdraw.

Men. Would either Magnum or Bailey have requested her blessings for anything?

Entering her house, Brooks froze in the doorway. Her jaw dropped. She mouthed, "Oh, my, god."

Standing still, Brooks contemplated what to do next. Should she call Morgan and ask her to have the driver bring her back? Should she dial 9-1-1? Instead she closed the door, got in her car, and drove a mile to her neighborhood grocery.

She powered off the engine before dialing his number. "I need you to meet me."

"I can't talk right now," he said. "I'm on the other line with my wife."

Her voice trembled. "I need you now. Please."

"Hold, on," he said.

The phone went silent for a moment then he was back. "Where are you? What's happening?"

They'd been together long enough for him to know the tone of her voice when she was scared. It'd only happened once in their relationship and his response was the same, except that time he hadn't been on the phone with Morgan.

"Meet me at my house right away," she said.

"Be there in thirty minutes," Magnum said, ending the call.

Brooks hoped if Morgan found out that she'd called Magnum, that her friend would understand. Despite their ongoing argument, she still considered Morgan her friend.

Each minute that passed felt like an hour. Brooks waited until she had one minute to spare then drove back to her home.

Magnum's car was outside the gate. When she drove in, he

followed her then escorted her to the front door. She placed a finger over her lips, turned the knob, then stepped aside.

He stood beside her, stared at what she saw, then asked, "What?"

"What do you mean, what? Don't you see there are so many flowers in here it looks like someone died?" she commented. "I didn't order any of these."

"Neither did I. Obviously, you have an admirer."

"Not one with keys to my house. You don't even have keys to my house."

"But my wife does. You called her?"

"I was with her when this happened."

Magnum became silent. Shook his head.

"What?"

"Nothing," he said.

"Morgan knows I hate red roses. Reminds me of weddings and funerals."

"Shouldn't that be white roses?" he asked.

Brooks gazed into Magnum's eyes, closed the door behind him. "You know she knows about us. She's been making a lot of accusations lately. Maybe we should tell her the truth." Brooks checked each of the eight bouquets for a card but there wasn't one.

"And what exactly would you say to my cheating wife?" Magnum asked, not awaiting her response. "I'm more concerned about you dropping out of the race. That's the only thing you need to tell *my* cheating wife."

Now Brooks had to wonder what Magnum knew? What if the arrangements were from Bailey? Even if he'd figured out the code to her security gate how would he have gotten the vases inside her home?

Entering her bedroom, she opened her nightstand drawer. Her gun wasn't there and her spare set of house keys was missing. "Come here. Look at this."

Magnum looked inside the drawer. "What? What am I looking for?"

"You know I keep a spare set of keys in here. They're gone."

"Your gun is gone, too. You probably moved them and don't remember." His hands rested on her shoulders. "You're tense. You need to relax."

He helped her recall that she'd left her gun in the living room. She'd call the twenty-four-hour locksmith as soon as Magnum left, which hopefully wouldn't be any time soon. The feel of his strong fingers massaging her felt heavenly. Brooks's eyes rolled to the top of her head. She couldn't lie. She wanted and needed a man to take the edge off.

"Since you're here, please stay the night with me. I don't want to be alone."

"Neither do I. You know how I feel about you, Brooks. But after tonight we need to discuss our situation. We can't continue like this for the rest of our lives."

Whatever Magnum was contemplating was too complicated. Brooks would handle their situation delicately and sex him, one orgasm at a time, until he had to leave.

CHAPTER 32

Hope

"Why weren't you at your fundraiser?"

"I told you and Storm I had an emergency," Brooks explained.

"If you want me to continue financially supporting this business venture, don't let it happen again. You're making the girls look bad."

Being a politician was not a built-in excuse for running late. If Brooks had stayed in the car with Morgan, she would've been there. "Next time let the driver get you where you're supposed to be. We hired him for you. Let him do his job."

"As long as Morgan isn't in the car with me, okay," Brooks agreed. "If she's in the car, I'll drive the one you gave me. It's faster."

"I'm not going there with you. We're all doing our part. I'll call you later," Hope said, ending the call.

Storm had delivered her videos to Anthony and Randy. Now it was Hope's turn to give Johnathon a rude awakening. Bible-toting, bible-quoting men were sometimes the worst kind, using the word of God to justify adultery, infidelity, and fornication. Not that Johnathon was a believer in much more than himself, but if he had to explain the video to the public, Hope was sure, like most men, he'd swear he was entrapped.

Hope would laugh in his face if he thought voters were ignorant enough to believe she'd forced him to stick his dick inside her and cum. When no one was watching, married and single men would engage in unthinkable sex acts.

Was it the feeling of ejaculation or the false sense of power that dominated a man's desires? Some would stick their dick in a glory hole and let an unseen stranger suck it until they released themselves in that person's mouth. Others would solicit sex from minors and virgins. Men would fuck men in their wives' beds, have sex in public, screw their bosses, and do their own cousins if no one were watching.

Johnathon had flown to Los Angeles this evening to prepare for a Town Hall meeting that Hope had arranged for him in Beverly Hills. Convinced he could garner more financial support, he'd eagerly agreed to come.

Her pre-meeting with him was at the Thompson Hotel in Beverly Hills. Hope toned down her alluring attire, from her preferred signature halter dress to a dark pantsuit, with red lipstick, a red blouse, and two-inch pumps.

Reserving one of the cabanas for Johnathon would've been fun but inappropriate. Hope texted Stanley: *Hey baby, meet me on the rooftop at the Thompson Hotel right now. I've reserved us a private area and I have some new juicy political news that's making me horny.*

She didn't have the news yet but the details would be finalized once she witnessed the look on Johnathon's face.

Cool! he replied. *See you there in an hour.*

Hope smiled and sat at the bar, where she knew Johnathon

would maintain his composure even if he didn't want to. Opting not to have a bodyguard as Storm and Morgan suggested, she was confident she could handle Mr. Waters alone.

Johnathon strolled in dressed like he was a teenager in private school—blue suit, white shirt, and a solid red tie. "Hey, Hope. How are you? You look fantastic," he said, kissing her cheek.

A smile spread across her face. The world was made of all kinds. Men like Waters. Women like her. Problem was, there weren't enough women in the world that cared enough to out-think men.

"You look handsome, like a winning politician. I bet your charisma alone will get you votes. Have you been to a tanning salon?" Hope asked. His olive complexion gave him a gorgeous undertone more brilliant than before.

His dark wavy hair looked the same as at their first meeting: tapered on the sides, higher on top, accented with a few out of place strands feathered to the left side.

"Yes, yes, yes," he stuttered. "Glad you noticed. You think it'll sway voters in my direction?" Johnathon grinned.

"I know so." But what she was about to show him wouldn't yield support from voters—or his wife. "A bottle of your best champagne," Hope told the bartender.

"You're too generous. When I win, anything that you need, consider it done," Johnathon said with a wide smile.

She wished she could fuck him one last time. Feel his strong throbbing dick deep inside her, or his lips pressed against her pussy as she'd sit on his face.

The bartender poured two glasses of champagne. Hope held up her glass. "A toast is in order."

Johnathon held up his own flute and started grinning again.

"Here's to claiming you, Johnathon Waters, are the next governor of California," she lied.

"And here's to you being my personal travel assistant, if you know what I mean," he said.

Was he indirectly offering her the position of being his mobile sex buddy? Hope's lips didn't part until she said, "I won't be able to make it to the meeting tonight but I'm glad you've invited lots of press."

He frowned. "Why? What do you have to do tonight? I was hoping we could get together for a recap afterward."

"It's best. You'll need to scale back on your campaigning effective immediately," Hope said, sipping champagne.

Johnathon shook his head, sitting on the edge of his barstool. "What are you talking about? Do you know something I don't?"

"Not for long. Just do as I say and I'll make sure your reputation remains intact."

He shook his head again. His eyes shifted to the left then back at her, mouth tightening. "Women. Just give it to me straight."

"Since you insist." Hope plugged in the headset, handed it to him, then pressed play on the iPad.

Two minutes into the video, Johnathon stood as he yelled, "You bitch!"

The bartender rushed over. People at the bar stared at them.

Maintaining her calm, Hope told him, "Keep the computer. Enjoy the video. You're really good." She winked, stood beside him, then continued, "Have fun at the meeting. And don't forget to scale back on that campaign."

Walking toward the restroom, she didn't look back.

Johnathon scooped her up from behind, her feet dangling in the air.

"Put me down!" she yelled, punching him in the face.

He carried her to the pool and dropped in her at the deepest end. Her arms flapped as she gasped for air, fighting to stay afloat. Slowly she felt her body sinking. Her feet couldn't reach the bottom, but her head didn't rise above the water.

This was the first time Hope wished she'd known how to swim.

CHAPTER 33

Storm

Four months to Election Day.

Powering on her cell, the signal for new messages dinged seemingly non-stop, one after another after another. "Damn!"

She'd turned off her iPhone because she was outraged with Tony's new verbal threats. She tapped her voicemail icon. A series of unheard messages appeared.

She listened to the oldest ones first. "Your days are numbered. I'm not dropping out of the race over a piece of pussy that's not as good as you think, and if that video leaks to the press . . . you and your pussy are dead, bitch."

That call had come from a blocked number. The voice was muffled but she could tell it was Anthony's. Storm saved the message, listened to the next. Another blocked call in a long list of voicemails on her iPhone.

Her phone rang, interrupting her messages. Another blocked number. She answered, "Hello."

"Bitch, you and Brooks are playing with fire. It'd be a shame if Brooks Kennedy were to get assassinated before Election Day.

If she doesn't withdraw, if this video goes public, the two of you scheming bitches can be buried together." The call ended. He never said his name but she knew it was Tony.

"Enough!" Storm yelled, immediately calling Brooks. "What have we gotten ourselves into? I just received a ton of death—"

Brooks cut her off. "Threats. Yeah, me too. I'd expected mine to come from Bailey Goodman but the last threat he made was when he ran out of my house. My caller sounded like a woman. Maybe it was Laura. And I still haven't found out who left eight dozen red roses in my house. I've changed all the locks and the security code on my gate again. Everywhere I go I'm looking over my shoulders. This is not what I signed up for, Storm."

Things were chaotic. Hope was the lucky one. The bartender had saved her from drowning. Perhaps it was time for the Rich Girls to stop playing it safe, take these cheating-ass men down to their knees, make them crawl on all fours, beg for mercy, then beat their asses.

"You're not dropping out, so if that's what you're thinking, forget it." Storm crossed her fingers as she tried to comfort Brooks. "These men are bluffing. Have you ever heard of a political candidate knocking off their opponent? Now, changing the subject, why didn't you say something before about the roses? What roses?"

"It wasn't a bomb. It was flowers. Have you talked to Hope since she gave Johnathon his video?" Brooks asked.

"No," Storm lied. They'd agreed to silence about the pool incident until the next meeting. They didn't want Brooks to freak out so close to winning and cause her to change her mind.

"Can you call Chancelor and have him move in with you until after I win this race?"

"Good idea," Storm said, but knew that wasn't happening.

"Maybe Hope should do the same with Stanley. What about you? Who can we get to move in with you?" Storm asked, worried about her friend.

"Don't worry about me. I have someone in mind. In case that doesn't work out, let's put that topic on the agenda for tomorrow's meeting. I'm tired. I'm going to bed. I can't worry about this right now. Got enough on my mind. Goodnight."

"If you need me, call me. Double check your doors and be safe," Storm said, ending the call then dialing Chancelor. Four months had passed but she wasn't ready to give up. Maybe it was her pride reaching out for closure.

The phone rang several times. When she finally expected voicemail, he answered. "I forgive you, Storm. I miss you like crazy. I have to see you. We can work this out. Can I come over? Please."

Storm closed her eyes with relief and whispered, "Yes."

Tonight would be a good time to tell Chancelor she loved him.

CHAPTER 34

⌒

Morgan

The Saturdays were coming closer together and her marriage was steadily falling apart. A home once overflowing with love was now furnished with intolerance. Simultaneously being in love with and hating a spouse had always been something that happened to others until Magnum had caught her fucking Bo.

Morgan stood in the kitchen. "I need you to have everything set up today before the girls arrive."

Bo held her hand. "You okay? Each week you seem more stressed. Let me take the edge off for you right quick," he said, unzipping his pants.

"Put that thing away. I'm fine," Morgan said, pulling away. "What's it to you that my husband caught us fucking? In three months when the election is over, I'll be six months pregnant and back to being my normal happy self. That is, if I don't have an abortion."

Being next to Bo with or without her clothes on excited her. But their session at the spa had been their last. If she was going to work on resolving her marital problems, she had to abort Bo's baby and not have sex with him.

"Wait," he said, touching her stomach.

She moved his hand. "Don't touch me again."

"No disrespect. I thought we were just having fun. When were you going to tell me? I apologize for wanting to fuck you, I didn't know." Bo tucked himself in, zipped up his pants.

"Liar."

"True," he said. "I want to fuck you even more now. My dick is so hard I could bat this honeydew melon to Canada."

"I can't believe you showed up."

"I can. You haven't fired me. He's not my husband and it's not like you didn't ask me to fuck you in his bed. I'm just following your lead. I mean, if you're already pregnant for your husband what's the harm in having a little more fun?"

This wasn't the time to tell Bo the baby growing inside her was his, especially if she wasn't keeping it. She couldn't get mad at him when she was the one that had initiated their affair.

"Fine," was all she said.

"Well, if there's anything I can do in addition to cooking for you on Saturdays, don't hesitate. I'll even go with you to the doctor to terminate the pregnancy," he said, heading toward the clubroom with a cart filled with chafing dishes, china, and table settings.

Bo's biceps pressed against his long-sleeved white chef jacket. Morgan imagined sliding her breasts against his protruding chest and she unexpectedly had an orgasm. Her body buckled and she leaned on the island. Exhaling, she said, "Oh, my, gosh, that man is fine."

Morgan knew Bo hated when she'd taste food from his decorated dishes but his special crushed pineapple ambrosia smelled almost as irresistible as when her nose was buried in his nuts. Soon as he was out of sight, she stuck her finger in it.

"Um, um, um." Morgan closed her eyes for a moment, let her palate savor every shred of coconut. "Damn, that's so good." The melody in her mouth spread throughout her body, awakening her sexual senses.

Tonight she might have to make one final exception. Her pussy got moist remembering how Bo's naked body had felt next to hers in the pool. Tonight she wanted to feel like a rich slut. Have him dominate her. One more rendezvous and she'd let him go. She scooped the dessert again.

Bo entered the kitchen. "I know you're not doing what I think you're doing. How many times have I asked you never to do that?"

A cynical smile started on the inside then spread across her face.

"I can't serve that dish. It's all yours. Eat the whole thing if you want."

"You can and you will," Morgan insisted. "It's not like I have a disease. But I do have a request. We don't have much time before the girls arrive. And after we're done, and you're finished setting up, you can leave."

"You sure you want me to leave? I mean, the food will be warm but I have to put my finishing touches on it. You know what I mean?"

Morgan stood in front of Bo, unbuttoned his jacket, kissed his nipples. "I think you know what I need. Let's go shower in the guest bedroom."

Bo scooped her up in his arms. Navigating the way, Morgan said, "You can put me down now. Take me. Do with me whatever you want. And I'll do whatever you tell me."

"On your knees," Bo commanded. He unzipped his pants.

His boxer briefs had a huge hump in front. He slid his dick out through the slit.

Damn, she couldn't wait until tonight. Morgan sniffed his crotch. "Mmm . . . smells like the ocean is in there."

Bo smacked his head against her jaw, then stuck the eye of his head against her nose. "I want you to remember what I smell like when you're fucking your husband. Now open wide and taste me."

She did as he commanded. Took in as much as she could. Her lips circled the middle of his shaft.

Pulling out, he said, "Get your naughty ass in the shower."

It would serve Brooks right and make her jealous if she had to watch what was about to happen. Morgan tossed her clothes on the bed. Bo did the same.

He stepped into the shower behind her, bent her over, held her hips. Hot water beaded against her back as his dick slid inside her pussy.

"Wait, I need to get you a condom. Won't take but a minute," Morgan said, trailing water from the shower into her bedroom, to her toy chest. A gold packet was appropriate for Bo.

Hurrying to let him finish what he'd started, she put the condom on him with her mouth, then resumed her position.

"But aren't you—"

"Shut up," she said. There were important reasons to protect her unborn.

This time when Bo slid inside, he grabbed her hair. His pubic hairs slammed against her ass. "Take all of this dick. It's about time you gave me this pussy again. I want this shit every Saturday, you hear me?"

He pulled out, put in the head, then penetrated her slow. He forced his head deep inside her and paused.

Her pussy throbbed. Morgan massaged her clit. "Fuck me, Bo. Call me a slut and fuck me hard. Don't stop even if I tell you to."

This wasn't about making love or being romanced. Morgan's orgasm was filled with revenge for Brooks and Magnum. She wanted Bo to punish her for fucking him. At the moment she was a slut. Why was her husband giving away the good dick that should've been in her pussy?

She wasn't a slut. It was Magnum's fault she'd sexed Bo. But Bo had done her husband and Brooks a favor. Bo's taking control of her released her burning rage to physically harm two of the people she loved most.

CHAPTER 35

Brooks

I'm not going to die. Not like this.

The hardwood floor squeaked for five seconds, then quieted. The dark bedroom filled with silence, for a moment. Resurfacing, the crackling noise grew closer to the bed, abruptly stopped, then faded toward the bedroom door.

Here comes the drama I've feared. Whoever it was, they'd waited until eight weeks before Election Day to strike. But what they didn't know was she wasn't home alone. She was going to be the next governor of California and no man was denying her, including the one in her bed.

Lying still on her back, her heartbeat thumped deep in her throat, damn near choking her. She held her breath, covered her mouth. Struggling not to cough, she quietly sucked in oxygen, removed her satin eye mask, then slid her hand under the sheet to the opposite side of the mattress. She touched her lover's muscular thigh then swiftly pulled her trembling hand away. He remained motionless.

Eyes wide open, but the darkness surrounded her. She knew where everything in her bedroom was, including her gun. The

Smith and Wesson Sigma 9mm that she usually kept on her nightstand was...*Aw damn!* It was still in the living room. She usually concealed her protection inside the top drawer whenever one of her two lovers stayed the night.

Since her announcement, she was down to one man but had considered inviting Jason over. With the personal training skills listed on his business card Jason might be better suited to protect her but would a considerably younger guy be sexually pleasing?

The man in her bed was asleep. *That's best.* He was a man of action and very few words—when he felt threatened. Awakening him would unleash his rage, expose her filthiest scandal, and alert the intruder that *two* persons were in fact in her bed.

The major disadvantage Brooks had was that whoever was in her bedroom was no stranger to the layout of her home. There was only one person that knew the new code to her alarm system. Morgan would have a motive to sneak up on her in the middle of the night, but was she bold enough to do so? She'd scared Bailey so much, she knew he'd never show up again. She prayed she was right.

What did the intruder want? Why were they there?

Since announcing her candidacy, she'd made more friends than enemies. But it only took one spiteful person to end it all. Her first guess to the intruder's identity was still Bailey Goodman.

Brooks kept still. As she counted three hundred seconds in her mind, her heart must've beaten a thousand times. She heard nothing. She told herself she was not imagining things.

How could a day that had started out perfect end like this?

What she heard next...terrified her. *Click.* She'd definitely heard her bedroom door open. Or was it a gun's trigger preparing for release? She wasn't sure. Was there more than one person invading her bedroom?

Sunshine would not brighten her room for another hour or so, depending on the present time. She lifted her head from her down feather pillow, then tilted her left ear toward the door. Nothing. She froze, wanting to lay her head back down on the pillow. Go back to sleep, she told herself. But she couldn't.

Her lover scooted closer to her, wrapped his arm around her waist. Gently she lay on her back beside him. He pressed the front of his naked body to the side of hers. Brooks cringed. She placed her palm to his chest and held it there.

That was when she heard it again. The floor squeaked. This time she heard another click. Was the intruder moving closer to the bed, or leaving?

Brooks longed to dial 9-1-1 for real this time and scream, "There's a robber in my house and they have a gun! Send the police quick before they kill me or I kill them!"

She was no murderer. But in a life or death situation, she wouldn't hesitate to aim for the head or the heart then pull the trigger. That was, if she could get to her gun in time. What if they had it?

Brooks could no longer wait for the intruder to make the next move. Her trembling hand tapped her lover's chest. She needed him to do his job, to protect her. Protect them. She whispered in his ear. "There's someone in my house."

"Huh? What?" he mumbled. Rolling onto his other side, he faced away from her.

Brooks nudged him in the back. "Wake up. There's somebody in my house."

He pulled the covers from her side of the bed, wrapped his upper body, then resumed a comfortable position.

Brooks quietly inhaled, held her breath, prepared for whatever was next. Her vision went from being blinded by darkness to being impaired by bright, rapid camera flashes.

"Fucking bastard!" she yelled. "Get out of my house!"

Her lover sprang to his feet, stood beside the bed. More rapid flashes ensued. "What the hell is going on here?" He rushed the intruder, wrestled him to the floor, struggled to take the camera.

When Brooks turned on the light, her lover yelled, "Damn!" Then as if he'd seen a ghost, he raced from the bedroom.

She was in shock. Why did Magnum abandon her again? Was he afraid that if the situation got media exposure, Morgan would know the truth? Magnum could stay gone. He was no longer welcome in her home after leaving her to defend herself. The intruder stood three feet away, cloaked in an oversized coat and wearing a ski mask. Brooks couldn't identify the person before her.

What she could do was run to the living room and get her gun. Unlike the time with Bailey, this time she wouldn't miss. But would the intruder shoot her in the back? Being in the bed put her at a disadvantage. Brooks opted to do nothing. If he'd come to kill her, she'd be dead.

All she could see was that the intruder's eyes were blood red and that gloves covering the hands holding the gun pointed at her face. Brooks closed her eyes and prayed he didn't pull the trigger.

CHAPTER 36

Hope

Three months to Election Day.

At the break of dawn, Hope's cell phone awakened her. Sleepily she answered. "Hey, you okay?"

"Can you come to my house right now?" Brooks's voice trembled with fear. "I need you and Storm here...now!"

"Okay, honey. Calm down. I'll call Storm and I'm on my way now. Is Morgan there with you?"

"No, just hurry. I'll call her and I'll explain when you guys get here."

"Stay on the phone with me," Hope insisted.

Brooks became silent.

"You okay?"

"Yes. No. No. I'm not. Do I sound okay? I don't know. Please hurry," Brooks said, ending the call.

Hope's heart raced. She sat up, turned on the lamp. Stanley sat up, grabbed her. "What now?" he asked, pulling her toward him.

Jerking away, Hope explained, "Brooks needs me." She didn't have time to tell him what she didn't know.

Stanley held her wrist as she was getting out of bed. "I need you. What about me?" he said, tugging her in his direction. "I'm your man—not Brooks, Morgan, or Storm. Me. If I didn't know better, I'd think you guys were fucking one another. She's running for governor, not president. Every time something comes up I'm the one left hanging. You know what Brooks needs? A man. It's not your job to rescue her. You're not leaving and that's—"

Breaking his grip, Hope protested, "Let me go! It's not negotiable."

"But your being my woman is? I'm tired of this, Hope. I should come first!"

Hope hurried into a pair of sweatpants, put on a T-shirt. "I apologize, baby. I'll be back in a few hours and I promise I'll take care of your every need when I return."

"Don't bother," Stanley said, getting out of bed. He put on his jeans, shoes, and pullover collared short-sleeved shirt. "Don't bother. I'm out. And don't call me."

Perhaps that was best for both of them. He worked a nine-to-five so when he was off from work everything in his life centered around her. Next to his occupation, she came first. Hope didn't feel the same about Stanley. Her clients, her girls, her parents, depending on the circumstances, all came ahead of him.

She made no effort to stop Stanley. In fact, he needed to move faster. "Bye," Hope said, to encourage a quicker pace.

When any of the girls were in trouble, Hope was on the way to help. A man with millions might understand her loyalty if he weren't chauvinistic. As soon as Stanley left, she got in her hot magenta Ferrari California hard-top convertible, settled into the pink leather seat, lowered the top, shifted into first gear, and ripped out of her driveway. By the time she reached her fuchsia gate, it was already open. Stanley was a few car lengths in front of her and he was in her way. The gate closed behind them. As soon as he turned onto the main road she revved her engine and sped past him.

In thirty minutes, she arrived at Brooks house. The entrance gate retracted immediately. Morgan's and Storm's cars were already parked in Brooks's driveway. Hope rushed inside. The girls were in the kitchen, all seated around the island.

"I got here fast as I could," she said, rushing in. "What is it? What's happening?" Hope asked, sitting on the stool as she gasped for air.

"I have to show you guys the latest footage from my security camera." Brooks turned on the wall-mounted HDTV and raised the volume. The morning news was on. Johnathon Waters stood behind a podium surrounded by the press.

"Turn that up. What's he up to?" Hope said. "I know he's not coming out of his panty-wearing closet."

Storm laughed.

Brooks interjected, "This meeting is about me."

"Wait a second. We need to hear this. Turn that up," Morgan said.

Johnathon announced, "First, I want to thank all of my supporters. Those of you who worked diligently at my campaign headquarters. The volunteers across the state that made phone calls on my behalf." He looked directly into the camera and continued, "Those of you who generously contributed financially, every penny was truly appreciated. Unfortunately, I have to withdraw my candidacy for governor of the state of California. I'm not at liberty to say why at this time but I promise you I'll be back next election. You have my word." He said this with tears in his eyes. "I'm backing the incumbent, Bailey Goodman, and ask that you do the same."

"This is not what we wanted! Blackmailing him is useless now," Storm said. "We needed him in this race. Hope, what happened? You were supposed to make sure he scaled back on campaigning, not dropped out to support Goodman. Damn!"

"He didn't throw your ass in the pool." Hope laughed. "Relax. We'll be fine. We've got footage on Goodman."

"Do we?" Brooks asked. "Has anyone seen the video Morgan claims to have? And Storm is right. Johnathon was not supposed to drop out."

Morgan remained and Brooks became silent. Was this meeting really about their unresolved issues? Hope prayed it wasn't. If it was, it was certainly no emergency and she could've stayed in bed with Stanley.

"You need to back up, Brooks. Everyone has done everything they were supposed to do. I can't control Johnathon's dick or his decisions. Maybe he told his wife. Maybe she insisted he drop out. Maybe Goodman paid him to swing his votes. Who knows?"

Storm sat down. "I apologize, Hope. You're right."

Quietly Brooks said, "Maybe I'm the one who needs to withdraw. I shot at Bailey Goodman when he came here and threatened me, and last night someone broke into my house and pointed a gun in my face."

Storm sprang from her stool. "Aw, hell no! Oh, my, god! And you waited until now to tell us that? Why aren't the police here? I'll call 9-1-1 right now." Storm picked up her cell.

Calmly, Morgan told her, "Storm, wait. That's not a good idea. Yeah, Brooks. Why didn't you call the police instead of calling us?"

Brooks stared at Morgan. Morgan stared at Brooks.

"What the hell is going on here?" Storm asked, holding her cellular in mid-air.

Hope's eyes shifted back and forth between Morgan and Brooks. The energy between the two wasn't about hatred; it was of disappointment and sadness.

Hope told Storm, "Put your phone down and be quiet for a moment."

The girls sat in silence. Morgan's bond with Brooks remained intact.

Five, ten, fifteen minutes passed. Storm's lips parted. Hope turned to Storm, pressed her pointer finger against her lips.

Morgan broke the silence but not her stare. "Yes, Brooks. Answer my question. Why did you call us and not the police?"

Tears streamed down Brooks's face but there were no whimpers, sniffles, or attempts to dry her sadness. "I'm sorry," was all she said.

Two months before Election Day. Mayhem was an understatement.

"What the hell is going on between you two now?" Hope asked. "I demand the truth or count me out of this plan."

"You can already count me out," Morgan said before walking away.

CHAPTER 37

Storm

"Morgan, get back here and sit your butt down. You can't be serious about not supporting Brooks."

Storm sat on the sofa in a semi-private area at Trés restaurant facing a wood-burning fireplace. It wasn't cold enough in LA to have flames sparkling but the ambiance made for a cozy environment. The awkwardness between the three of them was obvious.

Hope was seated in a high-backed espresso cushioned chair to Storm's right. Morgan was in a slightly different chocolate-colored seat to Hope's left. Morgan had agreed to meet with them only if Brooks was not invited.

Morgan's behavior had instantly become that of a toddler's. Her willingness to embrace the all-for-one and one-for-all bond the girls had established had diminished significantly.

"I'm dead serious," Morgan said, digging into her lavender designer purse.

"Why? Why now? Why all the secrets?" Storm asked. "That's what I want to know. That and how long have you been doing Brooks?"

Hope told Morgan, "More importantly, you devised this plan and if you want out, forget it. You will not abandon this mission until it's complete."

"Are you dictating to me?"

Calmly Hope replied, "Someone needs to and I have no problem speaking my mind. You know this. You're the one being evasive. Evasive about your relationship with Brooks, about Brooks's alleged affair with Magnum, about the so-called baby in your belly. I don't mean to sound insensitive but it's not getting old, honey, it is old. All of it."

Morgan placed a camera in her lap. "Alleged, my ass. What would you do if Brooks was fucking your man?"

Storm and Hope became quiet. Storm glanced around their area. The nearest diners were two seating areas away.

"Pussy ain't never been my problem. Friend or no friend, I'd check my man," Storm said, scanning the latest news on her iPad. "Wait. Listen to this. It reads here that Randall Wallace is withdrawing from the race. He's giving his support to Anthony Dennison."

"Aw, hell no," Hope said. "You were supposed to make sure he scaled back on campaigning, not drop out and support Dennison. Damn!"

Nodding, Storm smiled. "I deserved that, but don't you see what's happening? They're uniting to beat Brooks. They think Randy's votes will give Tony a solid position for their party. We can't let this happen. Morgan, we have to revise the plan."

"Morgan, did you give Bailey Goodman his video?" Hope asked.

"That's right. Is there footage on him? Why haven't we seen anything?"

"Yes, there is footage," Morgan retorted. Handing Storm the

camera, Morgan told them, "Scan the pictures and tell me what you would do about this."

Hope relocated next to Storm on the sofa as they viewed the pictures. She was a bit surprised that Magnum was bold enough to get comfortable in Brooks's bed but none of the photos shocked Storm.

"How long have they been fucking? Brooks is starting to come across as a closet freak," Storm commented.

Hope cleared her throat. "Morgan, let's discuss everything or nothing. Are you sexing Brooks?"

"No, I'm not."

"Let me rephrase the question. Have you ever had sex with Brooks?"

Morgan exhaled. "What difference does that make? Look at the damn pictures!" Morgan lowered her voice, then continued, "You see her in bed with my husband?"

"Has your husband seen you in bed with Brooks? Dammit, Morgan," Storm hissed, "what is your problem?"

"Why do I have to be the one with the damn problem?"

Storm wanted to get up and slap Morgan but didn't. She wasn't a violent person but she swore Morgan's stupidity was testing her patience.

"Because you're acting childish," Hope said. "So it's okay for you and Brooks to have sex? Only god knows where or how long you've been doing this but now that Brooks and Magnum are doing the same thing, you're upset?"

Storm chimed in, "Seriously, Morgan. Brooks probably thought you were okay with it."

"Okay, my ass!" Morgan protested.

Storm shook her head. "Bring it down. I shouldn't have gone there," she said when she saw tears form in Morgan's eyes.

"Changing the subject," Hope said. "You want to confess you've lost our twenty-million dollar investment? Or do you want to keep procrastinating on providing a statement that doesn't exist?"

Storm worked hard for her money. She wasn't as wealthy as Hope. There was a huge gap between millions and billions. Hearing this accusation, she couldn't believe her seven-figure investment might be lost. Storm exhaled, rolled her eyes at Morgan. "I've given Randy and Tony a million each, which I now owe Hope's dad from my personal account, and you've done what? Please deny this. Say it isn't so."

Morgan shook her head. "I'll explain at the next meeting, which will also be our last. And you'll get your money even if I have to take it out of my personal investment account."

Hope exhaled. "So you managed not to lose yours but you're admitting you've lost ours?"

"Does Brooks know about this? I see what you're doing. Just know that if you've lost *my* money. I'm going to—"

Hope interrupted. "Storm, I'll take care of it. I'll cover your costs until Morgan gives us the report."

Morgan blurted, "I'm in love with Brooks."

"Not this again. Damn, let it go. You can't be serious." Hope sat on the edge of the sofa. "Morgan, you're sick, honey. You need professional help."

"What about Magnum?" Storm asked.

"I love him, too."

"So what is it that you're trying to do?" Storm asked.

"I don't know."

Hope interjected. "Who gives a damn about your personal life?"

"We're not letting Brooks back out of a campaign she's sure to win," Storm said.

"Fine, but do it without me," Morgan said, reaching for her camera.

Storm grabbed it, then stood and went to the fireplace. "You don't need this," she said, tossing in Morgan's camera.

"The only blackmail the Rich Girls will have is against our opponents. What you need to do, Morgan, is get your shit together. All of it," Hope said.

Morgan stood. Brushed off her slacks. "You dangle a carrot in front of Stanley, and as long as he does what you want him to, you're satisfied. But you don't have a clue what it feels like to give your heart to him…And you, Storm, you're so worried about what your parents think about who you marry that you're afraid to fall in love with Chancelor. What y'all don't understand is love is not something you plan for. If it were that easy, we wouldn't be having this conversation. Just like our investments, love is a risk you take when you trust someone with your heart. Love grows over time. You look up and realize it's grown roots and no matter how hard you try not to love someone, the roots keep spreading. And you're right, Storm. I don't need those pictures to prove what I already know. And you're right, too, Hope. I do need to get my shit together but it's going to take a while because right now my shit is diarrhea. These are my problems. I'll find a way to solve them. And I'll repay each of you your five million even if I have to liquidate my assets."

"Morgan, wait. Please sit. I apologize," Storm said.

"Me too, honey," Hope commented. "We need you to finish what you've started, then we'll support you on whatever decisions you make about Magnum, Brooks, and the baby."

"Like I told you before, count me out. I can't do this," Morgan said before grabbing her purse and leaving the restaurant.

CHAPTER 38

Morgan

Two months to Election Day.

Morgan powered off her cell phone, computer, and television. This was the first Saturday of the year that there was no meeting. No girls were coming to her home.

Magnum had gone from being confrontational about her catching him in Brooks's bed to cutting off all communications with his wife. He was no longer working at the spa. She didn't know where he was but prayed he wasn't staying with Brooks, and Morgan's pride wouldn't allow her to call Brooks to confirm what she didn't want to acknowledge. If Magnum was at Brooks's house, he could stay there.

"How in the world did I get here?" she asked herself while pouring herself a glass of champagne. She picked up the flute and the bottle, then went to the clubroom.

Sliding back the patio door, she stepped onto the balcony, took a deep breath. She set the bottle on the table and looked out over the trees. In the distance the mountains appeared to connect with the blue sky. Normally on Saturdays at this time, she'd be greeting Storm, complimenting Hope, and kissing Brooks.

Tears streamed down her face. Her house was no longer a home. This was not the life she wanted. This wasn't her first time being alone, but it was the first time since her childhood that she'd felt lonely. Abandoned. Isolated. Ostracized.

She laughed, traded her flute for the bottle. She had it all. Everything that money could buy. And she was miserable and tired of being sick every morning. She knew what she had to do.

"That's my plan that Brooks Kennedy is benefitting from. Mine, you hear me!" she shouted toward the mountains. A faint echo bounced back.

Morgan gulped the contents of the bottle. She held her breath until she sucked air. "Forget them," she said, hurling the bottle toward her swimming pool.

She missed. Glass shattered. She'd call the groundskeeper on Monday to clean up her mess. She went inside, powered on her phone, called her travel agent. "Book me a flight to Sydney. All five-star accommodations and a personal driver."

"But of course," her agent said. "When are your departure and return dates?"

"Departing three days from now and I'm not coming back until Christmas Eve." Morgan turned off her phone, tossed it on the nightstand, then lay across her bed staring at the ceiling.

By Christmas Eve the election would be over, and if her marriage was still worth salvaging by then she'd do that. If not, she'd go home to her parents' for the holidays. One way or another she'd share festive moments with someone she loved.

Had Morgan alienated the people closest to her? Her solitude was a blessing and a curse.

Morgan grabbed her cell phone and powered it on. Alienation was a choice. All she'd done was her choice. She dialed Bo's number.

Immediately he answered, "Hey, you okay?"

"I will be. I'm calling my doctor first thing Monday morning. I've decided not to keep the baby. If you don't mind going with me, I could use the support."

"Just tell me what time you want me to pick you up and I'm there."

"Thanks, Bo." Morgan ended the call.

What Bo didn't know wouldn't matter in about forty-eight hours. It was easy for a man to say, "Keep my baby," but when it came time for him to be a real dad he'd probably develop a bad case of amnesia and become an absentee dad.

Her body. Her life. Her choice. She'd made the hardest decision she'd have to live with the rest of her life.

Morgan could initiate forgiveness. Call Brooks and apologize for intentionally making her best friend feel like shit. And if her man didn't want to be found, Morgan was not the type of woman to hunt him down.

Magnum would have to come to her. If he wasn't back by Christmas, all of his things would be in storage before the New Year.

"Hello." The voice was inviting.

"Hey, can you come over?" Morgan asked. "I'm hungry."

"I was hoping you'd call back. I'm on my way."

"Thanks. I'll open the gate and leave the door unlocked. Wear something sexy," she said, ending the call.

The simple connection lifted her spirit. Morgan showered, slipped into a sexy teddy. Brushing her teeth, then her hair, she smiled at herself in the mirror. The doorbell commanded her attention. "I said I'd leave the door open." She dabbed perfume behind each ear, strolled to the foyer.

Not peeping through the hole, she opened the door wide.

Her smile vanished. The person standing before her was not the person she'd called.

"What do you want? There is no meeting today."

Hope stepped inside. "I came for the video footage on Bailey. We don't need you but we do have to have that tape. I'm not leaving without it."

This was not the time to argue. She did not want Hope to see her invited guest. Morgan briskly walked until she was out of Hope's view then she ran to the clubroom, unlocked the file cabinet, retrieved the DVD, and ran back. Approaching the foyer, she took several deep breaths, slowed her pace to a stroll before Hope saw her.

"Here you go. Good luck."

"Thanks," Hope said, walking out the front door then getting into her sports car.

Morgan shut the door, watched through the peephole until Hope's car was out of sight.

Exhaling, Morgan thought, "Thank God they didn't bump into each another." She stood in the doorway until she saw the car and person she was expecting.

"Hey, you," he said, walking in with a bouquet of white roses.

Morgan shouldn't have had Bo deliver all of those red roses to Brooks's house. Her intentions had been the same as the night she'd caught Magnum in Brooks's bed . . . bad.

"These are beautiful. Thanks." Morgan closed the door and set the vase on the console in the foyer, then glanced up at the painting hanging over their heads.

"What exactly are you hungry for?" he asked, following her to the bedroom.

"If you don't mind, I don't want to talk. The wrong words might alter the moment."

His strong chocolate hands massaged her shoulders. His tender lips pressed against the nape of her neck.

Morgan released a long, slow, "mmm," when his hands traveled under her armpits then gently fondled her nipples. Her body quivered.

He led her to the sofa, faced her toward the wall. Pressing on her shoulder, he bent one of her knees to the floor, then the other. He leaned her forward onto the cushion. Her chin rested on her shoulder as she watched him brace himself on his hands.

Slowly he started doing pushups. Each time he came up he paused long enough to kiss her clit. Kisses transformed to licks, and licks to sucks. Just when she was about to cum, he slid his dick inside her.

He rested his body atop hers. Grinding on her ass, he humped deep with each stroke. His strong arms held her, gave her a false sense of security. His lips caressed the nape of her neck, his hand slid between her thighs, one finger lightly circling her clit.

Morgan buried her face in the cushion and screamed as her entire body exploded, releasing the emotional pain and welcoming the pleasure. His dick throbbed repeatedly. She could've fallen asleep right there with his dick inside her.

He led her to the bathroom, filled the tub with water, washed her body. Drying her body from head to toe, he tucked her in at noon, then left.

CHAPTER 39

Brooks

N ot having the meeting with the girls at Morgan's house
was painful.

Hope had brought the video of Goodman that she'd gotten
from Morgan. Storm had elected to stay with Chancelor, as opposed to coming to Brooks's for the Saturday meeting.

Storm professed her loyalty was intact when she'd told
Brooks, "I'm here if you need me." But for the first time Storm's
dedication to the plan appeared to come after her relationship.
She'd told them, "I need to spend quality time with my man."

Since when did Chancelor come before the girls? When did
any of their men take priority over the group?

There was no Bloody Mary and mimosa bar. No chef-pre-
pared meal. No clubroom in the West Wing. The two of them
sitting side-by-side felt awkward. Neither of them wanted a
drink. Brooks wanted to get through watching the tape then
move on with her day.

"It's not as adventurous as Storm's or my footage, but it's
enough to control Bailey."

Brooks didn't respond. She sat in her living room with Hope

watching the DVD of Morgan servicing Goodman. Brooks's sex sessions with Bailey had been different from what she witnessed on the flat screen. Suddenly she missed the way Bailey made love to her. She closed her eyes, imagining the last time he'd bathed her. In her mind his finger was pressing against her clit. Mentally she held it there, shivered, exhaled, then opened her eyes.

"You okay?" Hope asked, staring at her.

"Yeah. Just a little tired," she lied. The screen was black.

Hope said, "Well, I'm going to make copies for everyone and return the original to Morgan. I'll download this to a computer, set up a meeting with Goodman, and give him the footage. I have to do this within the next few days to make sure it's not too late for him to scale back his campaigning, especially since Johnathon has given Bailey his support. Can't let them build up too much momentum."

"What about Tony? You think he'll follow in Randy's footsteps, drop out and support Goodman?"

Hope's jaw dropped. "What the hell? Are you okay, Brooks?"

"What do you mean? I'm fine."

"Randall Wallace and Anthony Dennison are Republicans. You've got your facts twisted. Randy is the one that dropped out already and he's given Tony his support. There's no way Tony can drop out at this point and we don't want him to. Sweetie, you're still ahead of them all but Goodman is close . . . Lord, we'd better hurry up and get through this before you mess it up for all of us."

"What's that supposed to mean?"

"We need Morgan. I'm making an executive decision. As soon as I leave, you are going to go to Morgan and clear up whatever differences the two of you have. I can't do that for you. And I sure as hell can't do this without Morgan."

Brooks knew Hope was right. Strong as Brooks was, she was weak without Morgan. They were all weaker without Morgan. Magnum didn't matter. She did not owe him an apology nor had she heard from him since that intruder had broken into her house.

"How much do you know about what's happening between Morgan and me?"

Hope stood, retrieved the video, stared at Brooks. "I know that you, sweetie, are a selfish bitch. This plan started out as a good thing and it can still end up being great but not if you continue to sit on your high horse looking down on your girls. You take lies to your grave against your opponents, not us. We're busting our asses for you! We've sucked dicks for you! Fought for your ass! I almost drowned in that damn pool for you and I never complained. But what do you do? You sacrifice all of us. All of us, Brooks!" Hope jabbed her finger into her chest and cried. "Me! Storm! Morgan! And Magnum!"

And, Magnum? She definitely knew something.

Hope threw the DVD across the living room, then headed in the opposite direction.

Walking and ranting at the same time, Hope continued, "Make sure your locks and the code on your gate are changed, and since you refused ours, hire yourself a bodyguard until the election is over."

All of what Hope mentioned was already done except the bodyguard part. Calmly Brooks said, "I have someone in mind to protect me. I'll give him a call today. If he's not available, I'll need your help finding someone."

Hope stopped in the doorway, turned to face Brooks. "If you don't do what you know needs to be done, count me out, too.

This is not a game. In case you need a reminder, you're running for governor of California, for God's sake."

Another one of her friends had just walked out of her house. Hope got in her cranberry Corvette ZR1. The spinning of Hope's tires created a cloud of smoke right before she zoomed out of the driveway.

Brooks went inside, got her purse, and drove to Morgan's house. The gate was open. Unusual but hopefully a sign that she was doing the right thing. Brooks approached Morgan's door, which was slightly ajar. Her heart raced praying her best friend was all right. She tiptoed in.

"Morgan," she sang in a gentle tone.

There was no answer. She bypassed the kitchen, where nothing appeared out of order. She went to the bedroom. Morgan was covered to her neck with the sheet and comforter. She looked so peaceful as she slept but Brooks wasn't leaving until they resolved their problems.

She would've been more comfortable in the living room but didn't want to scare Morgan. Brooks selected a well-lit area, helped herself to a Bloody Mary, settled herself in the kitchen, and began reviewing documents on her computer.

Three hours passed. Brooks would wait all night if she had to, but if she drank one more Bloody Mary she'd have to get in bed with Morgan.

"Excuse me, what the hell are doing in my house?" The voice was loud, deep.

Brooks recognized the tone. She looked up and saw Magnum.

"I came to see Morgan."

He stood behind a stool across the table from her. "You've ruined our lives enough."

"I haven't ruined any," she paused. "You're right. I have. I apologize for the bad decisions I made but I wasn't the only one."

"You're sorry but you're not sorry. Why the hell did you let Morgan in your house when you knew I was in your bed? You wanted her to find out about us. I'm never going to be with you again. And I'm never going to divorce my wife. I love my wife."

Brooks gasped. "That was Morgan? You mean the person that invaded my house was Morgan? How do you know that?"

"He's right. It was me. Now I want both of you...out of my house. Now," Morgan said. She didn't wait for a response. She exited the kitchen through the same doorway she'd entered.

This was not the right time to tell Morgan everything that she'd done with her husband. The three of them confessing at the same time would only create a shouting match and make the situation worse.

Brooks didn't wait for Magnum to respond. She did as Morgan had asked and left.

CHAPTER 40

Hope

One month to Election Day.

United, the Rich Girls would persevere.

Relationships did fall apart. Deterioration was the natural order of every aspect of life. No one born and nothing built would last an eternity. If Brooks wanted to rebuild the friendship she'd torn down, she'd have to apologize.

Brooks's situation with Morgan and Magnum made Hope analyze her own truth. The words Morgan had spoken from her heart gave Hope inspiration. Did she love Stanley enough to marry him? Or was she keeping him around solely for her convenience?

"How do you feel about our relationship?" she asked him.

He glanced around as if someone else was lying between them in his bed. "You talking to me?"

Hope propped a pillow behind her back, leaned against the headboard. His sarcasm was annoying the shit out of her but rather than leave, she stared at him instead.

"It's just that you've never asked me that question. I feel it could be better...humph, a lot better, since you've asked."

"Continue," she said, not wanting to interrupt his thoughts.

Stanley pressed his back to the headboard, too, tilting his body to face hers. "You're a wonderful woman. Any man would be proud to call you his own."

The "but" dangling on the edge of his lips did not escape her. She patiently waited for him to continue.

"But honestly, Hope, you're selfish. Make that inconsiderate."

The one thing she wasn't was controllable. Hope didn't see value in doing things that would annoy her just to appease her man. She couldn't be in two places at the same time. If she could, she still wouldn't make more of a commitment to Stanley.

"You don't need to explain. I agree. But aren't we all at some point? Selfish, that is."

"Yes, but yours comes with a no-refund, no-exchange, no-compromise tag attached. It's like you have a take it or leave me attitude toward me. I've never treated you that way."

True. He hadn't. But giving someone your heart was no guarantee they'd do the same. That was a chance he'd taken. What did he want from her?

Hope asked, "If you could change some things about me, what would they be?"

He smiled as though she would do whatever he was about to suggest. That wasn't true. But she was curious to hear what he had to say.

"I'm the man. Let me be the man. I lost five grand on that trip to Paris. Five grand. And you acted as though it was five dollars. No real apology. You just shoved your sorry-ass 'I'm sorry' down my throat and solidified it with a 'take it or step' undertone. That still pisses me off."

Me too. She was tired of hearing about it. But there was one way she'd never have to hear it again.

"See, that's what I'm talking about. You ask me to tell you how I feel and I wish you could see how tight your lips are right now."

She didn't need a mirror. She knew he was right. She tried relaxing her mouth. Maybe Stanley didn't have enough backbone for her. Hope loved power. Her cars had more horsepower than Stanley. He had the pickup of an American-manufactured two-door hatchback.

Tossing back the cover, Hope planted her feet on the floor.

"Where're you going?"

This was the last time Stanley would see her naked. Hope eased into her cobalt blue halter dress and stepped into her thong. She picked up her purse, then wrote him a check for ten grand.

"Thank you for helping me to understand that I'm never going to love you the way you love me. But I appreciate you for encouraging me to step into my reality. We're not equally yoked. Never have been. Never will be."

Looking at his face, Hope felt sorry for him. He looked pitiful. Was that what she was sexing? Pity?

"What's that supposed to mean?" he protested. "Now you're trying to emasculate me? Cut off my balls?"

That wasn't her intention.

"Here, this should make up for your losses," Hope said, handing him the check.

His eyes turned red. "I don't need your damn money. Can't you see I love you? Nobody's going to love you the way I do," Stanley said. He balled the check into his fist, snatched pieces from it like he was picking cotton, threw chunks to the floor.

Softly, Hope blew him a kiss. "That's a chance I have to take," she said, walking out.

Getting into her eight-million-dollar, black-on-black May-bach Exelero, she gunned her engine, and ripped out of the driveway. Did some powerful women, like some powerful men, intentionally cling to those less successful than themselves?

The time had come for her to move on from Stanley...but she could never move on from her girls.

CHAPTER 41

Storm

The bottom line was, Chancelor made her happier than any man she'd ever dated. But was happiness enough for a woman to commit to marriage?

Sure, she could have a guy her age or an older man like the mayor. She smiled, shook her head. No, not like the mayor. But she could marry for prestige, companionship, or just to identify herself as a Mrs., or she could marry because society dictated and the bible documented that women should procreate.

Not a single reason for marriage could prevent her holy union from ending in divorce, or prevent her from becoming a single mom. In the end she'd have to give him half for having done what? That was the risk a rich girl would take if she married a poor man, and exactly why a woman with her wealth should never marry down.

Storm not only understood but also agreed with her parents' views. But having money didn't fulfill her the way loving Chancelor did. How could she have it all and be reassured it would all last forever, when most marriages ended in bitter divorce?

She loved Chancelor's youthfulness, his sexy body, his willingness to be by her side. She trusted and respected Chancelor. She'd never stuck a dick up his ass. He wasn't that type of man. At his age he had maturing to do but she loved his innocence, too. Working with her man on his personal development was one hundred percent better than trying to have patience for an older man that was opposed to trying new things.

"Why won't you tell me where we're going?" Chancelor asked, reclining in the passenger's seat. "Are we headed to the airport? Are you taking me on another surprise trip to Italy? I know you didn't buy me another car. Let me guess. A house! You bought me a house!"

Thanks, Chancelor. Storm wasn't focusing on the material gifts she'd generously given him, but what had he bought her?

"You'll see in a moment," Storm said. Exiting Sunset Boulevard she valet-parked at The Mondrian Hotel wishing she hadn't planned an extravagant night. Cancelling it all would cost her the same. Storm decided to improve her attitude.

Chancelor sat up straight. Smiled. "Whoa, this is where we met!"

And it was the anniversary of when they'd met. She wouldn't hold it against him for not remembering that. Most men were horrible at remembering details. Storm said, "Except we're not going to the SkyBar."

"Then where exactly are we going?" he asked, escorting her into the lobby.

Storm bypassed check-in. She'd reserved an apartment for them. "For the next twenty-four hours, my love, you are all mine."

"Not if I'm lucky," he said, entering the unit. "I want to be yours forever."

Storm exhaled, then responded, "This used to be one of my favorite places to stay in Los Angeles when I don't feel like staying at home."

"Are you still confused about what you want? Do you want to marry me or not? If I leave again, I'm not coming back."

Deciding to get married wasn't that damn simple!

Sliding open the doors leading to the balcony, Storm looked out over LA. The lights illuminating the city were spectacular. Inhaling the fall breeze, she leaned back into Chancelor's arms.

"I have a few surprises for you. Happy anniversary, baby."

"Aw, dang." He slapped himself on the head. "I didn't get you anything. I'll make it up to you tonight. I'm going to sex you crazy. You gon' beg me to stop, woman."

"Let's take a shower," Storm said.

Stepping under the water was like being in a rainforest. The aqua blue water flowed from the ceiling, showering them.

"This is crazy," Chancelor said, kissing her.

"Stay here," Storm said, exiting the shower.

She wrapped her body in an oversized white towel, went into the bedroom, dialed guest services. "Yes, you can send them up now. Thanks."

"Okay, I didn't mean for you to stay in the shower. Dry yourself off and go get in the bed."

Moments later the three women she'd hired were there. Storm opened the door, invited them in, and instructed, "He's in there," pointing toward the room. "Give my man the best massage he's ever had, then bring him to me."

While the ladies were fulfilling their duties, Storm lounged on the plush silver sofa in the living room and phoned Morgan.

"Hey, Storm. How are you?" Morgan asked. Her voice was peaceful.

Election Day was two days away. "Are you joining us at Brooks's headquarters on Tuesday?"

"No, I can't do that. I appreciate her apologizing but our relationship will never be what it once was."

"Nothing stays the same, but I understand how you feel."

Morgan softly said, "No, you don't. Because I don't."

"I hope you change your mind. The Rich Girls' Club isn't the same without you. We need you."

"Take care," Morgan said, ending the call.

"Excuse me, Ms. Dangerfield, Chancelor is ready for you. He asked that you come to him. We're leaving now."

"Thanks." Storm said, entering the bedroom.

Chancelor was on one knee. His arms were opened wide. "Storm, will you please marry me?" Tears streamed down his face.

Her heart could've said "yes." Her head was clear.

"Do you love me?" he asked.

She dried his tears with her lips. "Yes, I do."

"Are you in love with me?"

"Yes, I am," she said.

"Then say yes."

A few hours ago, perhaps, she could've accepted his non-ring proposal. Now that he'd brought to her attention just how little he'd contributed to their relationship, she felt sobered. Besides, who was she fooling? If she had to think this hard about making a lifetime commitment, she wasn't ready. Neither was Chancelor. Storm realized being with him didn't fulfill her the same as being with the girls. Maybe after the election was over she could entertain him. But right now she had to be where she was needed most.

"I have to make an emergency run. I'll send a driver to take you home."

CHAPTER 42

Morgan

This was the day she had planned. Tuned in to the election, Morgan lounged on her chaise in the clubroom. Storm was where she should've been, too, at Brooks's side. But where was Hope?

Morgan placed her hand on her stomach. There was nothing growing inside her. Not anymore. She'd made the right decision.

The last time she'd seen Magnum, he was in their bedroom. She needed time to think, so she went to the clubroom.

The Bloody Mary and mimosa bar was stocked. Although she was the only one in the west wing, her new chef had catered for four, set up, then left. Morgan missed her girls. Her only regret was not acknowledging her own faults when Brooks and Magnum had confessed and apologized to her.

Sipping on a spicy Bloody Mary and feasting on shrimp cocktail, she wondered what made her that way. Stubborn. Unwilling to apologize when she knew she was wrong. Seeing herself as the victim when she was also the culprit. She would not be alone if she'd remained an active partner in the plan. She should've given Goodman the tape but according to the polls

Brooks was in the lead anyway. The margin just wasn't wide enough for comfort.

"Why can't I let go and forgive?" she asked herself.

The sun had set. The polls had officially closed. Morgan was glued to her chaise. She'd be there until the final votes were counted and reported. She had to know if her best friend would be relocating to Sacramento.

Click. Clack. Click. Clack. The sound grew closer.

"Yoo-hoo! Are you back here?"

Morgan glanced toward the doorway.

"Get up. Let's go," Hope said, sashaying into the room. "I'm not accepting no for an answer. Get up right now."

Hope didn't have to ask twice. Fifteen minutes to freshen up and Morgan was kissing her husband good-bye.

"Baby, I'm leaving with Hope. I'll call you later."

"Give Brooks my blessings. Let her know I voted for her," he said. "Thanks, Hope." Magnum resumed watching the news.

Funny how the people that loved her, truly loved her. Morgan would never allow sex to destroy her marriage or friendships again.

"Girl, let's go," Hope said, tugging her along. "We can miss the final results." Revving up her engine, Hope ripped out of the driveway.

"Why did you come to get me?" Morgan asked.

"Because when one friend drops the ball, another friend, if they're a true friend, doesn't ask why. They don't point to the problem. They don't tell their friend what to do. They simply pick it up."

Their ride to Brooks's campaign headquarters was quiet. Morgan reflected on the past year. Breaking the silence, Morgan asked, "So did you give Bailey the footage?"

"No, I didn't. Things fell apart. But everything is in divine order."

"So you mean Brooks is beating him fair and square?" Morgan asked.

Hope nodded as she parked her car. "Let's go."

Hurrying inside, the room was filled with balloons inside of a net strapped to the ceiling. Wall-to-wall familiar and not-so-familiar faces filled the room. Eyes were glued to the big screen. The women from the Beverly Hills club were sprinkled throughout the crowd.

The moment seemed surreal for Morgan. She had actually orchestrated a plan that worked. Hope maneuvered their way to the front of the room. There was Brooks shaking hands and giving hugs.

Their eyes met. Morgan took the first steps to greet her best friend. She held Brooks tight. "I'm so sor—"

"Sssh," Brooks whispered. "I love you, too."

Side-by-side, the Rich Girls—Morgan Childs, Hope Andrews, Storm Dangerfield, and Brooks Kennedy—stood united. Morgan was thankful for each of her girls.

The room became quiet. Everyone listened for the final announcement.

"The governor-elect for the state of California is..." Morgan held her breath. The Rich Girls interlocked fingers. "...Brooks Kennedy!"

As Brooks stood behind the podium to speak to the press and the crowd, Morgan proudly stood one step behind her best friend.

THE DECEPTION OF DICK

Ladies, listen up. Read and hear what I'm about to tell you.

There is definitely a deception of dick.

Most men aren't in touch with their manhood but they're constantly stroking their dicks. They each devalue their dicks but somehow expect you to give it, not him, meaning and purpose.

Sad but true—a man will stick his dick in you, pull it out, put it in another woman the same or the next day and expect both of you to say, "I love you," to him.

A man that thinks with his dick has no conscience. He believes that all he needs to do is make you cum, cry, and commit because his dick is so damn good you'll never leave him. Scratch that. Most men couldn't care less if you cum. Some of them believe you can't leave him because you can't live without his . . . dick?

Feel me on this one, ladies, this derogatory behavior is real. These guys are so in lust with their own dick that if they could suck it themselves they wouldn't need you for shit. Why do you think they say, "The way to a man's heart is through his stomach?"

You've never heard anyone say, "Girl, sex him senseless and he'll never cheat." Face the fact. You can't satisfy a dick.

The deception of dick is . . . it has a conscience. That's a lie!

A man will stick his dick in another man's ass then bring that same dick home to you and stick it your mouth. You can find a shit stain in the front of his underwear and believe him when he says, "I don't know how that happened."

A dick doesn't have the muscle to tell you the truth. "I love dick as much as you do. I want to fuck your sister, cousin, mother, and brother, too."

It's hard when it's hard.

It's hard to tell which way he goes, and like E. Lynn Harris's novel, in most cases it's *Any Way the Wind Blows*. Most men are whores but they want you to respect them in the morning when they're on their way out the door to hook up with a stranger they met on Grindr, Craigslist, or someplace else online.

He'll show up, let another man fuck him in the ass, go to work, and despise gay men. This is often the man that constantly claims he's straight, as if he has something to prove to himself.

The deception of dick is ... it has a conscience.

A man will fuck you as many times as you will give him your good pussy, then turn around and marry someone else. But you thought he was yours and when he divorced his wife you assumed you'd be the one standing at the altar. You gave him your good pussy and wanted him to give you his last name. Oh, well. Actually he did you a favor.

Dick can do that for you. Favors.

I went out with this guy. I liked his ass a lot. He messed up things when he asked me, "Are you having sex with anyone else?"

I told him, "Absolutely. I'd be foolish not to. You're separated from your wife, you've got baby mama drama, and chicks on the side."

He said, "Baby, I can have any woman I want. I can have all the pussy I want. But I just want you."

Okay, the personal driver every time we went out was great. The fact that this man was top notch when we went out on dates was fantastic. Spending his money was never ever an issue.

But his dick had him confused, not me. He had the audacity to tell me he didn't want me sexing other men. I told him, "Look, if we're going out, we're fucking. If we're not fucking, we're not going out. I'm a woman. I don't have time for mind games."

Each conversation we had after that he started asking about how many guys I was seeing. I told him, "If I never see you again in my life, that'll be okay with me. But if I see you on the street, I'll speak." I was done with him.

Forget that *Act Like a Lady Think Like a Man* bullshit. If you don't fuck like a man, ladies, you will eventually get fucked.

Some women think this type of guy is all that. These are the ones that'll make you believe you're the only one he's sexing when the truth is he's wining, dining, and fucking another woman and telling her the same things he tells you.

You've been deceived by the dick. Admit it.

You thought that dick loved you. You thought that dick exclusively belonged to you. A dick is like a stray dog...constantly on the prowl for pussy. And he'll cum inside your pussy to mark his territory. And once you let him hit it raw he'll always believe he can get it again, and again, and again.

Why? Because in most instances he can.

Why? Because you feel you're better than the last and will outlast the next female that rides his dick. Your pussy is better, faster, tighter and can do flips and she's always got a new trick for his dick.

I wish dicks came with a speedometer so women could see how many miles he had. I wish there was a limit on how many times he could cum. Let's say two thousand shots max. Or I wish he'd lose an inch off his dick for every mile he tried to roll back on his dick-o-meter.

Like Pinocchio's nose, every time he lied his dick would grow not an inch but a mile. He'd have to call ahead and phone an elephant to say, "I'm only going to put the head in," because getting pussy would be like *Mission: Impossible*.

The deception of dick is...it has a conscience.

A dick will fuck up your heart, tear your insides and world apart. Your heart will tell a man's dick, "I love you," when he's beating your ass, spending your cash, and he won't even take out the trash.

The more he fucks over you, the more he fucks you, and the more you believe he loves you when he doesn't love you at all. Why? Because he doesn't know what love is or how it's supposed to feel.

He's got you whipped and now you want to whup every other bitch's ass. Not because you think she wants him. You know that dude is trifling. He's flirting with the next woman and you're afraid he's going to leave you to get with her, and you're probably right. But it's not her fault.

It's your fault that you've allowed yourself to fall in love with a dick. Get a clue. A dick should fuck you, not fuck with your head.

Okay, I'ma say this and leave this topic alone. A woman who can deceive a dick, is queen of the throne.

The deception of dick is...whatever you want it to be.

READING GROUP GUIDE

1. If you were to organize the Rich Girls' Club with your girlfriends, who would you invite to join and why? What would be the purpose of your club?

2. Which of the four girls do you identify with most and why would you love to have her lifestyle?

3. As a group, devise a campaign strategy to have one of your book club members elected for a high political position. Which member would you select to run? Why?

4. Ladies, do you believe pussy is best served ice cold? Could you serve your pussy ice cold? Just for fun, create a mission to lure or outsmart a man. Explain how you will accomplish your goal by using your female power.

5. What's your favorite sex scene? Just for fun, share with the group your fantasy or create a sex scene you'd like to see in a book.

6. In my opinion, infidelity is overrated, because most men who cheat try to justify their actions by blaming the woman. Would you agree or disagree? Could you forgive your mate if they cheated on you?

7. In the sex triangle between Brooks, Morgan, and Magnum, what do you feel the outcome should be? Should Morgan

stay married to Magnum? Should Brooks and Morgan remain friends? Which affair do you believe will end?

8. Do you think women who have sex with women can con-
tract sexually transmitted diseases? If so, what diseases and
how?

9. Should women with money date like men? Under what circumstances would you date like a man?

10. What politicians do you believe would have sex with the
same sex if no one was watching? Which married politicians
do you think are cheating on their spouses?

11. Should a married man have a vasectomy without his wife's
permission?

12. Why aren't women publicly humiliated for having affairs?
How many women can you name that have been exposed
in the media for having affairs?

13. Do you prefer to date younger or older? As long as the person is of legal age, is there a limit on whether someone's too
young or too old for you?

14. Chris Rock said, "Women would rule the world, if women
didn't hate women." What do you think he meant? Do you
agree? Are there any women you're jealous of or don't like?
Why?

15. If someone wrote you a check for one million dollars, what
would you do with the money?

16. Do you think married couples should spend time apart
from one another on a weekly, monthly, or yearly basis, or
not at all? (From Chapter 2)

ACKNOWLEDGMENTS

Life is an awesome journey through the unknown, a priceless adventure of countless experiences. We are the pilots of our passion. We never control the outcome of our choices but with each step we navigate the road ahead. What you do with your life is up to you and nobody else. It's impossible to be everything to everybody. Please don't die before you decide to live life to the fullest. Release your sexual inhibitions. Dance naked in the rain. Love and make love to yourself; you'll be happier.

Remember, no man acquires success independent of another. For my achievements I'm thankful to the Creator, my publishers, editors, agents, family, friends, and to each of you. I acknowledge and appreciate your emotional and financial support. You are a blessing to me and I pray somehow, even in a small way, that I too have or will positively influence you.

The main reason I smile is because of my son, Jesse Bernard Byrd, Jr. Honey, you're the best. I'm proud to be your mom and I love you unconditionally. Another reason is my guardian angels—my mother, Elester Noel; my father, Joseph Henry Morrison; my great aunt, Ella Beatrice Turner; and my great uncle, Willie Frinkle—always lift me up when I need them. Wayne, Andrea, Derrick, and Regina Morrison, Margie Rickerson, and Debra Noel are my siblings. Thanks, guys, for always believing in me.

I genuinely appreciate all of my Facebook friends and fans, my Twitter followers, my MySpace crew, and my McDonogh 35 Senior High alumni. Happy thirtieth reunion to my class of 1982!

To Latoya Smith, Karen R. Thomas, Linda A. Duggins, and Jamie Raab for supporting my career at Grand Central Publishing. Latoya, congratulations on your accomplishments. I look forward to working with you as my new editor and enjoyed getting to know you better during our time in the Bay Area. You're a brilliant woman. I wish you the best of everything.

Thanks to my editor and friend, Selena James at Kensington Publishing Corporation. To Steven Zacharius, Adam Zacharius, Laurie Parkin, Karen Auerbach, Adeola Saul, Lesleigh Underwood, and everyone else at Kensington for growing my literary career. In loving memory of Walter Zacharius. It is my honor to be a part of your undying legacy to the world of literature. Your spirit will dwell within me forever.

Well, what's an author without brilliant agents? I'm fortunate to have two of the best agents in the literary business, Andrew Stuart and Claudia Menza. You are appreciated.

By the time you read this, *Soulmates Dissipate* the movie will be scheduled to premiere in theaters. I thank everyone that is making this seven-film project possible—Leslie Small, director/producer; Jeff Clanagan, CEO of Codeblack Entertainment and producer; Dawn Mallory and Jesse Byrd, Jr., producers; Richard C. Montgomery (my best friend and business partner); and all of my fans.

Wishing each of you peace and prosperity in abundance. Visit me online at www.MaryMorrison.com, sign up for my HoneyBuzz newsletter. Join my fan page on Facebook at Mary Honey B Morrison, and follow me on Twitter @marybmorrison.

IF I CAN'T HAVE YOU

by Mary B. Morrison

PROLOGUE

Granville

"I came to tell you something," she said softly.

Loretta sat across the table from me at our favorite restaurant, Grand Lux Café, on Westheimer Road. Her naturally chocolate lips were perfectly painted with that sweet gloss I'd tasted twenty-three times. I wanted to lean over the table, suck it all off, up my count to twenty-four.

Her big brown eyes connected with mine. When her thick lips parted, my dick got hard, making me reminisce about the first and last time she'd given me fellatio. Loretta had said, "I'm never sucking your dick again," because I came too fast. Hopefully she'd change her mind, but if not, that was okay with me as long as she kissed me somewhere.

Her wide pink tongue peeped at me. The scent of fresh bubblegum traveled from her mouth to my nose. Loretta's mouth was always inviting. I winked at her, then smiled.

"You know what you just did to me, right? You gave me another woody," I whispered. "My dick is hard."

I lifted my brows twice, narrowed my eyes, kept smiling at her. She made me feel sexy, had done things to me no other woman had. She'd once tied me to my bed, naked except for my cowboy boots, then rode me like I was a bucking bull. My head banged against the headboard as I screamed her name.

My woman exhaled, rolled her eyes to the corners, then returned her gaze to me. Her stare was dreamy.

If she said she was pregnant, she'd make me the happiest man in the world. I swear I'd jump on the table and shout to everyone in hearing range, "We're pregnant!"

Yelling too loud would hurt my throat. But the announcement of my son would be worth the joy and pain. Twenty years ago I was shot in the shoulder and the bullet grazed my vocal cord. The damage was permanent, my voice forever deep and scratchy. When I first met Loretta, she thought I was hoarse. The louder I tried to speak, the more it hurt, but I loved to talk. Some women actually thought my voice was sexy. But not Loretta.

My baby scratched the side of her nose. "I don't want to go out with you anymore. You're nice and all, but I can't. I met you here to let you know that this is our last date."

Generally, I'd want to ram my tongue down her throat and give her one of my juicy kisses, letting the saliva drain from my mouth to hers. Now, all I wanted to shove in her mouth was my huge fist. Lucky for her, we were not alone. That, and I didn't hit ladies, even when I felt they deserved a slap or two.

An affectionate pat on the back from me had sent a few grown men stumbling. "Watch your heavy hands," Loretta would scold when I touched her face.

"I don't understand. I thought things between us was getting better."

"For you," she said.

"For me? I've done everything you've asked me to do. I even went to that sex therapist you recommended. You can't deny the sex between us is the best you've ever had. Right?"

"For you," she said again.

The heel of my left boot lifted then thumped to the floor. Again and again. I shook my leg sideways, rubbed the denim covering my left thigh.

"What about the lingerie I just bought you? You using me? You gon' put my shit on for some other nigga?"

Loretta opened her oversized purse, handed me a red plastic Frederick's bag. "I thought you'd bring that up. I never wore them. Everything is there, including the receipt."

I didn't want no fucking refund. I wanted her!

"Tell me what your problem is. Give me a chance to fix it," I pleaded. This woman was making me look like a guest on an old episode of *Jerry Springer*. What was I supposed to do with the engagement ring in my damn pocket?

"I'm tired of telling you that you talk too much. Your voice is annoying. You don't listen to what I have to say. Your shoving your tongue down my throat, draining your bodily fluids into my mouth is horrible, but you think each kiss is 'the best kiss ever.' You think we're in a relationship when I keep telling you...we're not!"

"We are in a relationship!"

"I'm not your woman."

"You are my woman. We talk on the phone every day. We go out every other day. And we've had great sex. What's wrong with you?"

"You. I've only known you for three weeks and my stress level has gone from calm to calamity." Loretta pushed back her chair. "As nice as you are, you are not the guy for me. You're not the guy for any woman, Granville," she said. "Take care."

There was someone for everyone and Loretta was mine. I couldn't let the love of my life walk away from me. I grabbed her wrist. "But we haven't eaten. Look, I'm sorry. I apologize. I love you, Loretta. Sit down. Let's have lunch. You talk. I'll listen. You're right."

"And you're desperate. Let me go."

I wanted to release her. I couldn't let go. What if she was serious? What if I never saw her again? My fingers tightened. Worse, what if I saw her with another man?

Loretta picked up a glass of water, tossed it in my face. This was one of those few moments when a woman made me want to hit her.

Why was Loretta treating me this way? All I tried to do was take good care of her. Treat her with respect. Buy her nice things.

I dug deep into my pocket. Pulled out a twenty, placed it on the table. Dug into my other pocket, pulled out the ring, flipped open the box, kneeled on one knee, stared up at her. "Marry me, Loretta."

I continued holding her wrist until she shouted, "Let me go!"

The people staring at me were supposed to be cheering for me, for us. I dumped the ring in my palm, snapped the box closed, jammed the box in my pocket, staggered to my feet. The baby I wanted us to have wasn't growing inside her? The woman I loved had to have a reason to love me too. Anger festered inside me as she broke my grip, stomped out of the restaurant.

I trailed her to her car. "Wait, give me one more chance."

Loretta faced me, waved her hands in front of my face. "What is wrong with you?"

"What's wrong with you, skank ass bitch? You'd better get your hands out my face. You gon' need medical attention if you don't. I told you I'd put you on my insurance. You'd rather be a hometown ho, spreading your pussy around Houston like pollen, than to let me take care of you?"

Calmly, she said, "Yes."

"You trifling bitch! You're not going anywhere," I said, blocking her driver's side door.

"You need to get your fucked up, crooked yellow teeth, nasty-ass crusty feet, slobbering like a dog in heat self away from me and my car."

"You're right. I apologize. Please forgive me. Will you marry me?"

I fought to put my ring on her finger. She yanked her hand away.

"Officer!" Loretta shouted. "Help me!"

I hadn't noticed the cop getting out of his car until now. I wasn't looking for trouble. I stepped aside, hoping Loretta would get in her car and go home. That way we could continue our conversation in private.

"Is there a problem, sir?" the officer asked me. His hand was on his gun.

"No problem. Just a little lovers' quarrel with my girlfriend."

"I'm not his damn girlfriend. He's harassing me. I'm trying to leave, but he won't let me."

"Sir, let me see your identification."

"What did I do?" I asked. My eyes narrowed toward Loretta. "She'll calm down shortly. Women always exaggerate. Soon as you leave, she'll be begging me to come over to her house and you know what, man."

"I'm not going to ask you again, sir."

Fuck! I eased my wallet out of my pocket, handed my license to the officer. "Here."

"Wait right here. Better yet, you come with me. Ma'am, you wait here."

Women could fuck things up in a heartbeat. When shit didn't

271

go their way they wanted the police to rescue their ass. Just like that, Loretta was about to know what I didn't want her to find out. Ever.

The policeman got out of his car. "Put your hands behind your back and turn around."

"Why? What did I do?"

"I'm not going to ask you again...sir." The officer unfastened the latch securing his stun gun, pulled it out.

I faced the fuckin' patrol car, did as I was told. I knew the routine. The officer placed his hand on top of my head, shoved me in the car, left the door open.

I sat there feeling like an idiot. Watched him escort Loretta to the patrol car like I was in a lineup and she needed to ID me. I stared at her. After all I done for her, that bitch didn't have an ounce of empathy for me. Just like the rest, she'd get hers.

"Let me see your identification," the officer asked Loretta.

She opened her purse, handed the cop her license.

"I don't know your relationship to this man, but there's something you should know," the officer said. "Granville Washington has three restraining orders against him filed in Houston by three different women. If he's harassing you, I suggest you do the same, Ms. Lovelace. This man is dangerous."

"Arrest him! He's insane. I want to press charges."

"Wish I could, ma'am, but I don't have cause to arrest this man. He hasn't violated the law."

Watching Loretta walk away, I smiled on the inside. It would be in her best interest to take the officer's advice. I'd never violated a restraining order. Better to get another woman than to go to jail and become someone else's woman.

I wasn't finished with Loretta Lovelace yet. If she were wise, she'd never turn her back on me again.

CHAPTER 1

Madison

"Y ou can't see it . . . it's electric!"
The music moved through me like lightning. Happiness filled the room. My hips swung to the beat. I sang, "You gotta feel it . . . it's electric!"

My man got down on one knee. I gyrated in his face.

"I love you, Madison Tyler. Will you marry me?"

In the midst of grooving with over a hundred people doing the electric slide, I stopped dancing. The moment I'd been waiting for had arrived in style. I couldn't hold back the tears. What girl didn't want a husband to love and adore her for the rest of her life? I was positive I wanted to get married.

"Yes! Yes, I will marry you, Roosevelt!" I wasn't sure if he was the one, but he'd do for now.

Roosevelt didn't like his first name, but I appreciated it more than what everyone else called him, Chicago. I found southerners strange in many ways. Roosevelt had no middle name, so his family gave him one when he was a toddler. They weren't from Chicago and he hadn't visited the Windy City until he was an adult. The only rationale was that the Bears were his father's favorite team.

The ice cube he'd slid on my ring finger blinded me. Damn! I held my hand in front of my face and cheesed the widest grin ever. I pulled Roosevelt to his feet by his lapel, leapt into his arms, smashed my lips against his.

The Electric Boogie faded from blasting to silence. "Did Chicago just propose to Madison?" the DJ asked.

"He sure did!" I flashed my ring to all the bitches at my girl's wedding reception. All the single females' eyes melted. It didn't matter who caught the bouquet now; I was the envy of them all.

Stealing the spotlight from Tisha wasn't planned. How was I to know my engagement ring would be a bigger solitaire than all the chips in her wedding band and engagement ring combined?

Not my problem. I gave Tisha a big hug because she had to be feeling really small right now.

I'd turned to kiss Roosevelt again when someone snatched my bicep. The grip was that of a blood pressure machine about to explode. My fingers automatically curled into a tight fist.

I didn't fight, but I swore if I turned around and saw one of those desperate bitches that wanted my man trying to ruin the moment, I was going to lay their ass out, then glide over them as though I was on the red carpet.

They were beneath me. All women were beneath me, including my best friends, Loretta and Tisha. When I saw it was Loretta, I uncurled my fist.

Loretta had dated that loser construction worker, Granville Washington. He worked for me. I told her not to do it, not to do him. Told her that misfit had a big dick—saw it myself when his lazy ass pissed outdoors on my property. And he had nothing to lose because outside of work, he had no real interests other than trying to get laid.

Granville was a clumsy brute. Six-feet six-inches, two-hundred and seventy-five pounds of muscles. Worst combination for a man is to be good looking, great in bed, and think he knows everything when what he truly is, is ignorant. Loretta should've taken my advice, took the dick, and kept shit moving. But no. Loretta always had to find the good in every man until he treated her bad.

"Girl, let me——" Before I finished protesting, I was being dragged off the dance floor, out the back door.

"What the hell are you doing?" Loretta asked.

I flashed my ring in her face. "Duh. Trying to enjoy the moment. What's wrong with you?"

"You can't accept Chicago's ring. You're going to ruin another good man. You've already got what, six engagement rings collecting dust. It's women like you that mess it up for women like me."

"Correction. It's eight. And see, that's where you're wrong. It's women like you that allow men to dictate to you instead of you training them like I've taught you. That's how you end up with fucked-up men like Granville. By the way, have you filed that restraining order like I've told you?"

"Have you fired him like I've asked you?"

"He's not my problem. Granville is an excellent worker. Hell, he does the work of ten men. I'd be stupid to fire him."

"Well, don't marry Mr. DuBose. What are his mother and father going to say about this? If he marries you, our entire football team is going to hell."

Not my problem.

So what if his parents hated me. Roosevelt appealed to me because he managed a professional football team. He was unquestionably a man of power, in charge of everyone around

him, except me. I'd make sure I'd marry him right before he in-
herited the ten million his grandparents had willed him.

"Look at it like this, Loretta. Now, I'm responsible for all
sixty-one players and the assistant coaches and the head coach.
You should be nicer to me. I might hook you up with a millionaire, girlfriend. Stop hating because you can't find the right
man."

"Fine, if you want to ruin Chicago's life, go right ahead,"
Loretta said, flinging my arm toward me. "But don't overshadow
Tisha's wedding day."

"Not my problem. Tisha should've married a man with more
money."

Loretta shook her head. "Girl, you're lucky you're my friend
or else."

"You've got that one twisted. The soon-to-be Madison DuBose
is going back inside to celebrate her engagement. I suggest you
stay your ass out here until you cool down. Trust me, you don't
want me to blast your business in front of Tisha's guests."

"Okay, Ms. Thang. Wait a minute," Loretta said. "Since you're
so great at training men, I bet you that you can't train Granville
Washington."

I stared at my girl. She must've been insane giving me a dare.
Nobody gives Madison Tyler a dare and wins. I'd show her how
good I was at getting my way with men. "This'll give me something to do while Roosevelt is on the road. But before I agree,
what's in it for me?"

"Whatever you want."

That wasn't specific enough. I could become Loretta's worst
enemy by the time I won this bet. I threw my hands up. Why
was I entertaining her? "Look, I'm not sure you have enough to
lose for me to charm that loser."

"Just what I thought. You're all talk. You're not all that, Madison," Loretta said, walking away from me.

"Fine, I'll prove it. But I'm not having sex with him."

"That's the only way you can prove it to me."

I was so good I could open an obedience school for men, but sexing Granville would go against my principles. Not sexing him would give Loretta bragging rights. I'd show her ass. I was going to break this Granville guy in one weekend.

"Fine," I said, walking away.

"One more thing," Loretta said.

"What? Girl, what!? You are ruining my moment."

"Better for me to ruin yours than for me to stand by and let you do the same to Tisha. If I win, you'll call off your wedding with Chicago."

I shook my head. "Fine. Because I'm not going to lose. You are."